Samantha M Thomas

CONTENTS

To all the awkward kids that never quite grew out of it:
Own it baby, because you are all kinds of special.

CHAPTER ONE
AINSLEY

*M**oving back home is the right decision.*

Maybe if I keep repeating it, I'll believe it. It's not like it's even all that far from where I was living, it just feels like I've ... failed.

My sister, Larkin, would say none of this is my fault. Deep down, I know she's right, but I'm still too angry and raw to think logically about the situation.

Exploited. I feel exploited.

I'm currently driving from Austin to my small hometown of Bluebell Falls, about two hours away, because my direct supervisor harassed me at work and then got me fired because of it. In this day and age, I wasn't expecting to have to defend myself against a raging narcissist who thinks women are only there to please him. The worst part is I was passed up for a promotion, for the job he actually got, and I had seniority on him—yet, I'm the one who got fired.

Good 'ol corporate America strikes again.

I sigh as I pass the sign telling me there's only thirty more miles until I'm home-sweet-home. Population of 2,739. God, I fucking hate small towns. It's the reason Larkin and I moved to Austin for college and never came back. In a small town, everyone is always in your business and there is zero privacy.

Good thing I don't plan to stay here.

I guess that's why I'm renting a small-ass house on the outskirts of town, in hopes that people leave me alone. I don't want to have to explain why the previously ultra-responsible Ainsley is back home to lick her wounds and start her life from square one. Talk about anxiety-inducement.

I guess the only positive is I'll have my parents close, although, that could quickly turn into a negative, depending on how invasive they are. Lord knows I was vague as hell when I explained I was moving back home. And I know my dad is going to be butting his nose into my business the second he can. My mom will tag along, but my dad is the one to watch out for. He's worse than the group of octogenarians playing Phase 10 every week as an excuse to exchange town gossip.

Moving home is a good thing. Admitting defeat isn't weakness—it's accepting that things didn't turn out the way I thought they would. And I'm one hundred percent okay with that.

Yep, keep telling yourself that.

I'm trying to stay positive.

My inner devil-and-angel argument is interrupted by my phone ringing through my car speakers.

"Hey."

"Where are you at? Did you make it yet?" Larkin's anxious voice hits my ears.

"I'm, like, thirty minutes out. Calm down."

"Sorry, you know I'm just worried about you."

"It's the mother hen in you now." I chuckle.

"Possibly. I had no idea how fearless a thirteen-year-old boy could be, but let me tell you, it's not for the faint of heart."

Her and Theo, her husband, adopting Gavin out of foster care will forever be something I'm beyond proud of her for. It's also the reason I cried the first hour of this drive. I won't be close to my nephew or niece anymore. I can't just go pick him up from school and have a "fun aunt" afternoon. And my heart is still breaking because of it. His little sister is awesome too, but I've always had a deep connection with Gavin.

"Tell him I miss him," I whisper, trying to hold the tears in.

"Oh, Ains. I promise we'll make trips to come see you. Hell, he and Maddie can even spend the weekend if you really want. It's not like Theo and I would say no to a quiet house once in a while." She says it barely over a mutter, so I have to assume my sweetheart of a nephew is close by, or the tornado that is Maddie. It's a toss-up, really.

"Deal. I'll come steal them myself if I need to."

"You really think this is the best move?" she asks me for the tenth time.

"I do. Lance is going to blacklist me from any financial firms in the city. Hell, he already is, and staying means starting a completely new career. At least with this new job, I can work from home and get my bearings back."

"But you could stay here and do that too," she offers.

"I could, but I need the change of scenery, Lark." I could explain that staying in the same city as Lance makes me feel dirty and used. That the circle of work friends I had sided with him and left me in the dust. But right now, I don't really want to examine too closely how I feel about that. Running away from it all feels like the easiest option.

"Okay, well, we're not that far if you need anything. And text me when you get there, so I know you aren't in a ditch on the side of the road!"

"Yes, Mom." I smile as I hang up the phone.

My smile instantly drops as I think about what I'm doing.

When did I start running away from my problems instead of facing them head-on? Will I ever feel sure of myself again?

I pull into the driveway of my little rental and stare at it. The house is not awful. In fact, it could be really cute if I added some flowers to the front and tidied up the yard. It's a little, 900-square-foot bungalow with a good-sized backyard that backs up to a greenway. It's the sole reason I jumped on it so fast. I imagined sitting on the back porch and staring out into the wildflowers, thinking about how happy I am with my life.

Yeah, right. It'll take a lot more than wildflowers to be happy with my life right now.

I hate this so much. I'm thirty-four years old. I should have my shit together. Instead, all I want to do is hide out in my new home and ignore the world and my problems, hoping they magically disappear. Adulting is overrated anyway.

Well, that's exactly what I plan to do for the foreseeable future.

I hop out of my car as I nod to the imaginary devil on my shoulder and grab the suitcase from the back seat. The POD with all my other shit should be delivered in the next couple of hours, so until then, I'll check out the wildflowers.

The house is actually in great shape. You can never really tell online when you're just looking at pictures, so it's a relief to see it's not falling apart at the seams. It consists of one large open area that contains the kitchen and living room, with the bedroom and bathroom off to one side of the house.

I beeline it to the French door and see a large deck that spans the entire length of the house, and my heart starts to feel ten times lighter. Walking through the doors, I drop down on the edge of the deck and swing my legs as I peer up at the sky. Vitamin D is supposed to cure all, right?

Moving home isn't something I ever thought I would do, and coming to terms with the decision is harder than I thought it would be.

The only good thing is it didn't take me long to find a new job. It's nowhere near the ambitious and demanding financial advisor career I had, but maybe a change of pace is a good thing. Plus, the company is based in Bluebell Falls, so it just makes life easy all around right now.

Sure, being a virtual assistant and someone's lackey is definitely better.

I roll my eyes, annoyed with the pessimist currently infiltrating my mind.

I don't have much of a choice at the moment, so bitching about it won't actually solve anything. I honestly don't know if I want to solve anything. Being in a demanding job in a male-dominated field was fucking hard, but I was excelling. Until Lance got that damn promotion, and his true, asshole personality came through. Do I even want to stay in a field that prioritizes misogynistic assholes like that? At the moment, hell no. And when I took a step back and looked at the life I had created in Austin, the only bright spot was Larkin and her family. I never went out with friends, always too busy working. I never really got past date three with anyone recently, so it's not like I had a thriving love life there, either.

Those realizations about my life are the reason I'm back here, in a town I wanted nothing to do with for years. It's why I chose this little bungalow on the outskirts of town, away from neighbors and people. People haven't been a positive in my life in a long time, so hiding away from them seems like a great option to re-prioritize my life.

Maybe I should pick up a hobby... Knitting? Is that still a thing people do? Or maybe I'll get a gaming console and play video games with my nephew.

I pull out my phone and text Larkin, asking what console they have. When she answers me, I immediately go online and order one, along with some games I've heard Gavin talk about non-stop. I can still be the cool aunt from two hours away, right?

God, I hope so, because I desperately need a distraction.

Tilting my head back, my eyes close, and I soak in the dying warmth of the day.

Who needs a booming career and amazing food all within their fingertips? Not this girl. I'll just find those copycat recipes online and try to replicate all my favorites.

The closing of a car door interrupts my cooking plans.

"Annie?" my dad calls out.

A smile creeps onto my face at the nickname he's always called me. That didn't take long. "Back here, Dad!" I yell out.

"There she is! Your sister called us to tell us you made it. I brought your favorite pizza from Mullin's," he says as he plops down next to me, and my mom shuffles through the gate, holding a basket of God knows what.

Mullin's is that greasy, cheap pizza I survived high school on. It's nostalgia, through and through.

The smell of small-town, fresh air, and greasy memories makes me think this move might not be so bad.

CHAPTER TWO
LEDGER

Driving past the bungalow that's closest to my house on the way home from a job site, I see a familiar car in the driveway next to one I don't know. The Mathewses. I slow down as I pass and look to see if I can figure out why they're at the house that's been empty since the Clarks moved away, when I spot a figure standing off to the side of the house, and my heart stops.

Ainsley Mathews.

The girl I was too shy to ask out in high school. The girl I've crushed on for as long as I've had an interest in girls. The girl who's never quite gotten out of my head, no matter how much time or distance was between us.

And she's back.

Is she here for good? Is she just visiting for the first time in far too many years? I may have known she'd be a part of my life since I hired her to be my virtual assistant, but I also knew that didn't necessarily mean she would be anywhere near Bluebell Falls.

I don't have a ton of answers, but I do know I'm not the same shy kid I used to be. I've been through some tough shit, and I've grown a lot in the almost two decades since then. If Ainsley is in town, I'm shooting my shot.

CHAPTER THREE
AINSLEY

Why I thought I didn't need much time to unpack my life before I started my new job, I'll never know. But Past Me has to be having a laugh right now. I'm currently sitting in an office chair with boxes forming a makeshift desk. My bed is a mattress on the floor, and I've been living off of the pizza my dad brought over a couple of days ago. I'm pretty sure my entire bathroom is packed in one of these boxes I'm working on, including my vibrators, which is a bit of a downer if I need any form of stress relief in the next few days.

I used to be so organized and on top of everything in my life. This is decidedly the opposite, and I don't know how to cope with it. I feel frozen. Like there are too many things to do and not enough time to get everything done. As if starting one project feels like too much for my brain right now. On top of that, today is my first day as a virtual assistant. I'll be honest, the job duties were a little vague, and I've only communicated with my boss, Mr. Hutton, twice. I know nothing outside of the fact he owns the nursery in town and his landscaping business, and he needs help with the administrative side of things. The salary wasn't total shit, and it had immediate availability, which sold me more than anything.

Now, I'm wondering if it was smart to just jump into a random job while my life is literally up in flames. It's too late now, though, as I login to my email and see one from my new boss waiting for me.

I'm not a quitter, so I might as well suck it up and jump in.

Subject: Today's List

Good morning, Ms. Mathews,

I'd like to start every morning by sending you a list of tasks to accomplish for the day. I might add some things as they come up, but I endeavor to keep it as close to the list I send you in the morning as possible.

This morning, I wanted to start light, so we can both get used to this system and adjust as needed.

1. *Go through emails and mark anything urgent that needs my immediate attention. (Ongoing through the day.)*

2. *Go through receipts on the company drive and organize them into months.*

3. *If possible, go through our current advertisement and liven it up. Make it more appealing, and send it to me when you are done.*

Please let me know if you have any questions,
Ledger Hutton

Well, at least this seems easy so far, although "make the current advertising more appealing" leaves a lot of room for interpretation. I'm not a marketer by any means, but I'll give it a go and see where we get. Everything else is straightforward, so I follow the instructions he attached to log in to the company drive and start exploring, trying to learn about their current organization.

By lunch, I have all the receipts organized—the files were absolute chaos—and have gone through most of the boss's inbox—also a hot mess. I haven't heard another peep from Mr. Ledger Hutton, but this girl needs to eat some damn food before I keel over from starvation.

I really don't want to go anywhere, but my lack of planning has forced my hand. Heading to the diner downtown is probably one of my only options for a quick lunch, outside of the pizza I've been living off of. I look down at my galaxy leggings and black razorback tank, and shrug. Good enough. I'm not trying to impress anyone anyway. Besides, most of these people have seen me in the dreaded preteen phase, so I think I'm okay. Grabbing my keys and my sunglasses, I jump into my car and drive the ten minutes it takes to get to Sal's Diner.

Sal's Diner is an institution. Run by Kelly Adams, who—according to my dad—took over from her parents when they decided to retire. Shockingly enough, no one in the family is named Sal. The story goes that the family ran into a dog in the alley when they first moved here and decided to open the place. They took him to the vet and found out the dog's name was Sal, and he liked to wander the town. The Adams family decided that if he was a dog of the town, they should name the diner after him. The rest, as they say, is history.

Kelly and I went to school together. Hell, we practically grew up together, but after I moved away, I did the shitty thing and ignored any connections from Bluebell Falls. Aside from my parents, I didn't keep in touch with anyone, and the only information I got was from whatever gossip my dad got that week. I'm ashamed to say I didn't always do the best at keeping up with my parents, either. I'll be honest, I forgot a large amount of the people I grew up with. I remember some names, like Kelly's, but it's like I disassociated when I moved, and my brain forgot about the people I grew up with. I'm not sure what the general reception will be, but this is something I knew I would have to deal with when choosing to come back here.

Now, it's time to put my big-girl pants on and face the people of Bluebell Falls.

Walking into the diner is like walking out of the Tardis after traveling back in time and having an obscure adventure. Nothing has changed—not the chairs, not the booths, and not the menu board hanging from the ceiling. A wave of nostalgia runs through me, and a small smile tips up the edge of my lips.

A voice from behind the counter draws my attention. "Well, I'll be damned. I thought your papa was joking when he said you were back in town."

"Nope, here I am, in the flesh." I gesture down my body.

Kelly has changed a lot in the almost fifteen years since I've been back, but she's still rocking her ice-blonde hair in French braids and wearing the standard Sal's uniform of jeans and plaid shirt.

"Well, grab a seat, and I'll get you some food," she says like I didn't disappear for years.

"Actually, I was going to grab it to go. I've still got some work to get done, so I need to head back." I'm not sure why I feel embarrassed, but her genuine hospitality has me struggling with my decision from all those years ago to cut everyone out of my life. I feel uncomfortable in my own skin, and it gives me even more reason to get out of here quickly. That out-of-control feeling is swarming over me, and it's making my skin itch.

"Alrighty then, what'll it be?" Kelly asks, holding no animosity towards me.

"Umm, just a cheeseburger and fries please," I say and hand her some cash. I move to sit at a table off to the side to wait.

She nods as she turns around and puts the order in, giving me the opportunity to look around. It's fairly busy. Most of the tables and booths are filled, and I catch the occasional look as my eyes travel across the room. I've never felt quite as much of an outsider as I do right now. No one is outright giving me a dirty look. It's more curiosity than anything, but I can feel my anxiety ratchet up. That is, until my eyes catch onto the brightest blue eyes I've ever seen. They spark a vague recollection, but I can't seem to place them. The man behind the eyes is just as distracting. He's huge. Even sitting, I can tell he's well over six feet tall. I trail my gaze lower and see untidy scruff along his jaw, and his T-shirt, which barely contains his biceps.

He clears his throat, and my eyes dart back up to his. A sexy-as-hell smirk spans his face, and I can feel the blush taking over my own.

"Alright, cheeseburger and fries. I threw in some onion rings too since you used to live off of those." Kelly steps between me and the hottie. Thank God too because I definitely don't need to get involved with anyone right now. My life is enough of a mess, thank you very much. Even looking feels like too much at the moment.

And I'm not staying here. Right, there's that too.

"Thanks, Kelly." I give her a genuine smile.

She isn't lying. I think my primary food group for most of my adolescence were the onion rings here and pizza from Mullin's. I grab the bag from her hands, and speedwalk to the door.

The drive back is maddeningly quiet, and the smell of those damn onion rings is making my mouth water. I finally pull into my driveway and head inside. Sitting on my couch, I shove papers to the side of my coffee table and lay out the feast Kelly sent me home with.

I scarf down my food, hoping that if I'm able to jump back into work quickly, I can finish up my day early and start unpacking this hell hole so I'm not living in boxes.

I send my boss a quick update, letting him know what I accomplished this morning, before pulling up the ads I found on the drive. They are definitely basic, and it makes me wonder what he's using these for. It's not like you need real advertising in this town. Everyone knows who the best person for literally every job is. The company name, Bluebell Landscaping, gives me a lot to work with, so I run with that idea as I pull up pictures and fonts to play with.

I get so engrossed in making this ad eye-popping, that I don't realize how late it is until an internal message pops up from my email.

Ledger Hutton

> I noticed you're still logged in and just wanted to make sure you sign off shortly. You're already past a normal eight-hour day.

I read it twice, trying to decipher his tone. It doesn't seem like he's upset, and I get paid a salary so it's not like I'm getting overtime, but I can't tell if he's mad that I'm still working.

Ainsley Mathews:

> I was so engrossed with this ad, I didn't even realize what time it was. I apologize. Let me just finish this up really quick, and I'll send it your way and sign off.

Ledger Hutton:

> No need to apologize. I just didn't want you to get into the habit of working late.

What kind of boss is this? Are there really employers out there that don't want you working a shit ton of hours to get your work done?

Hello, small town job. We're not in the big city anymore.

Ainsley Mathews:

> Well, I appreciate that. I'll be sending this over in a minute.

I buckle down and finish what I was working on before sending it to my boss, then pop back over to the messaging system.

Ainsley Mathews:

> All finished and sent.

Ledger Hutton:

> Thank you. How do you feel the day went? Does sending an email in the morning work best for you?

Ainsley Mathews:

> It was perfect. I'm pretty flexible, so if you ever need to change things up, just let me know. And I'll be sure to tell you if I'm unable to get something done for the day.

This conversation is making me nervous. I'm used to the cutthroat world of finance, and no one would ever ask what works best for someone else. He seems genuine, but I can't completely trust it. My brain is screaming that it's a trap, and I don't know how to change my thought process.

Ledger Hutton:

> I'll take a look at all of this tonight, and I'll have an email waiting for you in the morning. Thanks for all the hard work today.

I shut my computer and stare blankly at it. I've never had a boss tell me to stop working. Granted, I actually got everything done, but it didn't seem like he cared if I did either way. Doing this entire job virtually is also strange. I could just as easily go into the office and work, so if things come up, I'm able to adapt as needed, but he was very firm that this stay virtual. He said it was because he was rarely in the office, always at job sites, so it didn't make sense to for me to come in if I could do the entire job from home. While it's nice, it's just not something I'm used to.

But you left that life behind, so you better start getting used to it. This is your life now.

Sighing, I lean back against my chair. I guess I should get to work unpacking some boxes. Dwelling on my first day of work won't really get me anywhere, so I might as well try to be productive. I need to give this job an actual chance because, at the moment, I don't have another option. I have a decent nest egg, but it's not enough to feel comfortable without employment for long.

Decision made, I get up and start unpacking the boxes I used as a makeshift desk today.

CHAPTER FOUR
LEDGER

Last night when I messaged Ainsley, I was so fucking awkward. I was trying to get her to see that I don't want nor expect her to work past her regular hours, no matter what is going on. I pride myself on taking care of my employees and making sure they feel appreciated. But my stilted conversation probably came across as too blunt.

Maybe I'm overthinking this. Hell, I know I'm overthinking this, but it's *Ainsley.*

It's been a long time since a woman caught my eye, and that's mostly due to my ex, who did a number on me. I haven't felt the need to be with anyone since her, so I'm very much rusty when it comes to talking to women. To top it off, Ainsley is the girl I crushed on hard in high school. I was two years older, but I always had my eye on her. When I moved away for college, I never quite forgot about her—an ever-present memory, keeping me company when I got lonely. Meeting Jenna in college was a whirlwind. Proposing felt like the right thing to do, what I was *supposed* to do. My plan was to go back home after graduation, and I was sucked into her spell, willing to change all of my plans for her. And it never quite broke until I caught her cheating on me in our bed, three days after I'd proposed.

Shaking my head to clear the memory, I climb out of bed and go to the kitchen to make a protein shake. I try to go for a run every morning—it helps clear my head and start the day fresh, ready to tackle anything that comes my way. Building my landscaping and nursery business from the ground up took a lot of work, and I knew pretty early on that I needed to branch out of Bluebell Falls if I wanted to make the business successful. Sure, all the residents know they can come to the nursery and get whatever they want for their botanical needs, but there aren't enough residents to sustain the business year-round. I've been slowly growing and advertising to the surrounding towns, but now it's time to think bigger.

It's one of the main reasons I put up the job listing for a virtual assistant. I needed someone to help keep me organized as I try to expand my business.

What I didn't expect was Ainsley Mathews to apply for the job. I didn't second-guess my decision; I hired her on the spot when we did the phone interview.

After looking at the ad she revamped, I know it was the best decision. She turned a boring, dry ad into something eye-catching and witty. It blew me away when I pulled it up last night. This job was intended to take care of mundane things, but seeing her work makes me want her to work her magic on all the advertising.

My phone rings as I make my way on my usual running route, and I answer it while putting my headphones in.

"What's up?" I ask.

"How's the new hire?" The smugness in my younger brother, Lennox's, voice immediately irritates me.

"Great. Why are you calling me?"

"Damn, Ledger, chill out. I was just curious." He barely holds in his laughter.

"Sure. Is that why our lovely sisters had you call me? Because they thought you could get more information out of me?"

His belly laugh makes me reluctantly smile.

"Willow and Marina should know better than that." I tsk at him.

Our parents had a unique theme while naming the four of us. They named us all after the places they conceived us. It's a fun fact I think the four of us could live without knowing, but our parents never let an embarrassing detail go to waste. My brother, Lennox, was the "oops" child, so they named him after the bar they were at before the deed was done. A fact the three of us tease him endlessly for. Although mine wasn't much better, on the ledge on the outskirts of town, overlooking the little valley we live in. I hold back the shiver that runs down my spine every time I think about it.

"They do, but you know they're nosey as hell. How is Ainsley, anyway? The rumor mill is buzzing in town about her. Old Man Walter was at the diner yesterday and is making up all sorts of shit."

"Of course, he is." I roll my eyes. Walter is known for telling tall tales and making up obscene stories. I think it's just because he gets bored and likes to stir the pot, but everyone is convinced he believes the baffling rumors he spreads.

"Ainsley is good. She's entirely more capable of this job than I anticipated, so I'm trying to come up with more things for her to do. Use her skills to benefit the company more."

"That's good. You know..."

"Nope. Don't even go there. I don't need your advice on women. Lord knows the ladies of this town have enough to say about you."

He chuckles. "You're too easy to rile up, man. Well, I'll see you at dinner tomorrow night."

He hangs up unceremoniously. It's not uncommon. We see each other almost daily, so the need for formalities isn't there.

I'm distracted thinking about how I'm going to navigate our weekly family dinner tomorrow when I run right into someone.

"Oh, shit. I'm sorry!" I grip the person's arms and pull them back to make sure they're okay.

Ainsley.

"Oh!" she squeaks.

"I'm so sorry. Are you okay?"

"Totally fine. I didn't realize there were more people that lived out here, so I wasn't paying attention."

"I'm about three miles that way." I point to my left. "And there is another house, over there, that's been empty for a while."

I'm not sure why I felt the need to tell her that.

"Well, that's good to know."

I realize I'm still gripping her arms, and I awkwardly let my hands drop and take a step back.

"I'm Ainsley, by the way." She holds out her hand, with a small smile on her face.

I panic. That's the only way I can describe it.

She clearly doesn't know who I am, and all my insecurities from when I was younger rear their ugly head.

"Dean. Nice to meet you, Ainsley. If you need anything, now you know where to find someone close."

Dean? Why the fuck did I give her my middle name?

There is seriously something wrong with me. How did I just revert back into a damn teenager around this woman?

"Well, I'm going to head back in now. I've got to start work soon." She takes a step back but not before I see her eyes trail down the length of my body.

A quick glance down tells me my athletic shorts aren't doing a great job of hiding anything, and my sweat-soaked shirt is clinging to my body.

I stand frozen as she turns around and heads back inside the house.

What the fuck is wrong with me?

As soon as her front door closes, I look at my watch and realize I need to race back home so I can send Ainsley her tasks for the day. I'll deal with my poor decisions later.

I make it back to my house with just enough time to spare to send Ainsley an email fifteen minutes before she starts working.

This day has been so hectic. I should have known it was going to be a shitshow when it started with telling Ainsley I was Dean, but I didn't realize that would set the tone for my entire day.

Two of my bigger jobs right now had major setbacks, and I had to explain the added timelines to the owners. Let's just say, both owners were not very happy with the added time on the project, but when a very specific plant they requested had to be special-ordered, we're at the mercy of the supplier.

The group text with all my siblings has been blowing up too, but I haven't even had time to check it. It's six at night, and I'm just now pulling into my garage. I'm starving, irritated, and just want to take a shower and crash into bed. Unfortunately, I need to check my emails and eat before I call it a day.

I love my job and my company, but some days, it takes its toll. When I started, I didn't have intentions of growing past our town and the few surrounding ones. I thought it would be enough for me. But as I've gotten older, my goals have changed. The nursery is already getting some regional attention, but I only started it to make it easier for me to supply the landscaping business. My goal now is to grow my business regionally too. I believe we're the best and, selfishly, I want to be recognized for that.

Tossing a frozen pizza in the oven, I plop down on the couch to open my laptop.

I stare at my email, confused. There are only a handful and all of them are potential new clients. My messaging system pops up in the corner, and I see a notification from Ainsley.

Ainsley Mathews:

> Finished up all the tasks for today. I took it upon myself to go through your emails a little more and answer questions that got sent to you if I could. I managed to get your email down to only new inquiries. If that isn't okay, let me know and I'll go back to marking things that need your attention as urgent. I also played around with a couple of new ads. I added them to the drive, so take a look when you have time.

I was not expecting her to go above and beyond, and take it upon herself to make some actual changes to my damn near-nonexistent system. I can already feel the stress lifting off of my shoulders. To come home and not have close to a hundred emails to go through every single day is a game-changer. I turn my focus back onto her message and realize she's still logged in.

Ledger Hutton:

> Are you still working?

Ainsley Mathews:

I'm just finishing up a little organization on the drive, then I'm calling it a night.

Ainsley Mathews:

Did I overstep by tackling your email?

I shake my head. My bluntness is making her think she did something wrong.

Ledger Hutton:

You didn't overstep. I think I'm more in shock that you managed to get my emails down so low.

Ainsley Mathews:

Most of the emails you get are people asking pretty straight-forward questions on their landscaping projects or about the nursery. It wasn't too complicated to answer them for you so you could focus on new clients.

Ledger Hutton:

Well, I appreciate it more than I can say. It was a pleasant surprise to come home and not have a million emails to go through.

Ainsley Mathews:

Perfect. Well, I'll keep that system going then.

Ledger Hutton:

I haven't had a chance to look at anything else yet, but I'll give you any feedback I have in the morning, if that's okay. You've already worked long past your workday.

Ainsley Mathews:

You're a real stickler for a traditional workday, huh?

Ledger Hutton:

It's more that I'm a fan of not overworking my employees. Nothing we do is life or death, so nothing about this job needs to be done right this second.

This is something I've always been passionate about. I told myself, when I first started my company, that I would never push my employees to the point of burnout. I wanted to build the company but not at the expense of my employees. Making sure everyone keeps a good work-life balance is important to me. I know Ainsley came from the world of finance, but the way I run things is drastically different. She'll eventually get used to the slower pace of small-town life.

Ainsley Mathews:

That's a new concept for me, so it might take me a minute to break my old habits.

Ledger Hutton:

As long as you don't mind me bugging you in the evenings while you're still on the clock.

Ainsley Mathews:

I think I can handle that. *wink*

This feels very close to flirting, but I'm sure it's all in my head. It's not like you can tell the tone from a bunch of text on the screen. I'm her boss. I know I'm not that lucky.

Ledger Hutton:

> Thanks for all your hard work today. I'll talk to you tomorrow.

I stare at my screen until I see the little circle by her name turn red, just as the timer on my oven dings. Putting my computer on the coffee table, I get up and get my dinner.

Even the thought of Ainsley flirting with me has my heart rate up. I know she wasn't actually flirting. I'm her boss, and she just got this job. I highly doubt she would jeopardize that with toying with me. It's just wishful thinking on my end. But I need to get my head on straight if I want to pursue her. I need to figure out why the hell I didn't tell her my first name when we ran into each other.

My old insecurities and old hurt from my failed engagement seem to haunt me. I thought I was past all of this, but my actions prove I'm not. The other thing I didn't anticipate was figuring out how to maneuver her working for me. I didn't second-guess hiring her because the thought of being in her orbit blinded me. Now, I'm not sure this is a line she would cross, even if my team and I wouldn't have a problem with it. Hell, a bunch of guys that create gardens sure as shit won't care about who I'm dating.

Maybe, if I just find a way to show her, we can separate the two.

I shove a slice of pizza in my mouth and contemplate just how to accomplish all of this.

CHAPTER FIVE
AINSLEY

I don't understand Ledger.

I've been on this job for two weeks now, and every time we talk through our work messenger, I can't figure him out. He's blunt and straight to the point, but there's something else there I can't figure out. The actual work has been smooth sailing. I'm slowly getting used to having a normal schedule, even if it's taken Ledger messaging me multiple times, telling me to stop working.

The bigger thing is I'm bored. I'm not used to a lighter work schedule, and I'm not super keen to go into town and socialize. I'm still very much in my reclusive stage of life, hiding away from everyone I turned my back on all those years ago. I haven't quite come to terms that this is my life now.

The one thing I'm thankful for is having my parents close. My dad may be the biggest gossip in town, but since the day I moved back, he's been subtly taking care of me: dropping off groceries at my front door, inviting me to go with him to his gin rummy group, and just checking in to make sure I'm okay. Outside of Larkin, I never had this kind of support in Austin. I built my life that way, though. I never relied on anyone, always took care of myself, and didn't let anyone in. Letting someone in meant they could hurt me, and I never wanted to sign myself up for that willingly.

I shake myself from my deep thoughts and take a sip of my coffee. It's Saturday, which means I don't get to distract myself with my job or binging Netflix, like I usually do at night. There are only so many shows to watch, and I'm cruising through them entirely too fast right now.

I was able to get my house unpacked last week, so now I guess I need to find a *hobby*. My lip curls up thinking about it. What is a hobby for a grown woman, anyway? Maybe I should get some adult coloring books with the inappropriate words and pictures. Tilting my head, I think about actually sitting down to color a book. *Nope, I can't picture it.*

I walk out the back door, and my eyes land on the beautiful patch of wildflowers. I wonder if I could work in my yard. Maybe start a garden. I mean, hell… I do work for a landscaper. It would make sense to utilize that connection, right?

I look around and spot the side yard that isn't growing much of anything right now. This would be a brilliant area for a vegetable and herb garden. I grab my phone from my pocket and pull up Larkin's number.

"Hey! How's small-town life treating you?" Her voice is like a balm to my unsettled heart.

"Oh, it's small." I chuckle. "But seriously, it's not so bad. I'm trying to find a hobby."

"A hobby," she deadpans.

"My boss makes me stop working at a regular time, and he won't let me work on the weekends, so I need something to do. There's literally only so many shows I can watch."

"I'm not going to lie. This is a weird problem to have."

"Right? I don't even know what to do with myself. It's so stupid. How can someone have too much time on their hands nowadays?"

"I have no clue, but I have a teenager and a two-year-old, so I don't know the meaning."

"How are those perfect nephew and niece of mine?" My heart aches thinking about how it's been nearly three weeks since I've seen them.

"Oh, you know, he's a raging ball of hormones who wants nothing to do with his parents right now. But he's doing great! And Maddie is full of attitude and independence. It's testing my patience to the fullest." The sarcasm in her voice makes me laugh.

"Do you need me to come down for the weekend? Do you and Theo need a break?" I ask seriously.

"We're doing fine, Ains, I promise. Would Gavin and Maddie love to see you? Honestly, I have no idea because he's in this 'too cool for shit' stage, but I bet he would be happy. And Maddie is honestly a toss-up. She may love to see you or completely ignore you. That's not to say we need you to come visit. Focus on your life and what you want from it, okay? Stop worrying about everyone else."

Hard truths from my sister.

"Okay. Tell Gavin to text me when he's on his game tonight, and I'll jump on and play with him."

"I will. And Ains?"

"Yeah?"

"Start a garden. The answer is always plants."

I laugh because my botanical-loving sister is right. I totally forgot that was the reason I called her in the first place.

"Great plan, Lark. Thanks." I hang up the phone with a giant smile on my face.

God, I miss them, but I know leaving was the right move. Now, I just need to figure out how to live my life the way I want to. How does one go about living the life they want to live? Do you just make a list of shit you want to happen in your life? Like, manifesting it? I have no clue.

I step off the porch and walk to the side of the house, inspecting the land. I could totally turn this into a garden. I'm not Larkin, so I don't exactly have a green thumb, but I could make a vegetable garden. How hard could it be?

Looks like it's time for a trip to Bluebell Falls Nursery to see what I can get to make this happen.

It takes me ten minutes to throw on some cutoff jean shorts and a tank top before driving over to the nursery. It's down the street from my house, and if I wasn't planning on getting a shit-ton of plants, I would have just walked here.

An overly cheery voice draws my attention. "Good morning! Can I help you find something in particular?"

A petite woman with bright blue eyes, tattoos over most of her exposed arms, and a wide smile walks toward me.

"Actually, that would be great. I'm trying to set up a vegetable garden, maybe some herbs too."

Her eyes remind me of someone, but I can't place them.

"Oh, that's fun! Follow me, and I'll show you what we have. If you are looking for something and we don't carry it, let me know, and I can get the boss to special-order it."

"Awesome." I give her a genuine smile.

"I'm Marina, but everyone calls me Rina. I just saw Old Man Walter walk in, and he's going to need some attention." She winks. "But I'll be back in a minute."

"I'll be fine, thank you." *Rina, Rina, Rina... Why does that sound so familiar?*

It's not a common name, and if she grew up here, there is a good chance I at least know of her, but I can't figure it out at the moment.

Strolling through the aisles, I find a ton of options. I pull a few plants aside and look around for a cart or wagon to start my collection.

"Need a hand?" a deep voice says.

I look up and see those same bright blue eyes that Rina has, and now I know why they looked familiar. *Dean.*

"Hey! If you happen to know where I can find a wagon, that would be great."

"I do indeed." He turns and heads to the back, and comes back a minute later. "Do you have a pile started?"

I nod to the makeshift pile of plants I made.

"Do you work here?" I ask, confused.

He hesitates, and I see ... a flash of guilt, maybe? It's gone too fast for me to decipher.

"I see you've met—"

I turn toward Rina, but she has her eyes on Dean. Confusion is written all over her face.

"Dean," he finishes for her.

I look between the two stuck in a silent conversation as they stare at each other.

"Umm, yeah. We're actually neighbors," I add, trying to defuse the sudden tension.

Rina crosses her arms over her chest and tilts her head to the side, lifting one eyebrow. "How interesting."

"Yep, very interesting. I was just helping her get a wagon for her plants," Dean adds.

"Uh huh." Rina stares so hard, I wouldn't be shocked if Dean reduced to ash at this point.

"So, I'm just going to grab some more plants. Thanks for the help." I sidestep them both and pull the wagon behind me as I head over to the lettuces.

That was strange, but I'm not trying to get in the middle of any drama. I would assume they are siblings, just based on their features, but I could be wrong. Maybe they are dating, and I have been drooling over a man that's actually taken. Honestly, with my luck, it wouldn't shock me at this point.

I hear them whispering on the other side of the aisle, so I move farther away. This is why being semi-reclusive is my jam right now. I hate getting involved in drama. I've never really had good friends in my life, so I don't know how to not be awkward. Larkin is used to my tough love and lack of filter, but everyone else just assumes I'm a bitch. It's just easier to avoid people and not let them see the squishy inside.

Soon, I forget all about the awkward encounter and am immersed in too many options for my garden. I'm debating the merits of different peppers when Rina steps up next to me.

"Sorry about all that. Are you finding everything you need?"

Guess we're just brushing over the entire conversation. Fine by me.

"Absolutely. I think I'm probably getting too much, but everything sounds so delicious. Now, the real challenge will be to keep everything alive." I let out a self-deprecating laughter.

"I'm sure you'll be fine. Now, let's get you set up with everything you need to actually plant all of this and get them thriving."

When all is said and done, my car is packed to the brim with plants and soil. Making the drive home, my mind turns to Dean again. Rina and he have to be siblings. There was definitely something else going on with the two of them, but I'm not sure I even want to know what it is. Curiosity has never boded well for me, and I don't plan on sticking my nose in anyone's business anytime soon.

Unloading my car doesn't take long, and when I'm done, I decide to save the actual planting for tomorrow. It's officially evening, and I have a video game date with my nephew.

"You really suck at this game."

"Language!" I laugh.

"Oh, please. You talk like a sailor. I'll make you put a dollar in the next time you're here."

When Gavin first came to Larkin because of a child protective services case, he was shy, compliant, and on his best behavior. It didn't take long for him to come out of his shell, though, and I'd like to think I had a little influence on it. Lord knows Larkin blames me for some of his language habits, which is why it's become a running joke with us. He's less of a stickler on the Curse Word Jar now, but it still pops up now and then.

"I think I should pick the game next time we play," I say into my headphones as I try to shoot make-believe bad guys. Apparently, my video game aim is shit, but if it means I get a little time with Gavin, I'll do whatever he wants.

"Yeah, not happening. You'll pick some dress-up game or something equally as horrible."

I snort out a laugh at his assumption.

"When have I ever been the girly one? If I remember right, you used to dress up like that character from the book series you loved so much. I have some good blackmail pictures whenever you get a girlfriend, so she knows exactly what she's getting into."

He chuckles, and his voice cracks a little when he talks, "Do your worst, Auntie Ains."

My heart clenches tight in my chest when he uses the nickname he used to call me when he was a little younger. *God, I miss this boy.*

"So, how is Bluebell Falls?" he asks.

"It's ... okay." I sigh.

"Just okay?"

"Just okay, little man. My job is pretty good though, so that's a win." It's taken me a while to get used to the fact that Gavin is growing up, but he's been through a lot, so it's not shocking that he's more mature than your average thirteen-year-old.

"Mom says you're trying to plant a garden. She said some less than savory things about your skills."

In the background, I hear my sister say, "I did not say that, Gavin! Geez, who's side are you on, anyway?"

I burst out laughing. "Tell her you're on mine, always."

"Hel— Heck no. I'm not telling her that. Do you want me to be grounded?" His serious tone makes me laugh again.

"Fair point. So, how's school?"

"It's ... okay."

I smile at his repeat of my answer. "What's going on?"

"I don't know. High school is so drama-filled. Like, who is dating the sports star and who is going to be class president. I just want to get through high school and move onto real life. I hate all the cliques."

"Same, Gav, same."

"I just don't understand how kids think high school is the best it gets, ya know? Like, there is so much out there to explore and see, and they all think high school is, like, the peak of their lives."

"Yup, I do know. I couldn't wait to be done with high school. I couldn't wait to leave this small town."

"But you went back," he observes.

"But I went back. Sometimes, the best laid plans don't always pan out, and you have to roll with the punches."

"Are you happy, Auntie Ains?"

My heart thumps in my chest and I rub it, trying to ease the intense insecurity that comes with his question.

"I'm trying to be," I whisper.

"I think trying to be happy is just a way to say you haven't figured out what you want in life. Dad always says it's okay to not have a plan but to always make an effort to be the kind of person you want to be. Even if you aren't where you want to be in life, being nice costs nothing."

"You have a wise dad, Gav." His words burrow themselves into my brain. I've been so caught up in what has blown up in my life, that I stopped being who I wanted to be.

Who do I want to be?

I always thought getting a good job and climbing the corporate ladder was what you were supposed to do. Eventually, I would have time to live outside of work, right? I could maybe settle down with a man. I never really thought about having kids, but they could be in the mix too, I guess. Being back in Bluebell Falls makes me see how messed up that way of thinking is.

I may not be one-hundred-percent happy here, but I already have a better work-life balance than I've had in over a decade.

"Well, Mom is giving me the 'it's past your bedtime, and you're about to be in trouble' look, so I've got to go. Can we play again next weekend?"

"We can play whenever you want to, Gav."

"Thanks, Aunt Ains. You know, you can always text me and talk if you need to," he says in his far-too-serious-for-his-age tone.

"I do. The same goes for you, bud. I'll talk to you later."

He signs out, and my eyes fill with tears. How is a thirteen-year-old my moral support right now? And how is he the best human ever, outside of his parents?

His words swirl around in my head. *Make an effort to be who I want to be.* Maybe it's time to embrace small-town living and figure out what I really want with my *life*.

CHAPTER SIX
LEDGER

Yesterday was a mess. Running into Ainsley at the nursery while my sister was working? Absolute shitshow. And Rina glared daggers at me the entire day after our awkward interaction, where I stuck to the name Dean.

What is wrong with me?

The answer is I have no fucking clue.

I want to be the guy I thought I was—the one who isn't the shy, gangly teenager without the balls to go for what he wants. But giving Ainsley my middle name and not coming clean sure feels like I'm back in high school. My thoughts turn back to the embarrassment that was high school for me.

Ainsley walks through the front doors, and it's like one of those movies where all the spotlights are on her. I've watched her all year, and she's mostly kept to herself.

It's not like she remembers me, anyway. If she had, she would have called me on my bullshit immediately.

So why am I so hesitant to tell her who I really am?

It can't be just because she works for me. She's virtual, and we don't see each other daily—just messages here and there throughout the day.

My phone dings on the coffee table.

Rina:

> So, you guys will never guess what our dumbass eldest brother did yesterday.

Fuck. They knew about my high-school crush on her and haven't let me live it down now that I hired her.

Lennox:

> Oh, this I gotta hear.

Me:

> What the hell, Rina?

Willow:

> Well, share the gossip. It's not often our good-ie-two-shoes brother has some dirt on him.

Rina:

> Ainsley came by the nursery yesterday to pick up some stuff, and Ledg walks out from the back and interrupts me from introducing him to say his name is *Dean*.

I shove my hand through my hair and sigh. I'm about to get lit up, and it's my own damn fault.

Lennox:

> OH MY FUCKING GOD! Seriously? She thinks your name is Dean???

Willow:

> Oh, Ledg, what were you thinking?

Me:

Clearly, I wasn't.

Rina:

Yes, dear brother, you weren't. Why the secrecy
about who you are?

Lennox:

I'm going to start calling you Dean the Machine.

Me:

We can kick him out of the group chat, right?

Rina:

Nope. You make stupid decisions. You deserve
to have his immaturity directed at you.

Me:

Fine.

Willow:

Well?

Me:

Well, when I first ran into her, I panicked. It was a
knee-jerk reaction, and now… I don't know how
to get out of panic mode.

Lennox:

Definitely can't call you Dean the Machine now.
That's just sad. Maybe Dean the Teen.

Me:

Seriously, we can't kick him out?

Rina:

Nope. If she doesn't remember you, why are you panicking? You could start fresh with her, and she wouldn't even know the difference because she *doesn't remember you.*

Willow:

You need to just come clean. The longer you let the charade go on, the worse it will be.

Me:

I know…

And I do know. But the fear of rejection has me paralyzed.

Willow:

What's going on, big bro?

God love Willow. She's the gentle soul in our family and always the one to go to for advice.

I take a deep breath and go for broke. The other two will give me a ton of shit, but if Willow has any advice, I'll take it.

Me:

What if she rejects me? What if she magically remembers who I am and decides I'm not worth the time?

I cringe at my message. I sound like I'm still in high school. Maybe Lennox *should* call me Dean the Teen.

Here are my thoughts: If she's going to reject
you, she'll do it regardless of your name. And
if she somehow remembers you—which I doubt
she will since she's been working with you for a
couple of weeks now and hasn't connected anything—and decides you aren't worth the time
because of who you were in high school, then
she isn't the woman for you. If you genuinely like
her for who she is now, then you need to give
her and yourself the chance to see if she likes
you for who you are now too. There isn't a point
dwelling on who you were almost two decades
ago. You both aren't the same people.

Willow, ladies and gentlemen.

I stare at her words, and I know she's right. It's just hard to get out of
that mindset. Not to mention, I haven't dated or pursued anyone since
my ex, so I'm rusty as hell at all of this.

Willow with the mic drop. I second everything
she said.

I disagree. You're definitely the same as you
were in high school.

Shut up, Lenny. The only one who is the same as
they were in high school is you.

Oh, good one, sis. *eye roll emoji*

I laugh at their banter. The four of us couldn't be more different, but we've always had a strong bond. When I opened up the nursery, they all chipped in taking shifts so I could save money and hold off on hiring anyone for a while. They still do work periodically, refusing to get paid for the time, but they all have careers for themselves now. I think they still do it because they actually like the nursery, contrary to what they've told me for years. I've slowly turned everyone into plant lovers.

Me:

Well, this was eye-opening and annoying, all at the same time. Willow, thanks for the advice.

I put my phone down on the table and sit back on my couch, staring at a picture of the four of us at Lennox's high school graduation. Willow gave me some good things to think about. The biggest thing I'm stuck on is that Ainsley and I really don't know each other. Sure, I had a crush on her in high school, but we're both completely different people now. My crush on her may have stuck around, but I don't truly know the Ainsley she is now.

Going for a run is the best way to work out my thoughts, so I get changed and head out on my usual route. It's a good loop around town, roughly five miles, and makes for a challenging-enough pace. If I'm feeling particularly stressed, I do it twice. Bluebell Falls is unique because although it is a small town and you can easily walk to places if you need to, the actual houses are spread out. It gives an air of privacy when you're at home, instead of feeling like your nosey neighbors are on top of you. Now, if you go into the town center, it's a different story. Everything you do in the town center is everyone's business. It's the main reason I kept our parent's house. The land has plenty of room for adding the nursery, and it helped keep our little family away from the town's eye while we figured out our new normal. Bluebell Falls Nursery is on the far end of my land, and my house is on the opposite. There is plenty of distance so that I can't see the nursery from my house, but I'm able to get there in a matter of minutes if I'm needed.

The run clears my head a little, and the main point that sticks with me is that adult Ainsley and I don't know each other. We've had a couple of conversations but nothing all that deep. So, my plan of attack is to learn more about her. If that's at work through our messages, awesome. If that's when I run into her in town, also great. The whole Dean/Ledger thing is still heavy on my mind. Being Dean and having no connection to Ledger feels safer. Like I get a clean slate when it comes to Ainsley. It might be a mistake, but I like the anonymity for the time being. And when—if—the time comes to come clean, then I will deal with it when it comes.

I'm at the end of the loop and just about to hit Ainsley's house when I see her in her side yard. I slow down and watch her haul bags of soil on her shoulder.

"Need some help?" I call out.

She startles, dropping the bag she was carrying, and I instantly feel like a dick.

"Oh! Hey, Dean. That would be great, actually."

I jog over and grab two bags. "Where to?"

"Well, I'm trying to turn this whole side into a vegetable garden, so I was attempting to disperse the soil all the way down." She tilts her head and gnaws on her lip in thought.

I'd like to nibble on that lip instead.

No, nope. I'm here to help her, not drool over her delectable body in cutoff jeans and a blue tank top.

"Are you just putting the soil straight on the ground?" I ask.

"Umm, yeah?"

I shake my head. She's just winging this whole thing. It's kind of adorable, but it's making my landscaping heart cringe.

"I'm going to run to the nursery really quickly and grab some supplies. Don't put any of the soil down yet, but if you want to organize the plants how you want them and loosen them from their containers, we can probably get this done in a couple of hours when I get back." I'm in full work mode now. If she wants a garden, I'll be damned if it isn't perfect.

"You don't have to do all of that, Dean," she says quietly, and I barely conceal the flinch at my name.

"But I want to." I hope the sincerity is written all over my face. I'd do a hell of a lot more, but at least this project will give us a couple of hours together. This gives me the opportunity to see who she is now, and I can't fucking wait.

"I'll be right back." I turn and start jogging toward the nursery.

It takes me twenty minutes to grab all the supplies I need. I'm not sure what tools she has, so I bring everything, just in case. Realizing that walking back to her place isn't going to happen, I grab my truck to load everything in the bed. I'm back in front of Ainsley's small bungalow in no time.

"That was fast," she calls out as she makes her way to the truck.

"Good thing about small towns. It doesn't take long to get from point A to point B." I grin.

"Ain't that the truth."

When we have everything unloaded, I walk around the space, visualizing the garden and how to make it the most efficient.

"This is the perfect place to grow some vegetables."

"Yeah?" she asks as her eyes light up.

"Oh, yeah. Good sun and shade, and some decent protection because of the house."

"My sister has the green thumb. I do not, so I'm just hoping I don't kill everything within two weeks." She smiles.

I'll come over every day to take care of this garden if it puts a smile on her face.

Woah, got a little ahead of myself there.

"I think you'll surprise yourself."

She claps her hands suddenly, and I see a slight blush on her cheeks. "Alright, let's make me a garden."

We get the space cleared and lay down the landscaping fabric before she steps back and looks at the space.

"I can't believe we got all this done so fast. Also, thank you for knowing what you're doing because I would have never done any of this."

"No worries. I enjoy this stuff." I shrug.

"My new boss owns a landscaping business. I probably should have asked him about some tips, but this was a little impromptu and he's a stickler for not working on the weekends."

I'm a stickler for *her* not working on the weekends.

"How long have you been in town?" I ask while I grab some plants and start placing them where it makes the most sense. I already know the answer, but I'm trying to take Willow's advice to heart.

"Just a couple of weeks. I used to live here, and then I moved away for college and never came back."

"What brought you back, then?" Now, this I am curious about. I remember talking to her dad about her once, a while ago, and he was adamant she would never be coming back to live here. I think a little corner of my heart cracked off hearing that.

Her shoulders stiffen, and I immediately feel like an ass for prying.

"I got screwed over at my job and couldn't work in my field in Austin anymore. It made the most sense to come back here to try to figure things out."

"Do you miss it? Austin?"

She stands up after dropping a couple of zucchini plants on the ground. She tilts her head to the side like she's thinking.

"I thought I would," she says, barely above a whisper. "But outside of a little boredom, I don't think I do. I was in a very fast-paced position, barely had enough time for a life outside of work, and had no real friends. I had my sister, her family, and my job. It was ... kind of sad." Her tone is melancholy. She clears her throat, burying any emotion that was threatening to come out. "So, what do you do?"

Shit.

I blink at her as my brain scrambles to come up with something.

Lennox's job pops into my head, and I run with it. "Umm, I'm a wildlife specialist and Park Ranger."

"What exactly does that mean? Do you just play with animals all day?"

I try to remember what Lennox does all day, and the only thing I can think of is him hiking in the state park next to our town and documenting the animals he finds.

"It's a little of everything, actually. I do a lot of record keeping on the animals in the surrounding areas and help the larger landowners with any wildlife management ." Close enough.

I hold my breath, hoping she doesn't ask for any specifics because I have none to give.

"That's cool. I've never heard of that before."

"It keeps me active."

It keeps me active? What the hell am I saying right now?

"I bet it does." Her eyes travel down to the sweat-soaked shirt clinging to my abs.

The corner of my mouth tips up in a smirk. So, she's not entirely unaffected.

"So, you ready to plant these?" I ask, and her eyes snap up to mine. A deep blush covers the bridge of her nose and cheeks, and I've never seen something so innocent and attractive at the same time.

"Yep, let's do this."

It takes us another hour to plant everything. When we're done, Ainsley steps back, admiring our work.

"I can't believe I actually have a garden. Thank you so much for helping me. I don't think I would have been able to do all of this by myself, let alone properly."

"You would have figured it out."

She steps closer and wraps me in a tight hug. I freeze, not knowing how to react. It's a hug of thanks—I know that, logically—but my body hasn't gotten the memo.

She abruptly pulls back. "I'm sorry."

"Nothing to apologize for. You just caught me off guard."

We stare at each other for a minute, and I can feel the tension snapping tight between us.

"Well, I should probably go grab a shower before I head over to my parents," she says, breaking the spell. "Thanks again, Dean."

She turns on her heel and heads inside.

I stand rooted in my spot, wondering how the hell I'm going to get out of this bind I put myself in.

CHAPTER SEVEN
AINSLEY

A sweat-soaked, generously helpful Dean is a dangerous Dean.

I was fully prepared to fumble my way through creating my garden, but I have to say, having his help was a welcome surprise. Seeing his muscled body through his thin shirt was no hardship, either.

I shake my head to clear my thoughts.

I'm supposed to be going to my parents' house for dinner, but I feel like I need to talk to someone before I go so I don't accidentally let my small crush on Dean slip to my dad. Lord knows he would make it his personal mission to hook us up, and that's the last thing I need right now.

I grab my phone and send a text to Larkin.

Me:

So, I need you to talk me out of my crush.

Larkin:

Crush? Who?

Me:

Dean. I don't know his last name. This hot guy I've run into a few times. He's like … drop-dead gorgeous. Dark hair, a little longer on the top. Bright blue eyes and a little dimple on his chin. And he's super tall.

Larkin:

Okay. Why do I need to talk you out of it?

Me:

Because my life is a shitshow, and I definitely don't need to be crushing on a man right now.

Larkin:

What if you just use this as an opportunity to get laid? Release some stress and take advantage of the situation presenting itself.

Larkin used to be a party girl until she gave Theo a chance, but that's a whole other story. When she wasn't with him, she had regular hook-ups and unapologetically left them as her booty calls. I've never judged her for the way she lived her life. If anything, I was jealous of how secure she was. My finance job didn't leave time for me to sow my wild oats, though. Vibrators have done me well so far in life, so I figured I'd just keep my routine going. But Dean is making me question things.

Me:

I don't think I can hook up with him. Hell, he may not even want that.

Larkin:

What's holding you back from 1) asking him, and 2) actually hooking up with him?

Me:

I don't have a suitable answer except that I'm a chickenshit and scared of fucking up my life even more.

Larkin:

A reasonable fear. You know, you don't have to decide right this second. You can take your time getting to know him and go from there. There is no right answer.

Me:

But logically, I'm not here to find a man. I'm here to get my life back on track. Hell, I don't even know if I'm staying here permanently, so what would be the point of getting to know him better if I don't stay?

Larkin:

There are a lot of what-ifs in there for just a crush. I think not focusing on the big picture might be good for you. You don't need to have all the answers right now, Ains. You just went through terrible shit at your old job. It's okay to just be in limbo and take the time to really think about what you want. If it's this Dean guy, awesome, if it's not, then that's okay too. It's okay to live a little and let loose.

I know she's right, but knowing it and doing it are two very different things.

Larkin:

Tough love: I think you're overthinking everything. This is your chance to really buckle down and find what makes you happy. Find your passion and do what you love. You're getting a second chance to live life the way you want to, and that's such a rare thing these days. Don't get stuck on what you *should* be doing. Do whatever you actually want to do. You know Mom, Dad, Theo, and I will support you, no matter what you do.

Sometimes I forget my sister is a social worker, but times like these make it clear she's in the right profession.

Me:

I hear you. I really do. *How* do I figure this all out? How do I figure out what I want to do? I'm in my thirties. It's not like I can go to the school counselor and do an aptitude test.

Larkin:

Write a list of things that you have loved to do at your job and things you hated. Send it to me, and we'll go through each point and brainstorm ways you can turn that into a career, or at the very least, something to look into.

Me:

You are the best sister a girl could ever ask for, you know?

Larkin:

I know. You're extremely lucky to have a built-in mastermind who figures out all the things and is superior in all the ways.

Laughter bursts free from me. She's being sarcastic, but she's not wrong. Larkin is one of the best people I know, and not because she's my sister. She would do anything for the people she loves, and she's proven that time and time again.

Me:

You were doing really good until then. The sarcasm just forces itself out, huh?

Larkin:

It's like a default setting, I swear. I'm just glad I have you and Theo to let it out on because I'm pretty sure I would have been fired from my job years ago if I told parents what I really thought of them.

Me:

Too true. Well, I have to get ready for dinner at the 'rents, but thanks for the pep talk.

Larkin:

Anytime, you know that. Seriously though, send me a list!

Me:

I will, love you!

Larkin:

Love you too. Tell Mom and Dad hi.

How our conversation turned into a soul-searching mission, I'm not sure, but she made some excellent points. It's something to think about, but right now, I need to take a quick shower and change before heading over to my parents' house.

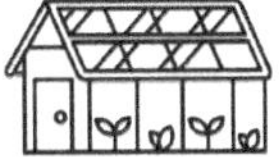

Less than a ten-minute drive later, I'm pulling into the same house Larkin and I grew up in. Nothing has changed in the almost two decades since either of us has lived here, but the nostalgia brings me back to a time when I was hopeful for my future. I want to feel like that again.

"Annie!" my dad calls as I climb out of my car.

"Hey, Dad. Long time, no see." I give him a smirk.

"I heard you were busy planting a garden today," he says as he pulls me in for a bear hug. It's one of those comforts you never realized you missed until you get one again.

"Oh yeah? And who told you that?"

"I never name my sources, honey." He *tsks* me.

I pull back from his hug and attempt to hide my chuckle. He takes his job as the town gossip seriously.

"Leave the poor woman alone, Jim," my mom calls from the front porch.

"Thanks, Mom. The harassment never ends with this one." I jab my thumb over my shoulder as I walk to hug my mom.

"You know him, dear. Retirement created too much boredom, so now he's in everyone's business. Come in. I was just finishing up the salad."

As I walk into the house, I take a deep breath of nostalgia. Growing up here, Larkin and I couldn't wait to get away. Now, it feels like more than just coming home. It feels like a blanket wrapped around you on a sick day, being spoon-fed chicken noodle soup, and watching Saturday morning cartoons. It's amazing how much your view changes as you grow up and mature. I don't particularly feel like I've grown up all that much, but being here makes me sad that I didn't make an effort to visit more often.

"Smells good, Mom," I tell her with a smile.

She beams at the praise. "I thought I'd make one of your favorites—chicken fried steak."

I immediately start salivating. I love to cook, but there are just some things you can't replicate, like her gravy for chicken fried steak. I've never been able to make it as well as my mom, and I've tried at least a hundred times.

Helping her finish the salad, I grab it and help bring all the dishes to the dining room table.

"So, how's it going working for the Hutton boy?" my dad asks.

I have to laugh at him calling my boss a boy. I don't know exactly how old he is, but he has to be at least around my age. I highly doubt there is anything boyish about him.

"It's pretty good, actually. I wasn't sure what to expect, but everything's been smooth sailing, and he's a stickler for not working overtime. Even if I'm just finishing up something, he messages me to just work on it tomorrow. It's very different from finance."

"He's a good boy, that one. Has a lot of responsibility on his shoulders, but he does a damn fine job."

I nod, a little confused, but it's not my job to know my boss's entire life story.

My dad starts talking about all the things he's heard in the last few days, and I start to tune him out. It's not that I don't love him—I do—but I'm just not into all the drama. I remember how hard it was to have privacy in high school, and I hated it. We couldn't take a step without my dad knowing about it.

We dive into the delicious dinner, and my mind starts to wander.

Ledger is sweet, and he's a good boss. He tells me almost every evening to stop working, and despite me having a hard time remembering that, he never gets annoyed or angry. In fact, he's gone out of his way to be nice about it.

My thoughts drift to Dean and an image of him—sweaty shirt sticking to his insanely built body as he practically built the entire garden himself. I never asked if he worked at the nursery as well as being a wildlife ... whatever it was. I just assumed he did by his knowledge and the way Rina talked to him. There was a weird dynamic between the two of them. I wonder if I could ask Ledger about him and see if he's single.

No, that's weird to ask your boss about another employee.

But if there was a way to find out more about him, I would jump on it. Maybe I should make my presence known in town. Quit hiding from everyone and see what kind of information I can find out.

"Have you talked to your sister lately?" My dad's voice pulls me from my thoughts.

"Yeah, I actually just talked to her before coming over."

"How's she doing? How are Gavin, Maddie, and Theo?"

I hear the twinge of sadness in my dad's voice when he talks about Gavin and Maddie. They would love to see them more, but traveling is hard for them with my mom's medical problems. She can't be in a car for very long because of vertigo, and an airplane is out because there isn't one close enough that actually shortens the trip for them.

"They're good. Gavin's growing up too fast and acts like more of an adult than I do." I chuckle.

"What about you? How are you doing?"

"I'm..." I think about my conversation with Larkin and try to be honest with myself. "I think I'm doing okay, actually. I didn't know what to expect with the job and moving back, but so far, it's been pretty good."

"It's really nice to have you back here, Annie. I know this isn't how you imagined things going, but we love having one of you girls back home."

Guilt wraps around my heart. It's not that I've ignored my parents, it's just that I got hung up on what my life was supposed to look like. Then my job became endless hours of work and barely any time to see my sister and her family, let alone driving the few hours to see my parents. It's a shitty excuse. I'm seeing that now, but it's what I thought I had to do to get ahead.

My dad continues talking, but I'm zoned out. Comparing my life before the move to my life now is eye-opening. I never realized how much my job in Austin sucked from me. I was a shell of a person, just doing their bidding and praying it was enough to climb the ladder.

Here, it's a slower pace of life. Although it's been hard for me to adjust to it, I feel calmer than I have in years. My anxiety has lessened, and my self-diagnosed ADHD has been a little more manageable. I'm not drinking coffee by the gallon and feeling heart palpitations halfway through the day. I'm not pulling all-nighters and then spending my weekend sleeping because my body can't handle them anymore, but unrealistic expectations and deadlines were the name of the game.

God, why did I put up with that shit?

Because it was what they drilled into our heads. If we didn't comply, if we didn't finish the next impossible task, our careers were over.

It's such a crock of shit. Ledger told me the other day that nothing we do is life and death, so there's no need to work ourselves to the bone. It hit home in a way I wasn't expecting. My job in Austin wasn't life or death; nothing we did had an immediate bearing on someone's physical life, yet we treated it as such. No wonder the stress was at a constant high. No wonder you see people having heart attacks at a young age in the finance field. It's physically unsustainable. Ledger's easy words opened my eyes to everything wrong with my last job.

Even if I don't stay on with Bluebell Falls Landscaping, I think those words will live on in my head.

CHAPTER EIGHT
LEDGER

Working with Ainsley for most of the day was the ultimate test in patience. She looked so fucking sexy in those cutoff jean shorts, that every time she bent over, all I could think about was stripping them off of her.

Needless to say, I'm racing home so I can jump in the shower and take care of my raging hard-on.

I pull into my driveway and barely get the truck door closed before running into the house. I strip as I go, fully naked by the time I reach my bathroom. Turning on the water, I wait for it to warm up. I lean against the counter, gripping my base hard. The image of Ainsley's strawberry blonde hair laid out on my bed has me harder than stone.

The shower finally starts to steam, so I rip open the door and rest my forehead on the tile as I go back to my fantasy.

I'd strip her down nice and slowly. Peel every inch of fabric off her body as she squirmed beneath my fingertips. I'd tease her for distracting me all day. Take my time circling each of her diamond-hard nipples before trailing lower. I'd put just enough pressure on her clit to get a little relief but not enough to get her off.

The hand on my cock moves faster, swirling the precum that's dripping from my head down my length. *Fuck, I bet she feels amazing.*

I want to hear her whimper for me, beg me for more. I want my name on her lips as I circle her clit in the way she needs me to in order to come.

I want to learn what she likes, learn what turns her on, and explore any fantasy she has.

My hips start thrusting as I squeeze a little tighter. I'm already so close, but I'm forcing myself to live in this false reality a little longer.

The need to hear her beg for my cock, to see her spread open and dripping for me, makes the pressure at the base of my spine ratchet up. I imagine lining myself up with her needy pussy and pushing in, hearing her gasp of pleasure. It's the image that finally takes me over the edge. I come against the tiles in my shower, watching as it goes down the drain.

It's anti-climactic. Sure, it took the edge off, but I'm not truly satiated. I want to see what she really looks like underneath me. I sag against the tile, worn out from working and keeping myself in check all day.

Dragging my tired ass out of the shower after washing up, I dry off before collapsing on my bed.

I need to figure out how to tell Ainsley who I really am. Every time I try, I panic and dig myself further into the hole I've created. I know the longer I wait, the worse it will be, but for the life of me, that fact doesn't register when I'm in her vicinity.

Today was exactly what I wanted. I got to learn more about her; we worked well together and talked about everything under the sun. My crush has turned into a full-blown infatuation. Now, I just need to pull up my big-boy pants and tell her the truth.

Sunday night dinners have been a tradition in our family for as long as I can remember. When we were young, my mom would rotate whose favorite meal she cooked, and it was a day we all looked forward to every week.

I've upheld that tradition ever since our parents passed away.

In my senior year in college, everything changed for our family. Rina was in college by then, Lennox was in eighth grade, and Willow was a junior in high school. Our parents wanted to finally take a vacation for themselves, so Rina came home to watch the kids while our parents took their first trip in far too many years. They were going to drive to the beach and relax. They barely got an hour away before a guy T-boned them going sixty-five.

It changed the course of all our lives. I was only a couple weeks away from graduating, and although I had plans to stay in the big city, grow my business, and marry Jenna, I had to go home to take care of my family. I've never regretted it, and catching Jenna cheating was a blessing in disguise. I did the best I could to help Willow and Lennox finish school, but I still worry about them. Especially Lennox. He still acts like a teenager sometimes, and I worry I've messed him up somewhere along the way.

The front door bangs open as I hear my siblings' chatter.

"I swear, if you put a hole in the drywall again with the doorhandle, I'm not making ribs ever again," I yell out to Lennox. He's like a bull in a China shop, and I know he's the one who threw the door open.

"You made ribs?" He pops his head into the kitchen.

"Had I known you were going to bust up my fucking wall again, I would have made that salad you hate."

"The strawberry one?" Willow asks with a smirk.

"Please stop putting fucking fruit in salads. I beg you. It's like a crime against food," Lennox whines.

"You are so dramatic. What do you need help with, big bro?" Rina asks.

"The ribs are resting, but you could throw together the potato salad." Rina has always been the one I've turned to when I needed help. We're only fifteen months apart, so we've always been close, but she helped raise Willow and Lennox when it all felt like too much for me.

"Have I mentioned you're the best brother ever, and I will come over here tomorrow and fix the dent in the drywall?" Lennox asks.

"You seriously dented it again? I was just giving you shit, but damn, Lenny." I shake my head.

"I know. I'm sorry." He cringes.

He walks over to the fridge and pulls out two beers, handing me one as he cracks his. I open mine and take a sip as I watch my family come together to share a meal.

This has always been my favorite time of the week. I love my job, but seeing my adult siblings still come together for a family meal always fills me with pride.

Willow starts bringing food to the table as Rina finishes the potato salad. Lennox does the table settings, and we all sit down. Part of doing this every week was to do a sort of check-in. We would always go around and say our favorite thing about the week. It was also a time when we would talk about any issues we had with each other. Our teen years weren't a walk in the park, so we had a ton of petty fights, and Sunday dinner was our time to talk it out and move on.

"Alright, who's starting today?" I ask.

"I'll do it," Rina says with a twinkle in her eye. "My favorite part of this week was witnessing our good brother make an absolute fool of himself in front of his high school crush."

"Wonderful. Glad I could provide entertainment." I roll my eyes.

"Mine was seeing the birth of twin fawns on Thursday," Lennox says as if it's everyday life. I mean, it kind of is for him, but it's still amazing.

"How did you manage not to scare the mom?" Willow asks.

"I know I'm loud as shit, normally, but it's different in the park. You never know what you're going to walk up on, so I pride myself on being slow and quiet. I was just walking the trail, trying to find this family of racoons I stumbled upon earlier in the week, when I heard the grunts of the birthing doe. I watched the whole thing from a log about thirty feet away. It was fucking amazing," he says in awe.

"Did you name them?" Rina chimes in.

Lennox scoffs. "Of course I named them. Marco and Polo."

I stare at him, amazed he's serious.

"We should really have a naming committee. Your names are getting worse and worse, I swear." Rina shakes her head as she starts plating up food.

"They're great names. You don't have to admit it." His smile is smug, and I hide my own behind my hand. I'll never admit this to him, but he's funny as hell, especially when he's not trying to be.

"Okay, Willow, you're next," I say.

"I think mine was killing off Daryl in my latest book." She smiles sweetly.

Oh yeah. Willow, the sweet and ultra nice one in the family, is an author, who writes primarily thrillers.

"Wasn't he the sweet old neighbor in the book?" Rina asks, tilting her head.

"Yeah. He found out my main character was murdering people, so he had to go." She shrugs like it's just another day in the office, and for her, I guess it is.

I let out a chuckle at her nonchalant attitude towards killing off a random guy in her story and continue to eat my food.

"And what about you, Ledger?" Willow asks.

"Mine was getting my emails down to next to nothing, thanks to Ainsley. She's taken on answering all the little tedious questions I get daily and just left me with new job inquiries."

"Damn, good for her." Rina's eyebrows shoot up in shock.

"I know. It surprised me too. I knew she would be good, but I had no idea she'd be this good."

"And does she know who you really are now?" Willow adds.

I shove a huge bite of potato salad in my mouth to avoid answering the question.

"Oh, Ledg," Willow says, with nothing but pity in her voice.

Lennox starts laughing. "Oh man, and you guys think I'm the fuck-up."

"We don't think you're a fuck-up. You're just immature as hell. There's a difference," I tell him.

"Whatever. At least I don't tell the woman I've been crushing on since I was seventeen my middle name instead of my *actual* name. You know, you could have just flat asked her on a date and seen how things went."

"Wow, I had no idea. Thanks for all your infinite wisdom," I deadpan.

"When are you going to tell her?" Willow asks, ignoring Lennox.

"Soon. Maybe... I don't know."

All three of them stare at me like I've officially lost my head, and hell, maybe I have.

"If you really want a chance with her, don't wait too long. You're a catch, Ledg, and any woman would be lucky to be with you," Rina says quietly.

I can feel the back of my neck heat with embarrassment. I'm the oldest—it's usually me who's taking care of them. This shift in our dynamic is hard to adjust to, but I'm also extremely proud of the adults all three of them have become.

I nod my head to acknowledge her words.

They're completely right. The problem is, I'm not sure how to dig myself out of this hole while still having Ainsley give me a chance. It feels impossible. But I know the longer I keep the truth to myself, the less likely I am to have a chance with her.

This week. I'll figure out a way to tell her who I am this week.

CHAPTER NINE
AINSLEY

Can I just say this new system with the emails is a godsend?

I'm glad it's working out. You get a lot of emails that are just a ridiculous waste of time.

I didn't mean that. They are just not what you could be spending your time on.

Jesus, way to insult your new boss and his business, even if it is the truth.

You're right, though. I'm used to running everything on my own, but we're growing larger and larger as a company, and I'm not great at delegating administrative tasks.

I think you're doing better than you realize.

What am I doing?

Ledger Hutton:

> That's just you being brilliant and taking the initiative.

Ainsley Mathews:

> So, what's on the agenda today?

Ledger Hutton:

> Well, I was thinking about throwing something new your way.

Ainsley Mathews:

> Perfect! I love a challenge.

Wow. Am I entirely too eager, or have I just started to enjoy talking to Ledger more and more every day?

Ledger Hutton:

> I'm trying to get into a conference for landscaping. National Landscaping Association is one of the biggest in the country, and they want presenters to send in their presentations early and they'll pick from whomever submits. They have thousands of entries every year, and only twenty get picked.

Ainsley Mathews:

> Bet that causes a ton of drama in the landscaping world.

I can't help but laugh and then promptly look around Sal's, making sure no one is staring at me. I'm not talking shit about his career, but

I never knew there was a competition aspect to it, even if it's just for a conference.

Ledger Hutton:

It's like being in high school again. I hate the politics of it all, but I'd like to grow the business, and this is one of the best ways to fast-track that.

Ainsley Mathews:

Did you grow up here? Sorry, bringing up high school triggered my curiosity.

The silence is deafening. I feel like I've been waiting ten minutes before his answer finally pops up.

Ledger Hutton:

I did grow up here. Moved away for college but was back after graduation.

Ainsley Mathews:

How old are you? I know the regional high school is bigger, so it's not like I knew everyone at school, but I don't remember your name.

Ledger Hutton:

I'm 36.

Ainsley Mathews:

Huh, that's probably why. Two years isn't anything once you leave college, but in high school, it's basically a decade gap.

It's not like I remember people from school, anyway. It's weird to live in a small town and only vaguely remember people you spent your entire childhood with. This mental block I have shows me just how disconnected I was in Austin. It's scary to just ... lose a sizeable chunk of my life because I was so determined to get away and make something bigger and better of myself.

Look how well that turned out.

Ledger Hutton:

Oh yeah, absolutely. So, the presentation. I'm thinking about going the sustainability route. Choosing plants that are sustainable for your area but also using what homeowners and business already have to create less overall waste on projects.

Ainsley Mathews:

Love it! What do you need from me?

Ledger Hutton:

Well, I'm thinking I can handle the actual source material, like how to find sustainable plants, and you could handle putting together the actual presentation. I'm shit at making things pretty, and this needs to be a blowout presentation.

Ainsley Mathews:

I can handle that. Give me all the must-have information, and I'll start putting it together.

Ledger Hutton:

Thanks, Ainsley. I'll have it to you by the end of the day. If you finish up all the other tasks early, just call it a day.

I still find it weird that he's so adamant on the schedule. It's been a few weeks, and I'm still not used to having an abundance of free time. And by free time, I mean babying my new vegetable garden and endlessly scrolling through Netflix for something to watch.

God, I should really figure out something productive to do with my life.

Turning my attention back to work, I start going through Ledger's email.

Ledger.

Our conversations have gotten more and more friendly, and less strict-boss/ employee. Although, I'm not sure he was ever a strict boss.

He's intriguing. Owning his own business takes hard work and endless dedication, yet he's still down to earth and incredible to work for. This may have been a means to an end—whatever end that is—but he's making me feel like this could be a new direction for me. I like what I'm doing right now. Is it sometimes boring? Yes, but I have freedom in this job. Freedom to take initiative and be recognized when I have a good idea. Freedom to really contribute to this business he's worked so hard to grow. It feels more meaningful. And a hell of a lot more fulfilling.

It makes me wonder why climbing the corporate ladder was ever a goal. They don't care about you. You're just another replaceable cog in an endless machine.

It's because you were told over and over again in school that it was the only way to be successful.

What a load of shit. I'm happier stuck in this small-ass town than I was in the last five working with a bunch of whiny dickheads.

The thought catches me off guard. Not about corporate America being the killer of souls but about being happy here.

Am I happy here?

I don't get a chance to contemplate it because a couple of women my dad's age plop down at the table I'm working at.

"Little Miss Annie, I never thought I'd see the day," the one with flame-red hair—clearly dyed—says.

"How is it working for the senior Hutton? He is just dreamy, isn't he?" the other one with long gray hair asks.

"Umm, hi. Yes, I'm back, and I wouldn't know because we haven't met," I respond, hoping if I answer their questions quickly, they'll just run along and leave me alone to work.

I knew coming out of my reclusive stage was going to be a bad idea.

"I'm Alice and this is Mabel, and we play gin rummy with your father. We've been waiting for you to come out of that little house of yours. We were about to go knocking and bring you a casserole. Of course, we can still bring you one, dear," Alice, the redhead, says.

I open my mouth, not even sure how to respond, when a shadow falls over our table.

"Ladies." He nods. "I know you're not over here disturbing this nice woman's workday, right?"

The two interferers gasp and clutch their imaginary pearls.

"Why, we would never!" Mabel says, positively aghast. It's comical, but I roll my lips inward to hide it.

"How about you two head up to the counter and ask Kelly for some fries on the house? Tell her I said it was a treat." I've never seen middle-aged women get up so fast in my life.

The chuckle I've been straining to hold in bursts out, and the man who saves me joins in.

"Sorry about them. They're nosey as hell. I'm Arlo, the sheriff in town." He holds out his hand for me to shake.

"Ainsley, thanks for the save."

"Not a problem. I'm usually around, so if anyone gives you trouble, just come find me. Most people don't seem to understand that people come to places to work sometimes, and it's not always social hour."

I smile at him. He's not flirting, just being genuine. "They don't know any better, unfortunately. Most people have never been outside of Bluebell Falls. But I appreciate you looking out for me. I should probably head out, anyway. It seems like there won't be much work getting done here." I look around and find almost every head in the place turned my way.

He nods, then steps back, letting me clammer from the old, sunken booth.

Grabbing my computer and throwing a ten-dollar bill on the table for taking up space and the soda, I make my way home.

My thoughts wander back to my earlier thoughts of being happy. I pull out my phone and text Larkin as I walk home.

Me:

There is something in the water here. It's slowly poisoning everything I thought I wanted in life.

Larkin:

That's very dramatic for ten in the morning.

Me:

If it's accurate, it's not really dramatic, now is it?

Larkin:

I feel like Gavin could handle this conversation better than me right now.

Me:

No, he would just tell me he has actual problems in school and I shouldn't complain so much.

Larkin:

...

Me:

Rude… Here I was, trying to get some advice from my favorite sister, and she's throwing me under the bus like this?

Larkin:

Jesus, there's something in the water there. You are way too snarky for me right now.

Me:

Okay, I'll tone it down. I apologize that some of us are younger and, therefore, more exuberant at all hours of the day.

Larkin:

Says the woman who crashed on our couch at nine o'clock last New Year's.

Me:

That's cool. Insult me all you want. I'll remember that the next time you need something.

Larkin:

Haha. So, what's really the problem? That you aren't having nearly as bad a time there as you thought you would?

Me:

Kind of. I mean, I'm still clueless as to what's next, but I think I really like my job and the slower pace of life. Even if I don't go out much.

Larkin:

That's not a bad thing, Ains. The whole reason you left was to find some stability and regroup. If you happen to find your next step there, then grab onto it with both hands. You know better than most that being unhappy doesn't make for a fulfilling life.

I know she's right, but sometimes you just need your big sister to knock some sense into you.

Me:

I know. You're right. Thanks for talking me off the ledge.

Larkin:

Anytime. Just know the next time you text me these dramatics, I'm sending you Gavin's way. Madison kept us up all night with some bullshit sleep regression, and I'm probably the last person who should be giving good advice right now.

Me:

Tell that little monkey to chill out. She may be the princess of the family, but that's no reason to be a diva. *wink*

Larkin:

Be right back. Going to tell her Auntie Ains just said she was being a diva.

Me:

NO! No, I take it back. She's the sweetest baby angel saint, who would never scare a soul.

I inwardly cringe. I'm not great with kids, and my only experience is with my sister's kids. But that girl is in a league of her own. She's fiercely independent, stubborn, and hilarious, all at the same time. No one needs to worry about her taking care of herself, that's for sure.

Larkin:

Liar. She could death-stare a storm trooper, and they would back down.

Me:

Too true. Well, as always, you're the best, but I've got to get back to work now. Sorry for my freakout.

Larkin:

You know I'm always here for you, no matter how much shit I give you. Love you, Ains!

Me:

Love you too.

I put my phone back and pull out my keys now that I'm home. I get set up at my desk and look at the thirty emails waiting for me to address them. This job, this time in my life, isn't as bad as I thought it would be. I still feel stuck, like I want to do *more,* but I'm starting to see how small-town life can be just as fulfilling as a high-paying, high-stress career.

I've already noticed subtle changes in how I feel, and it's only been a few weeks. I have less heartburn, less fatigue, and I haven't had a headache since I've been here. All three used to be an almost daily occurrence.

Letting out a heavy sigh, I decide the time for contemplating the big things can wait until tonight. Now is the time to get my work done and wait for Ledger to send over the information for the presentation.

I'm not going to lie—I'm kind of excited about the prospect of this conference. It's not like I'm going to get to go, but I wonder if it's like financial conferences, with all the stuffy suits and shitty banquet food. Is it a game to see whose output is higher? Or are people actually interested in bettering themselves and their company?

I'll have to ask Ledger one day. The way he was talking about it sounds like the biggest event for landscaping in the country, and somehow, that's intriguing as hell.

I contemplate what a bunch of landscapers getting together looks like as I go through emails, and it takes me all the way to lunch. I stretch in my chair, loosening up the kinks in my neck from being on my computer for too long in an uncomfortable booth before standing up and heading to my kitchen to get a drink.

I'm stopped by a knock at my door.

Who in the world would be knocking? My dad knows he can't just come over in the middle of a workday. We've already had that discussion—twice.

I walk over to it and slowly pull it open, revealing one of the last people I thought would be knocking at my door.

"Rina?"

CHAPTER TEN
AINSLEY

"Hi!" Rina says enthusiastically.

"Umm, hi."

"So, I realize you've been in town for a while now, and I don't really see you around, so I thought I'd come by and see if you wanted to get some lunch." Her large, blue eyes, so similar to Dean's, are filled with nothing but warmth.

"Lunch?"

"Yep, lunch. Sal's. Or Grind Time has great sandwiches and salads if you want something different," she offers.

"I was just at Sal's most of the morning trying to work, but I haven't been to Grind Time yet. I thought they only had coffee and breakfast stuff." Lunch with Rina could be fun. Making an actual friend here is probably something I should be working on.

"Oh, Grind Time is so fucking good—pardon my language. They have these super fresh paninis that are to die for."

Loud laughter bursts out of me. "Please don't feel the need to censor yourself. I'm the last person to care, I promise."

"Thank God, because I have been told I can curse like a sailor when the time calls for it. So, Grind Time?"

I realize we've been standing in my doorway, and I instantly feel unwelcoming. "Yeah, that sounds good. Come in. Let me just grab some shoes."

She bounces into my living room and plops down on my couch as I walk to my room to grab some shoes.

"I've never seen the inside of this place," she says loudly. "It's cute!"

"Thanks," I yell. "I haven't really had time to do anything more than unpack, but it's just enough space for me," I tell her as I slip some sandals on and join her in my living room.

"Well, if you ever need help, let me know. I'm a furniture builder, but I love decorating too."

"I thought you worked at the nursery?" I ask, confused.

"I help out when needed at the nursery, but it's not my day job."

"That's really nice of you."

She shrugs but doesn't say anything. It almost feels like she's actively trying to keep her mouth shut, even though she wants to say something.

We walk out the front door as I lock it behind us. Rina turns around and raises an eyebrow at me.

"Force of habit. I'm still not used to the whole small-town thing."

"I get it. No one's going to break into your house, though. If they do, they'll spend the night in the drunk tank being watched like a hawk by the sheriff." She rolls her eyes when she says 'sheriff', so I assume there's some bad blood there.

"Hop in. I'll drive." We walk up to her truck, and I have to hoist myself up into it.

Throughout the five-minute drive downtown, Rina chats my ear off. She wants to know about my life in Austin, and I give her the bare minimum. It's not worth it to get into the nitty-gritty of what my life was like before the downfall. It's over, so it doesn't really need my attention anymore. At least, I'm trying not to give it my attention anymore.

We walk in, and Rina waves to an older couple sitting by the door.

"How's the hutch working out?" she asks.

"It's just gorgeous, Marina. Better than I could have hoped for." The older lady beams.

"Aww. Thanks, Mary, I'm glad you love it. Let me know if you need any other pieces, okay?"

"We will. Tell that darling family of yours hello for us."

"You know I always do." She leans down and kisses her cheek.

I forget just how close everyone is here. And how *nice* everyone is to each other. It's something you take for granted as a teenager because it just feels like everyone is in your business all the time. But as an adult? This one interaction has successfully restored my faith in humanity.

"Alright, let's grab some delicious food wrapped up in delicious cheese and smacked together with glorious bread," she says, running her hands together as we look at the menu.

I can't help but laugh. I never expected a random meeting at the nursery to turn into a friendship, but I have to say Rina is right up my alley. She's hilarious, and I absolutely want to spend more time with her.

We place our orders and find a table at the surprisingly packed coffee house.

"I'm surprised my dad didn't tell me about this place. This wasn't here when I was in high school. I think I might have lived here if it was."

"Your dad is Jim, right? He's hilarious."

"If by hilarious you mean the nosiest gossip around, then I agree." I smile over at her.

"He definitely runs the rumor mill here, but he's sweet. I delivered a coffee table to him a couple of months ago, and he and Penny cooked me a full meal before setting me loose."

"Sounds about right. My mom's super quiet, so my sister and I give her crap for marrying Dad, but she's a hell of a cook."

"That's nice that you guys are close, though," she says with a wistful sigh.

"Rina, come get your food!" a deep voice yells.

"Oh, that's us. Be right back." Rina jumps out of her chair and heads to the front.

I take the time to look around, and table after table is filled with sunny smiles. No one has their head in their phone or is working on their laptop trying to get some work done while they eat. It's so fucking refreshing, even though I was attempting to do all of that earlier.

Rina slides my sandwich over and holds up two bags of chips. "Preference?"

"I'm partial to the jalapeño chips, but I'm good with either." I shrug.

"Good, I not-so-secretly want the barbeque." She winks as she sits down.

We dig into our lunch wordlessly, and I can't hold in the moan of deliciousness that comes out of me. These paninis rival those that are mostly overpriced in Austin.

"Oh my god, this is so good."

"Right? Oakley is from New York City. Was a big-city chef and got burnt out, and decided to make Bluebell Falls his home. Can't say I'm sad he dropped big-city life to grace us with Grind Time," she tells me before digging into her sandwich.

"That's amazing. This definitely rivals most places in Austin. It's nice to see the area grow a little."

"So, what's your story? What made you move back here?"

My chest clinches tight with anxiety. I knew this would come up. Hell, I'm shocked most people don't already know, thanks to who I have for a father, but I'm somehow grossly unprepared for it.

"Umm, I used to work in the financial field. It was super cutthroat, but I was climbing the proverbial ladder." She nods while maintaining eye contact as I continue. "I've always been good with numbers. It felt like a natural place to fall to with finance. Financial planning promised to be a great career—stellar pay and longevity within the company that hired me.

"They passed me up for a promotion not too long ago. The guy who got it had been with the company less time than me, and I had better numbers than him. I knew it was a boy's club, but shit, it was hard to live through it." I wipe my hands on my pants, wondering why I'm spilling the whole sordid story to this poor woman who's just taken pity on me.

"When I was in trade school, I was the only woman in my class. It's not often a woman dives headfirst into the furniture building department. It felt like I had to work ten times harder to get the same respect," Rina offers.

"Yes! You totally understand. So, that's not even the worst of it. The guy who got my promotion started harassing me. He wasn't technically supposed to be my boss, but the owners shifted him and he ended up being my direct supervisor. He saw it as an opportunity to take advantage of me—well, try to take advantage of me. He would walk by my office every day at the same time and try to hit on me. When that didn't work, he resorted to threatening me and my job."

"What an asshole!"

"Yep. I went to the partners in the company and told them what was happening. They said they'd look into it. Four days later, I was called to one of their offices. The asshole was standing there with a smirk on his face. I just fucking knew he managed to undermine me. I was in utter shock when they fired me. It wasn't until I was escorted out by security that the reasoning finally registered. He said I was harassing him. Borderline stalking, I believe was the term he'd used. None of what I said or did was ever going to matter."

"I have a lot of sharp tools. Austin's not that far away. You could just text me an address, and no one would have to know," Rina says with a gleam in her eye, and laughter so loud bursts from me, it draws the attention of the entire restaurant.

"Thank you for that. I don't think I've laughed that hard in a while."

"Well, my job here is done! But seriously, fuck that guy. And fuck that company!" She says it like a war cry, and I think I kind of love her. I didn't expect to make friends here, but she's kind of forcing my hand. I don't know that I *couldn't* be friends with her at this point. I mean, she just offered to do some physical damage to the asshole. That's like a blood bond, right?

"Thanks for making me come out for lunch. I've been a little cooped up lately, and this has been nice."

"Not a problem. I'm glad I could help. So, how is everything going? That's not exactly an easy transition."

"Honestly, it's going better than I expected. The little house I'm renting is quiet, and the job's actually not bad either. I think I came here wanting to hide away and figure things out, but it's going surprisingly well."

"You're working for Ledger, right?" she asks.

"I am. He's a great boss. I didn't know they made them that way." I chuckle.

She stares at me a beat too long. "He's a good guy. Hard-working, reliable, and always puts his employees first. He's built that company from the ground up during a really hard time in his life, and he's never let his success take over what's important to him." Her impassioned words just solidify what I know about him.

"He is a good guy," I whisper as we finish up our food.

"Alright, this was a blast, but I've got to get back to my shop and finish out this bookcase I'm working on." She grabs our trash, walking it over to the trashcan as I slowly stand up.

This is not how I expected my day to go. First, I'm getting more responsibility at work, and now, I've made a real-life adult friend. It's weird... When you change everything in your life, you realize just how hard it is to make friends as an adult. I have no willpower to do a whole get-to-know-you routine to figure out if we mesh well. Because what happens when we don't? You ghost them, and in a small town that's impossible to do. I wanted no part in it, but Rina just imbedded herself in my life, and I've never been happier to be dragged to something I wasn't happy about than I am about this lunch.

"Let's both get back to work. What are you up to this weekend?" she says as we both walk to the door.

"Umm, nothing?" I go to reach for the door, but it opens first.

"Oh. Hey, *Dean.* So nice to see you here. Will you be at the nursery this weekend?" Rina asks, but it's got a teasing edge to it.

"H-hey. I don't think I'll make it this weekend, sorry." He looks highly uncomfortable. His eyes keep darting between the two of us.

I throw him a little wave and move to the side so he can come in.

"Hey, Ainsley. It's good to see you." He smiles down at me as he passes. He abruptly gives a death-stare to Rina, but she smiles as if the cat ate the canary. Knowing what I know about Rina now, their dynamic makes a little more sense.

"Good to see you, *Dean!* Don't work too hard." She winks at him and then drags me out the door.

When we make it to the truck, I turn around and find Dean watching me with a small smile on his face. I can feel my cheeks heat, so I spin around and get into Rina's truck.

"Well, that was fun," she snickers.

Somehow, I don't think she meant lunch.

CHAPTER ELEVEN
LEDGER

W hat the hell is Rina doing with Ainsley? Are they friends now?

Shit. I need to come clean. Rina had that mischievous gleam in her eye that means she is planning something, and I don't need it fucking with my chances here.

You're already fucking with your chances because she thinks your name is Dean, you asshole.

Yep, I'm an asshole.

I walk up to the front counter just as Oakley puts my order up.

"Here ya go, Ledger. I added an extra pickle in there for you."

"Thanks man, you're the best." Oakley's a good guy. Mostly keeps to himself, but he's a damn excellent chef. He tells everyone the same story of how he came to be in Bluebell Falls, but there's something about it that feels too scripted. But it's none of my business.

"Rina was just in here with a cutie. She looked like she was looking for trouble." He laughs.

My shoulders instantly tighten when he calls Ainsley a cutie. *She's mine.*

"Umm." I let out breathy laughter, trying not to lose my shit on him. He's a nice guy, and I know he didn't really mean anything by it. I just need to remember that before I punch him. "When isn't Rina looking for trouble?"

"Ain't that the truth? Enjoy your lunch." He waves as he walks back to the kitchen.

I make my way back to my truck, and all I can think about is if Oakley hit on Ainsley and what the hell Rina is up to. Since when did my life become this complicated?

There's also the guilt. *Why the hell haven't I come clean yet? Am I really that scared of rejection?*

The answer is hell yes. I didn't realize the number my ex did on me. I mean, I knew it at the time, but I thought I had gotten over this. It's been over a decade—I *should* be over it.

Then why are you being a chicken shit with the one woman you've never gotten out of your head? How is lying to her going to get her to trust you?

Fuck. My head's a mess.

Trudging back to my truck, I set the bag of food in the passenger seat and head home for lunch. I have about forty minutes before I need to meet some of my guys at a house to start some landscaping, so I don't really have time to dwell on the shitshow that is my life.

As I walk into my house, my phone dings with a text.

Finally getting myself settled at my kitchen island, I lay out my food, then pull out my phone.

Rina:

Are you busy tonight?

So it starts. I knew she was up to something.

Me:

Not really. I'm starting a job after lunch and then wrapping up a couple of projects after that.

Curiosity gets the better of me. I want to know what she's up to, so I'll play her game.

Rina:

> Awesome. I'm stopping by around four, then. Be home.

I instinctually roll my eyes. I swear, the woman never asks me, just demands my presence when she has a problem or idea. And because I'm a sucker for my siblings, I cave every single time.

Me:

> Yeah, sure. Let me just work my day around you.

Rina:

> See you later!

I chuckle at her answer. She may give me a hard time most days, but she's still my sister and I know it comes from a place of love. At least, I hope it does.

I dig into my sandwich without continuing to analyze the reason Rina does anything. Pulling up my calendar, I make sure I'm able to be here at four. I see a new meeting has popped up, so I pull up the messaging system and start typing.

Ledger Hutton:

> Hey. I just saw that three-thirty meeting get added. Is there any way to push it to tomorrow? I have to be home by four today.

Yeah, I can move it. I'll call them and reschedule. I'll also block your calendar so nothing else gets put there.

You're a lifesaver, thank you.

Not a problem. Let me know if you need anything else.

Outside of my minor obsession with her, Ainsley is a hard worker. When I decided to hire an assistant, I was expecting the bare minimum in terms of work. And I certainly wasn't expecting someone to come in and make everything more efficient. She's gone above and beyond, and I'm impressed by her daily.

Now, you need to figure out how to come clean. The longer you wait, the worse it will be.

Fuck, when did my life get this complicated? When my siblings came into their own careers, my life got exponentially simpler. Now, it seems like things just went right back to muddled. I know it's by my own doing, but it's like a train crash that I can't stop watching. I don't quite know how to dig myself out here.

My eye snags on the clock on the microwave, and I realize I'm about to be late to my next job—and I'm never late. This shit with Ainsley is starting to affect my job, and that's how I know I'm running out of time. I just need to grow some balls and tell her.

I'll get on that, right after I talk to Rina tonight.

I'm barely able to walk through the front door when Rina pops up out of nowhere.

"You were almost late. I was about to send out a search party."

"That's dramatic," I murmur, dropping off my keys and sunglasses on the entry table.

"Okay, so I need a favor," Rina says with her owlish eyes that I can never resist.

"What?" I groan.

"I have this friend that I promised to set up, and the guy I had on the line canceled. You don't have to actually like her, but if you could take her out to dinner, I would owe you for my entire life," she practically begs.

"You owe me your entire life whether I do this or not," I say.

"You are absolutely right, all-powerful Ledg. I will ... make you that dining room table you've been bugging me about. And a new bed frame!" she throws in.

"Dining room table, bed frame, and an outdoor swing," I counter.

"Jesus. Do you know how many mechanics there are in a swing?"

"Take it or leave it, Rina. You want me to go on a date I don't want to go on to help you out of a bind. You're going to be working for it."

"But three huge-ass pieces of furniture? I have commissions out the ass right now. It's going to take me forever to get them done!" she whines.

I raise my eyebrow at her and cross my arms over my chest. Let's see how badly she wants me to go on this date.

"God, you're the worst sometimes. Fine, I will make a shit-ton of furniture in exchange for one date. This is ridiculously one-sided."

"It sure is. Send me the details." I walk past her and head to the kitchen. The twinge in my gut at agreeing to a date, no matter how fake it is, has me second-guessing saying yes. I'd do anything for my siblings, but with Ainsley in the picture, this feels like a betrayal, even if we are nowhere near together.

I hear the door slam, and my house turns blissfully quiet. My thoughts are screaming loudly in my head, though. This is a terrible idea. This poor woman is going to be expecting someone who actually wants to go on a date, and she's going to get me—a man hung up on another woman, who thinks my name is Dean.

I'll just be upfront when I meet her. I don't want to get her hopes up, and I'd rather just treat her to a nice dinner and leave as potential friends. Lord knows I don't need to lie any more than I already am.

Rina sends me the details of this "date", and I decide to spend the next hour taking a shower and cleaning up the house a little. The least I can do is not look like I just did eight hours of hard, physical labor.

Finally, feeling more like myself, I head to Sal's a little early. Rina said I was looking for someone in jeans and a white shirt. Apparently, she's newer in town, so I might not recognize her. What that tells me is to look for the only woman I don't know who's wearing a white shirt.

I reluctantly get in my truck and make the quick drive to Sal's. I also make a plan. After this date, I'm coming clean to Ainsley. If I really want to show her I'm a good guy, I need to start doing damage control. Because there's no way she'll let me off easy for the shit I've pulled.

Walking in, I see Kelly and throw my hand up with the number one to order a beer. Finding an empty booth that faces the front door is a stroke of luck, but now it's a waiting game.

Everyone that walks in sends me a nod, but so far, no one I don't know and no woman in a white shirt. I check my watch and see it's right at six o'clock. I'll give her fifteen more minutes, and then I'm out. Just as I make the decision, the door opens, and I catch a flash of white.

I plaster a smile on my face, and then she walks fully in the door.

My smile falters, and I'm confused. She looks around, and her eyes finally catch mine. Her brow furrows, and she slowly makes her way over here.

"Umm. Are you waiting for someone for dinner?" she asks quietly.

I say the only thing in my blank brain.

"Ainsley?"

CHAPTER TWELVE
AINSLEY

What in the fuck is going on right now?

Let me rewind. When Rina called me up a couple of hours after our impromptu lunch, it made me feel like the cool girl in high school. When she begged for my help, I didn't hesitate. Then I learned she needed my help because she set up a friend of hers on a date and she had to bail. She felt bad for the guy who put effort into the date, so she wanted to know if I could fill in. I wasn't committed to anything, just a free dinner with no obligations after.

She texted me thirty minutes ago with a description of what this guy was wearing, and I started getting excited. I like Dean a lot, but who's to say it's worth it to wait it out? I don't even know if he sees me like that. So, taking a chance on a blind date turned into an opportunity for me. Maybe this guy is perfect for me and if I turn down the chance, I'll never know if I lost out. Lunch with Rina made me realize I need to stop hiding all the time. It reinforced my plan to start working outside of my house at least once a week. This just came at a perfect time to start implementing that.

What I didn't expect was Dean staring at me like he's just seen a ghost, wearing the green flannel and dark jeans I'm supposed to be looking for.

"Ainsley?" His question comes out confused and breathy.

"Are you my blind date?" I ask. My brain doesn't have the capacity to figure out what exactly is happening here. I just want clear answers.

"Fucking Rina," he mutters and swipes his hand through his hair.

"I'm going to be honest. I'm very confused. Did Rina need me as a fill-in? Or is this actually the setup?" I feel stupid because none of this is computing in my brain.

"Do you want to sit down?" he asks, but I hear the uncertainty in his voice. He knows something I don't.

I eagerly sit across from him, wanting straightforward answers. If this is Rina trying to throw us together, I don't think I could be mad at her. It's extremely sweet. But Dean looks beyond uncomfortable, so I'm not sure if this is just one big mistake.

"Umm, I don't even know where to start." He looks like he's in physical pain, and it just amps up my confusion.

"At the beginning is usually a good start," I offer.

"Rina set us up. She created a story—I'm assuming she did the same for you—and guilt-tripped me into helping her out."

"Okay."

I'm not really seeing the huge problem. Sure, she meddled, but I like Dean, so I'm not sure why it's not a good thing—unless he isn't into me. *Oh God, he isn't into me like I am him. That's the problem here.*

"I'm not Dean—well, I am; it's my middle name—but my first name is Ledger, and Rina set me up so I would grow some balls and finally take the plunge with you, and now, I think ... everything is ruined." He says the last part on a whisper, but I can't focus on the pained look on his face.

All I can feel are my ears buzzing like there's static in my brain.

His name's not Dean, it's Ledger. And he was at the nursery, and he and Rina had that weird conversation without words, and Ledger is actually my boss. OH MY GOD, Ledger is my boss.

"Umm—"

"You both ready to order?" Kelly walks over with a giant smile on her face.

"Actually, could you give us a few minutes?" Dean—Ledger—says with a forced smile.

"Of course, just flag me down when you're ready."

"I'm sorry. I don't know why I lied about my name," he rushes out as soon as she leaves.

"But you're my boss," I say dumbly.

He cringes. "Yeah, I am."

"Why— I don't understand. Why did you say your name was Dean?"

"Would it help if I said it's a very long and embarrassing story?"

"No. It would help if you just told me the truth." The facts are finally settling into my head, and I'm starting to get pissed. I've dealt with enough lies and bullshit behind my back recently.

"We went to high school together. Well, I was two years older than you, so I doubt you even knew me."

"Rina is Marina Hutton. Holy shit, how did I not put this together?" I whisper as things finally start to click.

"Yeah."

"What does high school have to do with any of this?" I wave my hands around frantically.

The apples of his cheeks turn bright pink, and I'd say it was adorable if I wasn't so fucking mad right now.

"I had a huge crush on you in school. I was too chickenshit to do anything about it, so I just ... didn't. Then I went to college, you went to college, and I came back, but you stayed away. I had a lot of things happen in those few years that were my focus. When you came back, I thought it was this sign. I was so determined to not be the shy kid, the hesitant kid I used to be. But then I saw you, and it all went to hell. My brain blanked, and I panicked."

I can tell he's hopeful his explanation is enough to cancel everything else out, but it couldn't be further from the truth.

"So, you panicked when you first saw me? But what about after that? I've had multiple conversations with you as Dean, and as Ledger. You had so many opportunities to tell me who you were."

"I know." He drops his head. "I messed up."

"Yeah, you did." I'm so enraged that I can't even attempt to hide it. It's not even about potentially liking him—whichever version he actually did let me see—it's about the fact I've had to go through the lies and the deceit twice in just as many months. Why do people feel that it's okay to lie to me? To not respect me enough to just tell me the truth?

I shove away from the table, not caring that it draws the attention of the entire diner. I need to get out of here before I have an ugly breakdown.

"Ainsley..." I hear his voice; the deep baritone I usually love grates on my already frayed nerves.

"Nope. It was lovely knowing you, *Dean.*"

I speedwalk out of the diner and straight to my car. I will the tears to not fall. I'm not even sure why I'm so worked up over this. Does it suck that my boss lied to me and then made me have a sort of a small crush on him? Absolutely, but I shouldn't be crying over this.

I pull out my phone and dial Larkin.

"Hey, sis! How are things?" Her cheerful voice makes the tears fall.

I pull out of the parking lot and head back to my tiny, little house, in need of some privacy and ice cream.

"Do I have a sign on my forehead that says *Super gullable, please fuck with*?" I sniffle out.

"Umm, no? What happened?" Her tone changes to concern in the blink of an eye.

I take a deep breath and hope that I can put all that I'm feeling into words. If anyone can help me talk through all of this, though, it's my social-worker sister.

"Do you remember the Huttons?" I ask, figuring it's the best place to start.

"Umm, I think so. There's like three or four of them, right? I remember Ledger, and wasn't Marina in your class?"

"Yep. Well, Ledger is my boss."

"Well, that's interesting. I don't know why I didn't put two and two together on that one."

"It gets worse." I cringe as I pull into my driveway.

"Worse? Is he a shitty boss? I can drive down there and show him the Mathews women are not to be messed with."

God, I love her. She doesn't even know anything yet, but she'd drive here in a heartbeat if I needed her to.

"No. He's a great boss. Still conscientious of hours and how much I work, and is giving me more responsibility. I love it. Or I did."

"Okay... I don't get it."

I'm getting frustrated with myself for not being able to articulate things, so I just blurt it out.

"Dean is Ledger. Ledger is Dean!"

"What the fuck?" she yells.

I hear Theo yell in the background, "Language!"

Her voice gets further away, but I can still hear her. "If you tell me language right now, so help me, you will be sleeping on the couch tonight. This calls for language, good sir!"

The laugh that bursts out of me shocks me, but their relationship has always been goals for me. They are always like this; they argue, and then they love extra hard. They never take things too seriously, and they are both funny as hell. It helps me calm down enough that I feel like I can really explain the situation to my sister.

"Okay, so Ledger is Dean, Dean is Ledger," Larkin says at full volume again.

"Yep. So, let me explain everything that happened because it's just ... insane. Rina showed up at my door and invited me to lunch. We had a great time; she forced her friendship on me, and it was ... nice. She's really funny and blunt as hell. You'd love her. So, she texted me later, asking if I would do her a huge favor. She needed someone to fill in for a blind date because who she had lined up canceled and she felt bad. I didn't really have anything going on, so I said yes. Well, turns out she played me and Ledger, and set us up. Ledger was as shocked as I was, but he came clean. I was so upset, Lark, I just blanked and walked out. I don't even remember half of what I told him."

"I can understand that. Let me rewind a bit. Dean is—was—who you were crushing on, but Ledger wasn't so bad either. If they are the same person, that's not necessarily a bad thing, right?"

"I mean, maybe, but I'm not even thinking about that right now."

"What are you thinking about?" she asks.

"Why does everyone take advantage of me? What have I done to deserve all of this? I've put my head down, worked hard, never been problematic, so why does this keep happening?" I tell her, my voice quiet as the tears pool in my eyes.

"Oh, Ains. You don't deserve it. What people do is not on you. It's not your responsibility. People will always make selfish, stupid decisions, but it's not a reflection of you. You are so good and so hardworking that people, especially at your last job, felt threatened. Now, I'm not sure what Ledger's reasoning was, but I suspect there's more to it. He doesn't seem like the guy to just be an asshole for no reason."

"He said he had a crush on me in high school, which makes me feel bad now that I think about it because I don't remember him. And when we saw each other again, he just panicked and used his middle name. And he just kept going along with that decision."

"Well, can't say I saw that coming. Okay. I have some initial thoughts."

"Hit me. I need all the advice you can give me because, Lark, I feel like I'm drowning here. I left Austin to get away from shit like this. And now, this combines my job with my personal life."

"I hear you. I think the two situations are very different, though, even if they feel similar. Your dickhead co-worker in Austin used you as a stepping stool. It sounds like Ledger just made the wrong decision when it comes to a girl he likes. I'm not saying he was right in any way, but I don't think he was trying to use you. He made a mistake, and now he has to live with the consequences."

I think about what she's saying. She's not wrong. Even if it feels like the same thing, the two situations are very different. It still doesn't feel good. It still feels like a betrayal, so it's something I'll have to work through with time, I guess. At the moment, I just want to drown my sorrows in a cooking show and some ice cream.

"Makes sense. I think it'll probably take me a while to figure out how I feel about all of this, and shit, if I can continue to work for him." *Fuck, what if I need to find a new job? I actually like my job, and Ledger just ruined it in a ten-minute conversation.*

"Don't make any rash decisions, okay? Sit on it for a few days and see if you feel like you can still work for him. From what you've told me, you don't really talk in person, just message each other? You might be okay with just limiting how you communicate and keeping it professional."

"Good plan, Lark. Thank you."

"You know you can always call me for whatever you need."

"I know—" I'm interrupted by a knock at my door. "Hey, someone just knocked. I gotta go. Love you."

"Love you too. If it's Ledger, don't feel like you need to talk to him right away. It's okay to set boundaries and tell him you're not ready to talk."

"I will, thanks."

I hang up and take a peek through my peephole. What I find is not Ledger, but his same blue eyes are staring at me.

"What do you want, Rina?" I say through the door, not so much mad at her as I am tired of the entire situation.

"I messed up, and I just wanted to talk. I'm sorry, Ainsley." She sounds sad, and it pulls at my damn naïve heart.

Unlocking the door, I hold it open for her. "I was just going to dig into some ice cream. Care to join?" I don't want to be the person who holds grudges. I remember what Gavin told me: *Make an effort to be the kind of person you want to be.* The thought bounces around my head, and I realize I don't want to be angry and pessimistic all the time. I at least want to give her a chance to explain what the hell happened.

She holds up a bag from the market in town, holding what looks like four pints of ice cream. *Dammit, I'm supposed to be mad at her, but she's hitting me where I can't say no.*

I wordlessly walk into the kitchen and grab two spoons as she follows me and puts two pints in the freezer after we pick our poison.

"I'm so sorry, Ainsley. I didn't expect things to go like that. I shouldn't have interfered."

"Can I ask how you thought things would go?" I'm genuinely curious what she thought would happen.

"I thought Ledger would... I don't know, pull his head out of his ass and come clean. He talked about you so much when we were in high school, this all just felt like kismet. I didn't really think about how you would feel, and I feel really, really shitty about that. He's done so much for us. I just wanted to give him a little push to try to be happy. I didn't take into consideration how it would feel to be on the other end."

I get a huge scoop of ice cream in order to stall and get my thoughts together. I know her heart was in the right place. And I honestly don't know enough about their family to judge their dynamic a lot. I just wish I wasn't put in the middle of it like this.

"I'll be honest. This whole situation sucks. I wasn't expecting to be blindsided like that tonight." That sad, dejected feeling still stings.

"I know, and it was super shitty of me to do. I just … wanted to help him if I could. And I had so much fun with you at lunch. I knew you would be good for him. I already got a tongue-lashing from Ledger about not meddling. I really thought I was helping. I'm sorry."

"I'm not going to say it's okay because it's not. But I know you weren't trying to be malicious about it. How about we stick to our friendship and no more sticking our heads into other people's business?" I'm willing to give her a second chance because I know how it feels to never be given the benefit of the doubt, but I also need to protect myself a little here too.

She drops her spoon in her pint and holds her hand out to me. "Deal."

I shake her hand and we both turn to watch the mindless cooking show I put on. We don't talk any further, but we do finish our pints before she takes off to finish up some work.

"I really am sorry, Ainsley. I know it's not my place, but Ledger is a great man."

"Yeah, personally, that remains to be seen." I'm not trying to be mean, but I'm not ready to just forgive him yet.

"Well, I'll be around if you want to get lunch or dinner, or ice cream." She turns toward her truck, and I watch her drive away.

Sleep. I just need to sleep and wake up in the morning with a better idea of how to handle everything. Hopefully, I can deal with it and not have to look for a new job because I don't even know where to start with that.

CHAPTER THIRTEEN
LEDGER

What a fucking nightmare. I knew it would be bad news when it eventually came out that I had been lying, but I somehow convinced myself it would all be okay in the end. That she would already be madly in love with me, and it wouldn't be a huge deal.

Jesus, how delusional am I?

The problem is, I didn't think. I didn't consider what would happen if we got closer and how she would feel knowing I'd lied to her. I didn't think about anything except the fear of rejection and my own insecurities.

And here I thought I was past all of this bullshit.

Nope. Instead, here I am, sitting on my front porch trying to figure out how to get Ainsley to just talk to me again. Forgiveness? I'm not holding my breath. I certainly don't deserve it.

Now, I just have to figure out how to make her comfortable with me enough to stay on as my assistant. I don't want her to feel like she needs to quit because of my stupidity.

A truck pulls down my driveway, and I see it's Rina again. I already said my piece earlier. Talking to her again is just going to fray my already fucked-up head.

She parks and climbs out of her truck.

"Not tonight, Rina." I sigh.

"I know. But I brought beer." She holds up a six-pack. "Can I just sit with you?"

I motion wordlessly to the rocking chair next to mine. She plops down next to me and cracks a beer, handing it to me before doing the same for herself. We sit in silence for a while. That's the nice thing about the two of us—although I took on a lot of the responsibilities when our parents died, Rina really kept the younger two from going feral. She helped with routine and getting them places on time. Lord knows I couldn't have done any of it without her, but sometimes it was just overwhelming. So we would sit outside, drink a beer in silence, and internally reflect on the hard-ass days.

"I'm sorry, Ledg," she whispers, barely audible over the sound of crickets chirping in the field next to my house.

I sigh again, trying to figure out how to put how I'm feeling into words.

"It's not on you, Rina. Should you have taken it upon yourself to set this up? No. But the bigger issue is me not telling Ainsley who I was from the get-go."

I think about how I thought Ainsley was the ultimate girl back in high school. She was smart, pretty, and the limited times I interacted with her made me feel like I wasn't just some outcast. Made me feel like my shyness and awkwardness weren't going to deter me from having a life I wanted. I connected this idea of dating Ainsley with turning me into the man I wanted to be. And I clung to it. I fell into that habit when I realized she was back in town, and I fucked up. This isn't on Rina—it's fully on me.

"I just ... want to see you happy. You've taken care of everyone for so long, sometimes I think you've just given up on yourself. Ainsley is the first person since the nameless wench who's lit up your entire face. You've smiled more in the past few weeks than I can remember in the past few *years*. Willow and Lennox don't see the toll everything has taken on you, but I do. I just wanted to do something for you for once." She tips her beer can back and takes a long draw.

You know what's scary? Having your younger sister see so much of you. The parts you've tried to push down and not allow your siblings to see because you never want them to feel like a burden. The weariness in every decision, trying to make sure you don't fuck them up beyond repair.

Yeah, Rina's not the fuck-up here, I am.

"I don't know if I can fix this," I finally say.

"If it helps, I just spent a couple of hours at her house, and she forgave me."

I laugh at her sing-song tone. "Yeah, somehow, I don't think what I did is as forgivable as what you did."

"You want to talk about it?"

"Not really." I down the rest of my beer.

"You know, this closed-off act isn't going to win any awards. You want my advice?"

I don't, but she's going to tell me anyway.

"Think about where you see yourself in five to ten years. Do you want to be a lonely, old man whose only focus is his business and his slightly deranged siblings? Or do you want to have companionship, love, a family?"

Her questions make my heart clench painfully in my chest. Reaching up, I rub it, contemplating her words. I thought I wanted all of that. Then our parents died, and Jenna cheated on me. Everything in my world crashed down around me, and I haven't thought about my future in any other way except my business since. Maybe Rina is right. Maybe I need to figure out what I really want before I even attempt to beg for forgiveness. Because why put Ainsley through all of that if I'm just going to let her down in the long run, anyway?

"What about you? Where do you see yourself in five to ten years?" I ask, definitely deflecting but also curious. Rina's always been the extrovert, but she's never really had a close boyfriend that I've known about, at least. She's never put herself out there outside of friendships.

She heaves out a sigh. "Fuck if I know. Can't I just make a shit-ton of furniture, have happy customers, and call it a day?"

"I mean, you could, but if I'm going to do a deep dive into what I want in my future, it might be good for you to do it as well. You're not going to force me to be introspective without me dragging you along for the ride." I smirk at her.

"This seems like a very unfair situation. All I did was try to set you up, and now it's somehow about what I want in my life? Don't think that I don't know you're doing a hell of a lot of deflecting right now, old man. I'll allow it because I still feel like total shit for today. But that doesn't mean tomorrow I won't be on your ass about making it up to Ainsley." She gives me a small smile.

"Well, on that lovely note, I'm going to head to bed and hope to have a clearer head tomorrow to try to figure all of this out." Standing up, I stretch my arms over my head to try to get the kinks out of my back. Whether it's from stress or sitting too long, it makes all this talk about being an old man hit a little too close to home.

"Night, big brother. I'm sorry I fucked things up tonight." She ambles her way to her truck before I can get another word in.

I watch her drive away as the exhaustion of the day hits me hard. Grabbing the extra beer she left, I head inside, tossing it in the fridge before going to my room. Stripping out of my clothes, I turn on the shower as hot as I can stand it and don't wait for it to warm up before I get in.

The cold water pounding on my back feels like a penance for doing things so wrong with Ainsley. As the water warms up, my mind starts wandering to what Rina asked me.

Where do I see myself in ten years? Do I really just want to continue to focus on the business?

The answer is no. I know that with every ounce of my being. The second I saw Ainsley move back into town—hell, the second I saw her name pop up on her application—I knew the way I had been living my life wasn't the end-all for me anymore. So now, I just need to figure out how to get Ainsley to talk to me again. And then, from there, get her to see who I really am. Not the coward who lied about who he really was just because he was scared.

I'm still scared.

The thought flashes in my head, and I can't shake it. I am scared. I'm scared I've messed things up permanently between me and Ainsley. I'm scared I've lost the only chance I'll get at true happiness. Surprisingly, I'm not scared of putting myself out there again. Not scared that Ainsley will hurt me or cheat on me. I don't know if that makes me a fool or just optimistic.

I wash myself up and dry off before heading to bed. Sleep will be hard to find tonight, but maybe tomorrow I can start fresh and figure out how to fix all the damage I've done.

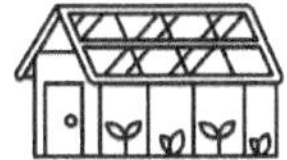

I'm a chickenshit.

What the fuck is wrong with me? Waking up, I was determined to—at the minimum—call Ainsley and talk about what happened. Instead? I emailed her the daily to-do list and acted like it was a normal day.

I don't know if it's a good thing or a bad thing that I haven't heard anything from her besides a confirmation of tasks, but I know I need to address this sooner rather than later. My time is already up, so I need to buckle down and figure out how to actually talk to her. *If* I can get her to talk to me again.

The problem is two of my clients have major issues with their projects, so I've been dealing with them all day. I haven't had time to stop and think about anything, let alone Ainsley.

It's just before five, and I'm finally walking through my front door. I don't even have the energy to cook, so I make a quick cup of noodles, letting it steam while I take a two-minute shower to clean off the layer of dirt on me.

Getting set up on the couch with my lame-ass dinner and my laptop, I'm finally able to check in with Ainsley and see how the day went. Hopefully, I can grow some balls at the same time.

Opening up my email, I see the usual stuff that Ainsley leaves for me, but I also see an email from her. My heart trips over itself, and I almost spill my cup of noodles all over me and my laptop, thinking this is her resignation letter. I take a few deep breaths before opening it up and tilt my head in confusion with what I see.

The presentation, the one I just told her about, is currently sitting in my inbox. I pull it up and scroll through all the slides, and I realize she's finished it. Aside from specific information I've yet to get over to her, she's got everything done.

What kind of mindfuck is this?

Is this her getting everything done so she can quit? Is this just over-achieving because she wants to stay? She hasn't said anything about last night. Is she just over it? *No, you idiot.* Even if she was over it, I have a lot of explaining and apologizing to do.

This email is ... confusing, and maybe I just don't have the brainpower to understand it all. I pull up the messaging system.

Ledger Hutton:

Did you finish the entire presentation?

Ainsley Mathews:

Umm, yeah? I mean, I still need to add some details you need to send me, but otherwise, it's ready to go.

Ainsley Mathews:

Do you not like it? I can change anything, it's not a problem.

Fuuucccckkk my slow brain right now.

Ledger Hutton:

NO! No, it looks amazing. I'm just shocked you finished it all today.

Ainsley Mathews:

Oh! Yeah, well, I like stuff like this, so it was ac-tually fun.

Ainsley Mathews:

Is there anything else that needs to get done today?

This conversation isn't going how I thought it would. She's acting like nothing happened, and if I'm completely honest with myself, it's making me angry. Which is irrational. If I don't talk to her tonight, it feels like I never will, like I'll just brush it all under the rug, never knowing if I could fix things or if I could actually make things right with her.

Fuck it.

I roll my eyes at myself. I sound like a needy teenager, which I guess tracks considering that's how I've been acting since she got back into town. Jesus, I need to get my head together.

Who the hell is she meeting? Is it Oakley? Did I just miss my shot?

It's all I can say at this point. Now, I just need to figure out what I'm going to say to her when she gets here.

CHAPTER FOURTEEN
AINSLEY

You know what I learned about myself today? I'm very, very good at avoidance.

After talking to Rina and thinking about this entire situation, I just … didn't want to think about it anymore. So, when I woke up, I didn't. I jumped into work and not only finished up all my usual tasks incredibly fast, but I also finished the entire damn presentation that was supposed to take the rest of the week.

Honestly, the sheer numbness I'm feeling right now reminds me a little too much of how I was back in Austin. I don't want to revert back to that Ainsley; I was just starting to like this new version of me.

When Ledger messaged me, acting like it's your run-of-the-mill workday, I followed his lead.

Did I purposely say I was meeting someone for dinner to irk him a little? I'm not above a little pettiness at the moment, but the reality is, I'm going to my parents' for dinner. He doesn't need to know that, though. Plus, I have an easy out if I go to his house instead of him coming here.

The bigger issue I'm avoiding is that I actually *like* Ledger. If I piece together the two versions of him I've seen, I like him. But the lying is something I can't get behind. My past has ensured that forgiveness is something I hold close and don't offer easily. But have I jumped the gun with Ledger? Larkin's words from yesterday echo in my head. *I'm not sure what Ledger's reasoning was, but I suspect there's more to it.* This is why I agreed to go talk to him. Because deep down, I'm hoping there's more to it.

God damnit, I can't just let him off the hook, though.

When I signed up for this small-town life, I didn't expect this amount of drama. I was leaning more towards the slow life with a gossiping dad, but not drama in my love life. *Can I even call it my love life?*

Shaking my head at my confusing thoughts, I grab my purse from the entryway table. I'm going over to Ledger's for ten minutes, then booking it out of there. I'll hear whatever he has to say but not make any rash decisions. I've done that enough recently, so maybe this is the time to really think about things. Think about what he has to say and see how it makes me feel. See if I can forgive him and not just say that I do.

I came back home to start fresh, and maybe that starts with the way I think about and approach things. Running away from everything and working myself to death to avoid my problems hasn't worked too well. But it's exactly what I default to when I'm overwhelmed.

True to his word, his house is two minutes from mine. I pull into his driveway and see him sitting in a rocking chair on his porch. *I want rocking chairs on my porch.* Nope, focus on the task at hand. Even if my brain wants to immediately jump to distraction.

I take a few seconds to clear my thoughts and think about what my goal is here before I get out of my car.

He stands to meet me at the steps.

"Hi." His voice is shy as he fidgets with his hands.

"Hi."

"Umm, do you want to sit out here or go inside?" Extra-awkward Ledger is strangely endearing.

"Out here is fine." I step up onto the porch as he motions for me to sit in the other chair.

We rock in silence. I'm not sure what he's waiting for, but he asked me to talk, so I'm waiting him out. I can tell he's extremely nervous, though, so I'll give him some time.

I wait another minute before I realize the silence is about to make me irrationally angry.

"I like these chairs," I offer.

He startles and looks over at me. "Thanks, Rina made them."

"No shit?" I look around at the construction and am supremely impressed.

He chuckles. "Yeah, she's really fucking good at her job." The blatant pride in his voice is the same as I feel for Larkin whenever she kicks ass at anything.

"Listen—"

"I don't need more explanations, Ledger. If you want to act like the whole thing didn't happen, that's fine. I will continue at work like nothing happened." I cut him off because I'd rather have an upper hand.

"Is that what you want?" he asks, but his voice is a little shaky, drawing my attention towards him.

He looks crushed. His eyes are downcast, and he's gripping the arms of his chair until his knuckles have turned white.

I sigh. "I honestly don't know what I want. I moved here to get away from my problems and figure out where I want my life to go, and suddenly, everything's gotten very complicated. And I don't like the lying. It's the one thing I can't stand, and I'm not sure I can forgive it."

I didn't expect to lay it all out there, but it's probably better this way. He should know where I stand just as much as I should know where he does. Especially if we're going to continue to work together.

"I respect that. My intention wasn't to lie. I hope you can see that. You just ... get me flustered to the point where I can't articulate anything, much less talk to you like a normal person. I just kept digging the hole deeper and deeper, not knowing how to get out. I don't want you to feel uncomfortable with me at all, at work or around town. So, however I can fix that, I will. I am truly sorry." He maintains eye contact, and I believe him.

"I believe you mean that, but I still need time to figure things out. I'm fine still working as your assistant if you are, but as far as friendship or anything else, I just need time." It's the best I've got. It's not forgiveness, it's not a complete write off, but it's a promise to not shut down completely.

"I can work with that." The determination in his voice and in his eyes makes me weary. I might have just issued a challenge I'm not quite prepared for.

But moving here was all about starting over. Maybe it's time to just go with the flow and see where things take me.

"I've got to get to dinner, but thanks for the chat." Standing up, I see his brow furrow and his jaw clench. I hide my smirk at the hint of jealousy showing unbidden on his face.

"Talk to you to tomorrow, *Ledger*." I make sure to emphasize his name to remind him that he's why we're even in this mess to begin with.

"Talk to you later, Ains," he says with determination.

Hearing my nickname from his very attractive lips has me thinking things I don't need to be thinking about right now. That means it's definitely time for me to leave. I bound down his front steps with a little wave over my shoulder before jumping into my car and hauling ass out of his driveway.

That man is dangerous in too many ways for me.

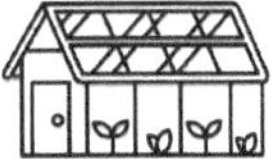

"Knock, knock!" I say as I open the front door of my parents' house.

"Annie!" My dad jumps up from his recliner to give me a hug.

I sink into it, feeling balanced for the first time since the blind date gone awry.

"You know, I thought we'd be seeing more of you when you moved back here, but it feels like we've barely seen you since you moved. Although, I heard you were dressed up last night for dinner. Special date already, Annie?" He pulls back with a smirk, and my heart sinks.

The gossip in this town is unreal.

"That was nothing, Dad. We probably need to get you a hobby or something. Your gossiping is getting a little extreme." I smirk.

"I agree!" Mom yells from the kitchen, prompting me to laugh.

"Didn't realize you two would be teaming up on me today, but that's fine." We both walk into the kitchen to sit at the bar top while Mom cooks.

"Oh, hush," my mom scolds my dad.

"That's not what you were saying to me earlier," my dad replies with a smirk.

"Oh God, no! My ears! I will literally leave and never come back if you keep that up." I fake a gag.

"You know, it's perfectly natural to have a healthy sex life at any age. We're not ashamed of it." My mom shrugs as she continues to stir the spaghetti sauce.

"Save me." I tilt my head to the ceiling. "Pull me down to hell, I don't care, just save me from hearing this conversation," I mutter.

"And I'm the dramatic one." Dad rolls his eyes.

"Can we just make it a rule that we don't talk about any of our sex lives over dinner? Or ever—I feel the need to clarify now," I beg.

"You're no fun, Annie."

"If not talking to my parents about their sex life or mine is no fun, then I will gladly take that title," I groan.

"So, what's new?" My mom gladly changes the subject.

"Nothing really, just working." I don't want to give my dad an ounce of ammunition, so sticking to work is a safe subject.

"Are you liking it? I know Ledger was running around like a chicken with his head cut off there for a while. He needed the help." My mom tsks.

"Yeah, his email was a mess." I chuckle. "It's good, though. Pretty straightforward and easy, so that's a huge change. I did have to create a presentation for him, though, so that was challenging, but I liked the creative side of things more than I thought I would."

Thinking about that more, I realize I've always been a numbers person. I've never had a creative bone in my body. But creating that presentation today was really fun. I *enjoyed* the work. I don't think there's ever been a time where I enjoyed my job.

Huh, that's eye-opening.

"I'm glad things are working out, honey. And Ledger is such a sweetheart. I'm glad it's helping both of you." My mom pats my hand as she starts plating up dinner.

The rest of dinner is our usual affair: dad gossiping about everything he's heard in the last week, me filling them in on all things Larkin and family. It's a level of comfort I didn't know I would love so much. And I had no idea how much I was really missing it.

I sit back after dinner, watching my dad do the dishes as he dances with my mom in the kitchen, and I realize how much I'm starting to like it here. My heart also clenches at the display of love spinning around together in the kitchen. *Could I have that?*

CHAPTER FIFTEEN
LEDGER

I t's been a long month.

Things have been ... civil, between Ainsley and me, but that's as far as it goes. She asked for time and I'm giving it, but damn, it feels like I've ruined every potential chance I'll ever get with her.

She's been working her ass off and hanging out with Rina, but the only reason I know this is because of my sister. Ainsley doesn't tell me about her days or what she plans to do on the weekends. Even when I try to make conversation, I get minimal in return.

I know this is my fault, but damnit, I want to find a way to sweep her off her feet and make her see me as something other than her boss who fucked up. Or as the high school guy who had a crush on her, but she didn't even remember who I was.

Pathetic. So fucking pathetic.

What happened to showing her I'm not the shy kid and that I go after what I want? Instead, I'm cowering in my office, waiting for her to reply to my message about some bullshit trees I ordered.

My phone rings, drawing me out of my Ainsley-induced stupor, and I answer without looking at who it is.

"This is Ledger."

"Hello, Mr. Hutton. This is Dan from the National Landscaping Association. How are you doing today?"

"Oh, umm, good. Hi," I stutter out.

"I'm calling to let you know you've been chosen to present at our conference this year. We were very impressed with your presentation and would love to have you as one of the main sessions."

I sit frozen.

I got the presentation.

I got a *feature* presentation.

Because of Ainsley.

My first thought is to hang up immediately and call Ainsley, but Dan's voice pulls me from my shock and excitement.

"Mr. Hutton?" "Yes, sorry! That sounds wonderful. Thank you so much."

"Great, we'll be emailing you all the information about the conference and lodging, so be on the lookout. Until then, if you have questions, this is my direct number so please feel free to call me."

"Thank you so much. I look forward to seeing you at the conference." I hang up and stare at my computer.

Holy shit, I did it. Well, Ainsley did it because that presentation was incredible.

This is something I've wanted professionally for years but have never been able to crack. I've gone to these conferences every single year and dreamed about being a presenter to really bring awareness to eco-friendly and regional-friendly landscaping techniques. It's not even about the exposure this would bring, although that's nice as hell, but this makes me feel like I've finally made it in my career.

I pick up my phone again, debating on who to tell first. Tossing my phone between my hands, my gut reaction is to tell Ainsley, and that's more telling than anything. Instead, I open up my family's group text and share the good news.

> I'm presenting at NLA next month.

Willow:

YES! Holy hell, that's amazing, big bro! Congrats!

Rina:

It's about damn time! I'm glad they pulled their heads out of their asses. You're going to kick ass.

Lennox:

Yay. Congrats.

Willow:

Lenny, you could at least pretend to care and be excited. That's a dick move even for you.

Rina:

I will kick your ass, Lenny…

I chuckle at the girls' responses. I would put money down that Lennox is just working and came across an endangered animal or some shit like that, so I'm not upset by his pretty standard message.

Me:

> Leave him alone. He's probably working and finding some magical animal.

Lennox:

Thanks, big bro. I was trying to catch a hurt armadillo, jerks. I am really excited for you, though! You've put a lot of hard work into this, and you deserve it.

Rina:

Armadillos are neither magical nor endangered,
so I stand by what I said.

Lennox:

You just don't have an appreciation for animals,
Marina.

Rina:

Excuse the fuck outta me. Guess that sweet-ass
new bed you wanted isn't going to get built… It
seems like you just don't have an appreciation
for furniture building.

Oh shit, here we go. I'm laughing my ass off reading this. They constantly fought as kids, and it didn't slow down much once our parents passed away. Now, they verbally spar more than they talk, and I'll say it's entertaining as hell. Willow and I usually just sit back with drinks and listen to them until one leaves out of frustration.

Lennox:

Jesus, you are a pain in the ass.

Me:

And on that note, I have to get back to work. But
great conversation, guys, and thanks for always
helping out at the nursery so I could grow the
company. It means a lot to me.

I've always made it a mission of mine, when I took over the role of sole guardian, that I would never shy away from showing my gratitude or expressing how proud I am of my siblings. I never wanted them to feel like they needed to prove anything to me. I just wanted them to continue to feel loved and supported, even though their world fell apart around them.

Closing out of our chat, I open up my email in hopes of catching the National Landscaping Association email before Ainsley does. A new email pops up, and I see it's exactly what I'm looking for.

I move it to my Needs Attention folder and open it up. I am unsure as to why I'm hiding it, but I want to surprise her with the good news. I want to be the one to tell her the presentation she single-handedly created made one of my greatest career aspirations come to fruition.

Reading over the details and the conference stuff is all straightforward and standard. When I get to the hotel information, I go in search of a long-ago sent email with my room confirmation. This conference usually fills up fast, so as soon as they announce it, many people book a room immediately, myself included. Now, I want Ainsley to come with me because she's been a huge hand in this and she knows the material better than I do at this point. I pull up the website and look at my options. Sadly, I'm fucked. There are only two options, and I'm not about to force her to share a bed with me. Calling the hotel, I change my reservation to the only option that will work.

It's a suite, technically, but at least she'll have her own space. Plus, maybe this will force her to talk to me outside of work shit.

And the business may be doing well, but it's not raking in the cash either. So, this is a logical move for the business too.

Sure, keep telling yourself that.

But maybe the close proximity will help her forgive me, help her see I'm not the guy who lies about his name to be malicious. I'm just a guy who never quite got over his high school crush and is learning the adult version of that woman is even better than he could have imagined.

When I get the new confirmation email, I stare at it and decide how to approach this whole situation with Ainsley.

Knocking on the door, my hands start to sweat.

Maybe I should have just called her or, shit, messaged her.

Ainsley interrupts my inner turmoil by opening the door.

"Ledger?"

"Hey, hi, umm." *Shit, get it together.* "Hey, Ainsley."

"Hi." She says it skeptically like she's unsure how to react to my presence at her door. And who can blame her, really? I can't even say a sentence confidently around this woman.

"So, I just got some great news and thought I'd tell you in person." There, simple and straightforward.

"Umm, sure. Do you want to come in?" She still looks unsure, but this is a positive step.

"That'd be great."

I follow her into the living room, where she sits in a chair, and I take the couch.

"So, I got a call today from the organizer of the National Landscaping Association, and he let me know that your presentation was picked. Not only picked, but they want to it to be one of the feature presentations."

She sits, staring at me wide-eyed.

"You got it?" she whispers.

"Yeah." I smile.

"Oh my god! You got it! Yes! I'm so happy for you!" She jumps up and claps before slamming into me with a bear hug.

I wrap my arms around her and breath her in. She smells like fresh air and wildflowers, and I want to drown in it.

She gently pushes away, and I hear a mumbled, "Sorry."

The only thing running through my head are the words, *Come back.* I haven't earned it yet, but I will.

"I came over to ask you to come with me, all expenses paid, of course. You know this presentation inside and out, so I think it would be a tremendous benefit to have you there with me."

"Yeah, whatever you need for work, I can do." She nods, and I can see her entire focus turning back to work.

"It's in three weeks. I've had the room booked for a while, but I upgraded to a two-bedroom suite, so you can come, if that's okay. It's the only option they had. I can send you the details." I can hear how stilted my voice is, but I liked seeing carefree Ainsley again, and I'm nervous she'll say no. It just makes me realize I have a lot more to do to show her the kind of man I really am.

"Shouldn't I be doing that? I mean, as your assistant?" She smirks.

"Possibly, but I booked the room right after last year's conference." I slap the tops of my legs before standing up. "Well, I guess I should go. I'll send you the travel details as soon as I have everything."

I want to stick around, but I know I need to slowly work myself back into her good graces.

"I really am happy you got it, Ledger. I know it was important to you."

Locking eyes with her, my heart starts to pound.

She looks sincere and genuinely happy—something I don't think I've seen on her since she moved here. I don't know the full story of what happened in Austin, but I do know she wasn't happy. But this Ainsley? This Ainsley is breathtakingly gorgeous. I want to tell her so many things right now, but I know the right step is to go home and plan an epic trip to Las Vegas.

"Thank you for making it happen. The presentation was what made this possible," I tell her before turning and heading to the front door. I hesitate for a second, wanting so badly to ask her to dinner, but decide against it. I need to figure out my head and how to not be a bumbling idiot around her before I jump again.

But now, I've got a timeline. Three weeks until the conference, and I'm going to plan the best damn time she's ever had.

CHAPTER SIXTEEN
AINSLEY

The last three weeks have been ... strange.

After Ledger told me about the conference and presentation, he went into planning mode and wouldn't let me touch anything. Being his assistant, it was weird to not be planning his trip and scheduling everything, but he was adamant.

Outside of work, I've been trying to be more social, although it's mostly Rina dragging me out to do things.

Getting to know my hometown as an adult is wild. All the things I hated about this place are things that I look forward to now. I love getting coffee and Oakley already knowing my order. I love knowing whose daughter is playing soccer this weekend and whose teenager is going on their first date, so everyone wordlessly bands together to keep an eye on them. I love to listen to Alice and Mabel contemplate wild scenarios that are almost always wrong.

I've always been close to my family, but this is something more. This is a group of people who will support their own in anything. Sure, the gossip is out of control, but at the heart of it, it's because everyone cares about each other. That care that felt so suffocating as a teenager is somehow the best kind of comfort as an adult. It's hard to wrap my head around it sometimes. I think about how all I wanted to do in high school was to leave.

I've wracked my brain, trying to remember Ledger for weeks, and have found nothing. The only thing I remember is the intense need to get away. To be this independent person, away from anything connected to Bluebell Falls. It honestly makes me feel ashamed.

So, things with Ledger may be totally up in the air. The clarity I've gained in the last couple of weeks has been refreshing. I've talked to Larkin about staying here, and it felt like a gigantic step. I was never going to stay here long-term, but somehow, this feels right. I feel more like myself than I have in a long time. And I want to keep that feeling so badly. There's still a chance I'll change my mind and not want to stay, but for now, this is enough.

I just need to make it through this conference with my boss—who I'm also still semi-crushing on—in one piece. I may still be mad at him for lying about things, but thinking about when I thought he was Dean and how much I *liked* him makes me realize how quickly I could fall back into just brushing things aside. And call me stubborn, but I'm just not ready to let him off the hook yet. I want to prove to myself that I'm strong enough on my own. All that lost confidence from the ordeal in Austin is at the forefront of my mind, and the need to make sure I can handle things on my own is too strong.

Today, we're flying out to Vegas, and I'm really excited. I've never been to Vegas, so I'm looking forward to seeing the strip and eating some damn good food.

The only thing I'm apprehensive about is sitting next to Ledger for the next hour while we drive to the airport, then another two hours in the air. But what could happen in three hours?

The answer: Apparently, a lot.

The drive wasn't so bad. We made small talk, and Ledger gave me the rundown of what to expect at the National Landscaping Conference. I figured it would be drastically different from the financial ones I had been to, and I was right. It sounded like a close-knit group somehow. There were the heavy hitters in the industry, but everyone kind of knew each other and kept tabs on how business was doing. It's bizarre that people who could be your competition were genuinely happy for your success. Just another way my life in Austin was not the sole definition of how life could be.

It made me think about the possibility of turning this job into *more*. It felt like I was part of something that made a difference, no matter how small, and it made me feel damn good.

As Ledger told me about some people I would meet, I sat quietly in the truck, contemplating my future. It was a strange dynamic, but Ledger seemed content to do all the talking and, for that, I was thankful.

When we finally arrive at the airport, things get confusing. Because it is such a quick conference, we both only packed carry-ons, so we bypass the check-in counter and go straight to the TSA line.

Everything is pretty smooth until Ledger walks us to the Sky Lounge.

"Umm, don't we have to go to our gate?" I ask.

"We've got some time, so I figured we could relax in here until then." He says it so nonchalantly, not like we're about to go into a section of the airport I've mentally reserved for the rich and famous.

How does one even gain access to this? Do you have to pay extra? Does it only come with a certain seating section on the plane? Is there a cover charge? Dress code? I'm too unprepared for this.

My anxiety is in full force with the number of questions running through my head. Sure, I could just ask Ledger, but we're still not on a really friendly basis. I'm still holding that grudge, and I don't want to let him in any more than I have to.

Because you know that if you let him in, it would be game over.

The devil on my shoulder needs to shut the hell up sometimes.

I awkwardly walk in behind him as he leads us to a cozy seating arrangement, plopping down on the cushioned chair and stretching his arms over his head. The little sliver of his stomach that shows as his shirt lifts has me wiping my mouth with my hand to make sure there's no drool.

"Do you have a favorite drink?" His voice pulls me out of my ogling.

I raise my gaze to his and see the hint of a smirk there. "Umm, just a glass of red wine." I feel so out of place, I don't even know what to ask for.

"Coming right up. Make yourself comfortable."

He seems so at ease right now, and it's throwing me off. He's been so hesitant and awkward for as long as I've known him, and it feels like the roles have reversed. I woke up this morning determined to keep this all business, but this entire situation is throwing me off my game.

I gingerly sit down and fidget with my bag, pulling out my laptop and then thinking better of it, and I sit back abruptly and huff out, just as Ledger sets down my glass of wine.

I watch the entire scene play out in slow motion like it's not actually happening to me. I throw my hands up in annoyance with myself just as Ledger moves the wineglass in front of me to take. My hand bumps it from the bottom, causing wine to splash all over him, leaving nothing behind.

"Oh my God! Oh my God, I am so sorry. Let me grab some towels or toilet paper to clean this up. Holy shit, I can't believe I did that." I'm whispering now, and I can feel myself on the verge of tears.

What the hell is happening to me right now? It's bad enough I feel very out of place, but then I spill wine all over my freaking boss? Kill me now. This is literally the worst-case scenario.

I spin in a circle, looking for anything that can help clean up this epic mess I've made when I feel gentle hands on my shoulders.

"Hey, it's okay. Shit happens. It's no big deal. I've got spare clothes in my bag." Ledger's voice is so soothing, it makes my eyes well with more tears.

What in the world is happening to me?

"I'm sorry," I whisper as I collapse back in the chair.

He kneels down to my level, wiping his face off with the bottom of his shirt and leaving me momentarily distracted. *Holy, happy trail, batman.*

"Hey, there's nothing to apologize for. It's just wine, and it'll wash out, okay?"

My eyes don't leave the phantom image of his bare stomach with the sexiest trail of hair I've ever seen. It's burned into my retinas, and the conflicting emotions I feel right now are about to send me down a spiral.

"Sir, here's a towel, and the bathroom is right through there if you need to change or get cleaned up," a bartender says, handing a towel to Ledger. He smiles gratefully, and I send him a self-deprecating smile. "I'll grab you another wine. Give me just a second." Before I can tell him I'm fine, he disappears across the room.

"I'll be right back. Did you get any on you? Do you need to change too?" Ledger's concern as he checks me for any wine spillage makes my heart pound too fast.

"I think I'm okay, thanks."

He nods, then gets up and heads to the bathroom.

Sinking down into my chair more, I feel mortified and strangely turned on. It's the weirdest combination I've ever felt, so maybe that wine is a good idea.

My wine is delivered with a smile, and I chug half the glass before I see Ledger making his way back over. He's changed into a pair of grey joggers and a black T-shirt, and the man looks fucking hot as sin.

Nope, no. You are still mad at him. There will be no eye-fucking.

"See? No worse for wear." He sits down next to me, way happier than he should be.

"I am still so sorry," I mutter again. I don't know if I'll ever be able to stop apologizing.

"Hey." He waits until I meet his eye. "Accidents happen. It's not the end of the world."

I nod robotically, still feeling out of place in my own skin.

In all this mess, I didn't even realize he had a lowball glass sitting on the little side table between us.

"What are you drinking?" I nod to the glass.

"Oh, gin and tonic, nothing special."

I pick up my glass, bringing it to my lips but pause as he does the same.

His lips, more plump than I realized, pucker against the lip of the glass to take a drink, and I'm frozen in place, watching. It's wildly attractive seeing his large, callused hand grip the small glass.

I see the smirk start to grow on his lips, and I drag my eyes up to his. The laughter I see there makes me jolt back and almost spill my damn wine again.

What in the name of role-reversal is happening here?

What happened to the shy Ledger? The one who lied because he panicked? That Ledger, I could deal with. This confident yet sweet Ledger? He's throwing me for a loop, and I don't know how to get off of it.

"So, first time to Vegas?" he asks so casually.

I take a much-needed sip from my wine glass and nod as I put it down on the side table.

"It is. What about you?"

"Nope. They hold the conference here every year, so it's become a little vacation, I guess."

"That must be nice. Every conference I went to for my old job was in places like Columbus, Ohio and Raleigh, North Carolina. Not terrible places at all, but not what I would consider vacation spots."

"How are you liking this job compared to your last one? I know it was quite the change, and we've never really discussed it." His tone is all business, but I get the sense he's trying to subtly dig into my past to learn more about me.

"Honestly?" I take a sip of wine as he nods, looking more serious than he's been all day.

"I didn't know if I would like this job. It's so different from what I've been doing, what I thought I would always do. But ... I love it. It's much less stress. There's more freedom, and I like seeing happy clients every single day. I love getting emails about how great of a job you did and seeing firsthand how happy you make people."

"It's not a solo endeavor. You make clients just as happy as I do."

"I don't know about that. All I do is answer emails or forward them." I shake my head.

"You do much more than that," he says quietly.

The serious shift in conversation has me feeling on my back foot again. I'm not sure I want to delve into anything this deeply with him, but I also love the conversation.

Before I can say anything else, he checks his phone and downs the last of his drink.

"Boarding is about to start. You ready?"

I sigh in relief and finish the last sip of my wine. Standing up, I follow Ledger to our gate, where we wait for our group to be called.

It's only when I realize we're Group One that I begin to question a whole lot of things.

When we take our seats *in first class,* I stare a hole through Ledger's head.

The man has explaining to do.

CHAPTER SEVENTEEN
LEDGER

Did I fuck up?

No, splurging for first class isn't a fuck-up, no matter how much of a death-stare Ainsley sends me from her seat beside me.

I try to hide my small smile, but this day has gone nothing like I thought it would, and I'm kind of loving putting her on her back foot for a change.

The spilled wine was unfortunate, but having her eyes on me as I wiped some of it off my face and body was well worth it.

"Ledger." A little growl in her voice makes my lower stomach tighten.

"Ainsley," I parrot.

"What in the fuck is this?" She doesn't look angry, more like genuinely confused and trying to figure out what my plan is here.

"This is what most people call first class." I go for casual. Maybe if I can get her to laugh or not be so focused on first class, she can get out of her head enough to enjoy it.

"Thank you. I can see that, smartass." Her response draws my eyes, and I can't help the smile that takes over my face because she's smirking back at me.

We hold each other's eyes for a minute before she shakes her head and bends down to dig through her bag.

Okay, that's better than being angry with me.

She pulls out a bag of Twizzlers and sits back in her chair. Carefully opening the bag so it doesn't rip down the side, she gets settled in before taking a deep breath and looking over at me again.

"Why are we in first class, Ledger?"

"Because this is a big deal to me." I decide to go for broke. "And because I want to treat you. I want to show you I'm not the guy you met when you first moved back."

"By buying my attention?"

"No," I rush out, combing my fingers through my hair in frustration. "No, that wasn't my intention at all. Fuck, I can't do anything right around you, it seems."

I'm agitated quickly because I can't clearly say what I mean. I'm already screwing this up *again,* when all I've been trying to do is get her to talk to me, at the very least. I thought we were making progress after the wine spill, and then I just fucked it all up again by upgrading our flight.

This woman makes me a teenager, and I can't pull myself out of it. I was doing so well too.

"Do you have other things planned in Vegas?" she asks calmly.

"Yes." I'm not lying to her anymore. If she asks me a question, I will always answer her honestly.

"I suppose you aren't going to tell me any of those plans?"

"I would prefer not to."

She nods her head as she takes a bite of a Twizzler, then twirls what's left around like a rope.

"I don't think I'm ready to just forgive and forget, but I also like the idea of enjoying this trip. I don't know where that leaves us, though." She points at me with the Twizzler, and I have a hard time reigning in my chuckle. She used to do this in high school, and it's nice to see that some things don't change that much.

"I get it, I really do. It's going to take time, and I know that." I'm not about to act like she needs to just forget about my stupidity. "So, let's have a fun trip, and we'll figure out everything else later." I need to continue to be confident. I know the plans I have for this trip will throw her for a loop, but I need to be secure that this will work, or all my insecurities will rear their ugly head again.

"Deal." She snags another Twizzler, twirling it so hard, it flies out of her hand and smacks the flight attendant walking by in the face.

"Oh my god! I am so sorry," Ainsley rushes out.

"No worries, miss." She smiles as she picks up the candy, throwing it away as Ainsley turns bright red.

"What in the world is happening to me today?" she whispers, burying her head in her hands.

I do chuckle then because she's right—this is very much unlike her from what I've gathered by just working together.

"Don't laugh! I just hit her in the face!"

I laugh harder at her outrage, and it makes her crack.

"You might need to steer well clear of me on this trip if this is any indication of how things are going to go," she says through laughter.

"Maybe I'll just take all the projectile objects away from you. That should do the trick." I smile over at her.

She holds my gaze for a second, and it feels like the mood shifts. The tension is palpable, and my dick starts to take notice.

Of course, I noticed when I picked her up how well her *Favorite Aunt* T-shirt fits her and how the leggings she's wearing look painted on, but it feels like I'm finally able to react to how good she looks. Until this point, I was trying to be respectful and more focused on talking to her, and not how she affected me.

But being this close to her, smelling her wildflower scent, it's damn near impossible not to react.

She looks back and forth between my eyes like she's looking for something.

"What is happening right now?" she whispers.

The pull is too strong, and I start to lean forward. She unconsciously does the same, and we're so close I can see flecks of gold in her eyes.

"Can I get you something to drink? Champagne?" The flight attendant's voice causes both of us to jerk back.

Ainsley clears her throat. "A red wine would be great for me, and a gin and tonic for him. Thank you."

My head feels fuzzy. We were so close, *so fucking close*. I swear it feels like nothing is going right between us. Everything that could go wrong has, and this time, it wasn't even because I was being stupid.

Before I even have time to think about what just happened, our drinks are delivered, and it's then that I realize Ainsley just ordered the same drink I had in the lounge for me.

"Thank you for ordering for me," I tell her sincerely. If she was paying that much attention, that has to mean something, right?

"Not a problem. I hope you didn't want something else," she says as she takes a sip of her wine, not making eye contact.

"This is perfect." I take a large swig, trying to calm my racing heart.

"So." She puts her wine down as she starts talking. "Did you always know you wanted to get into landscaping?"

Okay, back to neutral ground. I can handle that.

"Kind of? I mean, I've always been interested in the design aspect of it. I decided to get my degree in Landscape Architecture and kind of see where it took me." I'm not really sure I want to get into the details of how that plan didn't really work out because I needed to come back here in order to take custody of my siblings when our parents passed away.

"Interesting. So, what made you come back home?"

I suck in a breath and debate what to tell her. Telling her all the nitty gritty is the best course because I made a promise to not lie to her anymore, and even a lie by omission feels wrong. Even if this is something I don't talk about.

"My parents passed away right before I graduated. I knew immediately I was going to come back and take full custody of my siblings so they could keep the life they always knew, even with the loss of our parents. The business itself started small. Just helping out neighbors here and there. I'm not sure when the growth happened, but the business has blown up in the last decade. It's been a lot of hard work, and Rina and Willow are the ones that really grew the nursery, but it feels like I've finally gotten to a point where I'm happy with it."

"I'm so sorry, Ledger. I didn't know." She reaches over and squeezes my hand.

"I wouldn't expect you to know." My tone isn't harsh because I understand why she doesn't know.

"It just makes me realize how much I've blocked out Bluebell Falls. I mean, I vaguely remember my dad talking about a couple that passed away and left behind some kids, but I never put two and two together because I just didn't care enough to. That sounds really shitty, right?" She looks over at me with sad eyes.

"That's not shitty at all, and I didn't mean to imply that you leaving was a bad thing. Hell, I wanted to leave, but circumstances changed my path. I wouldn't change it for anything now, but it's hard as a teenager to see past the small-town life. I'll admit that dealing with my grief at the same time as I was forced to take care of Willow and Lennox was not a great time in my life. In the beginning, I was extremely resentful, and I hated it. It made me feel like I was a terrible brother and son. But I was determined to help them live as normal of a life as possible. And anything I wanted didn't matter." The painful lump in my throat reminds me of how hard that time was for me. I wasn't planning on spilling all the dark details of that time in my life, but here we are.

"And do you feel like you lived your life the way you wanted to? Don't get me wrong, it's extremely admirable that you jumped in without a second thought, but they're all grown now. Do you feel like you are living the life you really want to have now?"

I take in her words, and the first thought that pops into my head is I expected to be married with a couple of kids running around by now because that's what's expected. It's not shocking that hasn't happened since I locked that part of my life away after Jenna, but looking at the woman next to me makes me feel like some form of that is possible again.

"I ... don't know. That's sad, right? I should know the answer to that. At the very least, I should know what kind of life I want, right?" I look over at her, no doubt looking a little lost. I didn't expect this conversation, and I certainly didn't expect to feel like maybe I've been putting things I want on the back burner.

"It's not sad," she whispers.

"What about you? Are you living life the way you've always wanted to?"

She scoffs. "No. Hell no. I feel like the last decade of my life was a complete waste."

"How so?" I don't know the story of what happened in Austin. I just know the job she applied for is a job she's well and truly overqualified for.

"You obviously know I worked in finance." I nod my head, so she continues. "I was always good at numbers. They just made sense to me, so it felt like a logical step to jump into the finance world. And I enjoyed it, for a time. It was when I started wanting to move up within the company that things went south. You hear it all the time, that women have to work twice as hard in male-dominated fields, and for some reason

I just didn't believe it. I thought if I worked hard enough, if I just put my head down and was the best person for the job, the best financial advisor at my firm, that it would happen for me. Joke's on me because not only is that not the case, but the boys' club that was my old firm blocked me from any other equivalent position in Austin. They went with a guy who lied to get the job and then harassed me once he was my supervisor." She huffs out a sad laugh.

"What the fuck?" I'm outraged for her, and I realize just how much me lying was a direct connection to everything she went through in Austin. *God, I'm a prick.*

"Easy there, turbo. It's long past over, and honestly, I'm completely fine with it now. It took me a long time to come to terms with it, but I think I'm mostly okay with where I've landed. Who wants to work in that kind of atmosphere, anyway?"

"I'm sorry I lied to you. It was never my intention to do that," I blurt out. It feels imperative that I get her to understand I never meant to lie and make her feel like I used her, especially after hearing a little of what went down at her last job.

"I know you didn't."

"You make me so fucking nervous all the time. It's like I'm right back in my teenage years. You turn me into the shy, bumbling idiot who can barely complete a sentence around you. It's not an excuse; it's just how you affect me."

"You're doing pretty okay today." She smiles.

"Yeah, I think maybe I grew some balls last night and finally figured out how to talk to the girl I like," I say.

She bursts out a laugh. "Not exactly the imagery I was expecting, but thanks for that."

I want to tell her I'll say any ridiculous thing if it means she laughs like that again. If it puts that carefree expression on her face, I'll do anything.

But for now, just letting her know where I still stand with her is enough. I don't want to push her away again.

The captain comes over the speakers, informing us we're about to take off. We settle in for the whole safety speech and then off we go.

"So, tell me how your sister is doing," I say as soon as the initial take-off is over.

CHAPTER EIGHTEEN
AINSLEY

"Larkin is amazing. She's got the whole life right now. Met the love of her life, Theo, promptly hated him, and then when they were forced together for a case—they're both social workers—decided they actually loved each other, and that was that. They also adopted Gavin. He was the kid in the case they were working on, and he's literally the greatest thing to happen in my life. I love that boy more than anything."

"Hence the shirt." He nods down to the shirt Gavin gave me for Christmas a few years ago.

"Yep. I think I'll wear this until it has a million holes in it and is so worn down it's basically see-through." His eyes heat when I say it, and I have to clear my throat and focus.

This flight has been nothing like I thought it would be. First, there's all my clumsiness, then, there was the almost-kiss that I still can't get out of my head, and then all the talk about how he was forced to grow up and take care of his siblings. It feels like I'm meeting him for the first time, and I *like* him. A lot.

"So, her and Theo have Gavin. Do they have any other kids?"

"They do. Maddie is two and a little spitfire. I always thought Gavin was the one who was going to give them a run for their money, but he has nothing on his little sister. She's hilarious and annoys the hell out of Gavin, but he's the best big brother ever."

"I remember in high school, she was the biggest extrovert. Always the life of the party. I don't think I expected her to settle down, honestly," he says.

"Yeah, none of us did." I laugh. "But if you met Theo, you'd get it. He's beyond perfect for her, and he's just the best person." Talking about them makes me miss them exponentially more than usual. I'm going to have to see about making a trip to Austin to visit them soon. At the very least, I owe Gavin a video game night when I get back from Vegas.

"Hopefully, they'll come to town someday and I'll get to meet them," Ledger says.

I lose a little of my smile then because I'm not sure that'll ever happen in the capacity he's hoping for. I don't even know if I would want him to meet Larkin's family as anything more than a guy she went to school with.

He clears his throat, sensing my discomfort. "So, anything you're looking forward to in Vegas?"

I perk back up, grabbing onto the change of subject like a lifeline.

"This will probably sound lame, but I am so excited about eating. I grew up watching cooking shows—hell, I still watch them—so I know there are a ton of chefs that have restaurants there. I definitely want to hit at least a couple of my favorites."

"I feel like I only ever eat the catered lunches at the conference or the buffets," he says shyly.

Gasping, I turn to look at him.

"You haven't even tried one of the million-and-one amazing restaurants here? That's... That's a travesty. I don't know that we can be friends after knowing that." I shake my head in mock disappointment.

"Are we friends?" The serious tone of his voice pulls me from a light-hearted attempt at a joke.

I stare into his eyes and really think about the question. If you had asked me five hours ago, the answer would have probably been no. But now? Now, I'm more confused than ever.

Can I be friends with Ledger if that's all there will ever be? Am I seriously thinking about more when I just shunned him for God knows how long?

If I'm completely honest with myself, if I put the lying about his name aside, Ledger intrigues the hell out of me. Our conversation on this trip alone makes me want to know more.

"Yeah, I think we are," I say softly.

We spent the rest of the flight talking about the many chefs I'm obsessed with, along with some work stuff. Making sure Ledger feels comfortable with the presentation is my number one job, so I wanted to make sure he was ready.

This is a work trip, after all.

We're currently waiting as the plane taxis to the gate, and I can practically feel everyone's excitement on the plane. I've never been on a flight where you know people are traveling to have a good time, no matter the reason, and it's intoxicating.

A sports chant breaks out in the back of the plane, and I turn to Ledger in question.

"Hockey. I forgot there was a game this weekend. Fans fly in to watch their team play against Vegas because it's one big party and vacation all rolled into one." He smirks as they get louder.

"Wow." I laugh as the entire plane joins them. "Sounds like a good time."

"There's a beer garden right outside of the arena, and they have a good beer selection and their fries with beer cheese are probably some of the best I've had. It's one of the few places I've ventured out of the hotel for."

"Sold. How fast can we get there and grab some?" I'm practically drooling at the prospect of any delicious food at this point.

"Well, I'll look up when the game is, and we will avoid that area like the plague. Like the whole day."

"Seriously?"

"Seriously. The entire area is packed for most of the day, no matter what time the game is."

"Damn. Here you are getting my hopes up, and I'll probably have to wait to get my beer cheese fix." I slump down in my chair as Ledger's husky laughter meets my ears.

"I will get you beer cheese, I promise."

Somehow, I believe him. If I was absolutely craving it in the middle of the game when the place was packed, I feel like he would go get it for me, just to make me happy.

This Ledger, the one I suspect has been the real one all along, would do a lot to make the people around him happy. And while I'm still irked he lied, I think I understand it more now.

We finally pull up to the gate, and it's the usual shitshow of everyone standing up and deciding to make deboarding difficult. I swear, if everyone just chilled in their seats until it hit their row, things would be a lot smoother.

Lucky for us, we're in first class, so we are off the plane in five minutes flat, and I feel fancy as hell.

Walking through the airport, I take in everything that is uniquely Las Vegas. Slot machines line the center of the gates, and it feels more like a casino than an airport. We make our way down to the transportation floor and join the mile-long taxi line.

"This is like an entirely different world," I mutter.

"Yeah, it's definitely something to get used to. Usually, I would just ride-share to the hotel, but taxis are actually cheaper and faster here. This line," he gestures in front of us, "will move fast, and we'll be at the front in, like, ten minutes or less."

"You willing to make that a bet?" I ask with a smirk, feeling the atmosphere seep into me.

"What's the wager?"

"If we make it to the front in under ten minutes, you get to pick the prize. If it's over, I do."

"What sort of prize are we talking about here, Ains?" he asks as his eyes heat at the inflection of his words.

I think on it for a second, wondering how far I'm willing to let the innuendo go.

"Let's keep the prizes PG-13." There, nothing too crazy that can happen at a PG-13 level, right?

Famous last words…

Ledger won the bet, and on the drive over to our hotel, he kept coming up with outrageous ideas, like going to one of the Cirque du Soleil shows and seeing if I can be one of the stage acts. Or going to one of my favorite chef's restaurant and seeing if the chef is there to get a picture.

I should have put a time limit on when he got to cash in on this prize, because I get the feeling he's going to hold on to it until he deems it the perfect time.

All it's doing now is creating a shit-ton of tension between us.

We make it to the Vdara, and it looks fancy as hell. I'm wondering how a bunch of landscapers can put on a conference of such a caliber, but then I feel like a bitch for assuming things about their income. Who knows, maybe the group rate is fucking amazing.

"Good afternoon. Check-in for Ledger Hutton."

I spin around, taking in the giant glass façade and the luxurious lobby. It's by far the swankiest hotel I've ever been to.

"I see here you booked a suite, but it looks like we overbooked. I apologize for the inconvenience. I can get you set up at our sister hotel, Aria, with our Strip-view king room."

I whip around, confused by what I just heard.

"Umm… I—" Ledger turns around, looking like he's in a full-blown panic.

"That's our only option for a room?" I ask calmly.

"Unfortunately, yes. Between the game and the conference, it seems we're in a very short supply of rooms. I apologize. We'll be sending up complimentary champagne and food tray as well." She smiles at us. She seems entirely unfazed by the colossal mistake this is.

My heart starts pounding when I think about what this means.

Ledger and me … in one room … with one bed.

A couch is comfortable, right? This place is fancy. They've got to have a comfy couch.

"Umm, that will be fine, thank you." Ledger's stilted voice breaches the haze of my chaotic thoughts.

We don't really have another choice, do we?

I stand stock still, trying to calm myself down and rationalize that this will all be okay.

It'll totally be fine. Ledger and I can be civil, sharing one room, with everything open to each other. No door separating us beyond a bathroom. So, I definitely won't have to see him change, or shirtless, or when he comes out of the shower with his hair dripping down to his chest and watch it run down his abs as he grabs his clothes for the day.

Nope, won't have to see that at all.

And then a worse thought enters my head.

I only brought skimpy shorts and tank tops to sleep in. I'm literally going to be showing my ass and tits when getting ready for bed. There is absolutely no way to hide any of that if we're in close contact.

Can I handle seeing that much of Ledger? Can I handle him seeing that much of me? I only have so much willpower, and I did bring a vibrator because I had wishful thinking. Not that I could actually use it in this situation.

A hand interrupts my wild thoughts on my lower back. "You ready to go up?"

Ledger's voice is strained, and I imagine he's not super comfortable with the arrangements either.

We're both silent as we walk over to the other hotel and ride the elevator up to the thirty-ninth floor. I follow Ledger stiffly to our room, trying to come up with the words to tell him this is completely fine and not awkward at all. And how I'm *not* looking forward to seeing him shirtless at all.

Jesus, I'm screwed. Completely and utterly screwed. This close proximity is going to kill me.

The door clicks open, and we both walk in.

"Holy shit!"

"And this is supposed to be a downgrade," Ledger says, shock in his voice.

What we walk into isn't a normal hotel room. It's probably larger than my house, and everything is the peak of luxury. There's even a freestanding tub that looks like it seats at least three people in the middle of the bathroom.

We're not in Bluebell Falls anymore.

CHAPTER NINETEEN
LEDGER

My initial worry is drowned out by the ridiculous room we're staying in. I'm not going to lie and say I was completely un-affected by our suite being oversold, but for now, I'll bask in this nice-as-hell room and deal with the fallout later.

My gaze is drawn to the bed that backs up to the wall-to-wall windows.

It's completely okay to imagine Ainsley, palms on the glass, as I fuck her from behind, right?

Woah, not where my mind should be right now. I move my hand to shift my dick as subtly as I can and take a peek at Ainsley, to see her still looking around the room in awe.

She may not have an issue with our sleeping arrangements, it seems, but if my first thought is of the position I want to put her in first, I'm going to struggle heavily over the next couple of days.

She walks to the opposite end of the room and looks into the bath-room.

"Holy shit, you have to see this!"

I quickly walk up behind her and lean in to see past the door frame.

The bathroom is exactly what I would expect from the level of luxury in this room. A free-standing soaker tub and a steam shower, covered in what I assume is marble, take up most of the space.

Ainsley soaking in the tub with me on my knees beside her, trailing my touch over every single inch of her wet, naked body.

Jesus, I'm never going to survive this trip. I tip my head back, taking a deep breath in an attempt to get my bearings.

She spins around, only inches from my body, with her eyes lit up like the brightest star.

"This is fucking incredible. I didn't even know they made hotel rooms like this!" She walks out of the bathroom, looking at the entire space.

I'm so distracted by the sheer happiness radiating from her that I don't register her words.

"Ledger? You okay?" Her furrowed brow makes me want to do anything to bring back her smile.

I can't take my eyes off of how fucking gorgeous she looks right now: no make-up, hair on top of her head, and wearing leggings and an oversized T-shirt. And she looks so fucking happy, I can't even think past impulse.

Cupping her jaw with my hand, I descend on her lips. The soft press nearly undoes me.

I'm kissing Ainsley Mathews!

I can feel her shock for a split second before she melts into me and grips my wrist as she leans into me more. Her lips part, and I instantly take advantage, sweeping my tongue against hers. I get so lost in the intimacy, it takes me a second to realize she's pulled back and is pressing her hand gently against my chest.

"We shouldn't be doing that..." she whispers.

I feel like I've just gotten smacked by her words.

Taking a huge step back, I feel like an enormous piece of shit because she didn't want that. I got lost in the moment and acted on impulse.

"I'm so sorry—"

"No! No, not like that. I just mean you're my boss, and this is a work trip..." She trails off like I'm supposed to understand her logic.

I don't. At all.

Fuck work. Fuck the conference. If that's what is standing in the way of us kissing again, fuck it all.

But her pushing me away right now, sending this obvious message, fucking *hurts.* It's irrational, I know that, but my head and my heart are going haywire, and I can't get myself to think logically right now.

"I ... I can't do this," I barely get out before I step into the bathroom and lock the door.

Leaning against the door, I lightly tap my head on it.

God damnit, I finally got a taste, and she pulled back because I fucked up too much to overcome.

My heart is beating too fast in my chest—whether it's from the kiss or being supremely disappointed in her reasons for pulling back, who's to say.

All I know is I need space. I need to take the time to calm down and try to see this from her view because, right now, I don't get it. I don't understand how you can kiss someone like that and *still* walk away.

Ainsley is the one that never was in high school, sure, but *this* Ainsley that I've gotten to know over the past few months? I don't think I can handle more excuses of why we shouldn't be right now, when all I see is just how fucking right we could be. If she needs more time for me to show her I won't ever lie to her again, fine. But there's no way she didn't feel the connection in that kiss.

Maybe I should see if they have another room. It's going to be actual torture to share a room with her if she wants to keep the distance. I respect her and her decisions about us, but that doesn't mean I'm going to willingly agree and give up. My feelings aren't magically going to disappear.

What a fucking mess.

A knock at the door scares the hell out of me.

"Ledger?" Her soft, hesitant question barely permeates through the door.

"What, Ains?" I can hear the defeat in my tone, and I hate every second of it. I'm supposed to be stronger than this, be able to be the bigger person here. But all I can think about is her not wanting me. The crushing weight on my chest tells me I'm a lot more gone for her than I thought I was, and it sure as hell feels one-sided right now.

"Can we talk … about what just happened?"

"Not right now. I think I just need a few minutes."

"Oh, okay." I can hear the sadness in her voice, and damn it if it doesn't make me want to open the door and comfort her. But I know if I do, I won't be able to respect her boundaries, and I refuse to be that kind of man.

"Just five minutes, Ains," I say, hoping she grants me this.

I had an entire plan for this trip. Woo her, show her how things can be, how *I* can be. And within the first five minutes, I've fucked it up by kissing her when she didn't want it. A conversation is probably in order, but I need a much clearer head to do that.

Silence greets my request, and I breathe a sigh of relief that she's giving me this time.

Maybe a cold shower will do me some good.

Not thinking about the fact that Ainsley is still on the other side of the door, I strip and turn on the shower as cold as I can stand it.

Water cascades down my back, and my nervous system finally calms down enough to think about this entire situation logically.

My original plan was to take her out to dinner, and I think sticking to that is the best approach. We need to have an actual conversation about what is happening between us, so we're on the same page and there is no confusion about what I want. Whether she's on the same page as me is anyone's guess, but I know I need to lay my cards on the table. This isn't what I was expecting to do right away, but my impulsive kiss is forcing my hand.

My thoughts of slowly leading her into the idea of us being together and dating have officially been placed on the back burner. Clearing the air is the priority.

Finally, feeling like I'm on more steady footing, I shut off the water and grab a towel.

Hell, even the towels are ridiculously soft here.

After scrubbing the towel over my head to dry my hair, I wrap it around my waist and head out into the room.

Ainsley is sitting on the bed, twisting her hands together, when she hears the door open and then abruptly stands up.

Her eyes are comically wide as they trail down my body. I couldn't hide the smirk on my face for a million dollars as I watch her take me in. We may be in limbo at the moment, but her reactions don't hide her attraction to me.

Clearing my throat, her eyes snap up to mine.

"I was thinking we could go to dinner." I specifically don't address anything that happened before my shower because I think we both need to be on an even footing—and me, with only a towel around my waist, isn't it.

"Umm, dinner. Yeah, that sounds great."

"I'm just going to grab some clothes." I walk right up to her before reaching around and snagging my bag off the bed.

I am feeling much better now. My confidence is mostly restored, and hopefully after an actual conversation about us over dinner, I'll feel better overall.

She sucks in a breath as I lean around her, and that confidence boost grows exponentially.

"Do you want to change in the bathroom or in the bedroom?" I ask quietly, close to her ear.

"Umm, bathroom. Bathroom's fine."

She frantically digs into her suitcase, grabbing some clothes, and sprints to the bathroom. I barely hold in my chuckle as I drop my bag back onto the bed. She's definitely not unaffected, even if she did push me away. No more jumping to conclusions, though. She needs to know exactly where my head is at.

I grab a pair of black slacks and a black button-down, and throw them on. I'm in the process of rolling up my sleeves when Ainsley emerges from the bathroom. Rolling the last bit of my sleeve, I glance up at her and freeze.

Holy shit, I think this woman will always put me on my back foot. Regardless of how confident I pretend to feel, she will always take my breath away.

She looks gorgeous; her strawberry blonde hair hanging loose around her shoulders and minimal makeup affect me more than any dolled-up version of her she thinks will garner attention. My eyes trail down and see she's in a pale-yellow sundress with some straw-colored heels. I'm sure they call those something particular, but hell if I know what that is.

I look up and see her gaze looking down my body, and when she meets my eyes again, the pure heat in them makes me think we'll be okay.

"So, dinner?" I ask.

"Yep. Yep, dinner. I'm ready." She walks toward the door, grabbing her purse on the way.

"You have anywhere specific you want to go?" I ask, knowing she probably has, at a minimum, a few places she wants to go.

"I do, but I'll be honest. I don't really want to walk all over kingdom come for food. I'm starving."

"Perfect. We can just walk around the little restaurant center they have here and find something."

We make it to the elevator easily enough, although the restraint it took to not lead her with my hand on her back almost killed me.

The elevator ride is silent. I'm not sure why she is, but I'm desperately trying to calm my dick down and force blood back to my head so I'm able to think clearly. Her smell—somehow, she still smells like wildflowers—is surrounding me, and it's a damn aphrodisiac.

We finally get to the lobby, and I steer her to the side with all the restaurants.

"Holy shit, how many are there?" she asks.

"A lot." I let out a chuckle. "I think every big hotel has at least twenty restaurants now. It makes it hard to pick sometimes."

"No kidding." She's looking around in wonder, and I swear I'll take her to every restaurant she wants to keep her happy.

"So, what's your favorite food?" she asks as we walk along the hallway of restaurants.

"Hmm, that's hard to narrow down. But I do love homemade gnocchi with just a simple, spicy marinara. It's classic but so hard to get right."

"Sounds delicious. Oh my God," she whispers.

"What?" I look around, trying to figure out what's wrong.

"Julián Serrano... *The* Julián Serrano has a restaurant here." She's still whispering.

I look around and find the restaurant she's talking about.

"The tapas place? Does that sound good?"

"Good? It sounds phenomenal!"

"Okay, let's go then."

"What? No! I'm not dressed to go somewhere that fancy. Are you kidding me?"

I stop in the middle of the large hallway and spin her by the shoulders to look at me.

"You are beautiful. You could be wearing a damn sweatsuit, and no one would care. We're going to go eat at the tapas place, and we're going to enjoy the hell out of it, okay?"

She nods and I take her hand, leading her to the restaurant.

"Good evening. How many are in your party tonight?" the hostess asks.

"Two, please."

"It'll be a bit of a wait for a table, but the bar is free if you'd rather not wait."

I look at Ainsley, and she not so subtly nods her head.

"The bar works, thanks."

We head to the bar and get ourselves situated before I look over at Ainsley again. She looks awe-struck and so damn excited it's infectious.

"Oh my gosh, I don't even know how to act. I mean, there are nice restaurants in Austin, but I never had time to actually go to them. This is unreal," she rambles out.

A smile so big that my cheeks start to hurt spreads over my face. Dinner was a fucking great idea.

CHAPTER TWENTY
AINSLEY

This is like meeting a celebrity for me, and I just know I look like a damn lunatic right now. I pull out my phone and snap pictures of the menu and the kitchen you can see from the bar, immediately sending it to Larkin. My phone pings with a message from her.

Larkin:

> Holy shit! I'm so jealous right now. Theo says to get the octopus because he saw it on a show and everyone said it was their favorite dish.

Me:

> Sold! I'll take pictures of everything and send them to you guys.

Larkin:

> Yes! But also enjoy your work trip … with Ledger.

I put my phone down and feel my cheeks heat with embarrassment. Did I forget Ledger was even here for a moment? Maybe, but now I feel bad and wonder how I could ever forget about his presence. Especially when thoughts of what he looks like in only a towel pop into my head yet again.

Snap out of it, girl! We're supposed to be here for business.

I clear my throat, glance up, and see Ledger watching me with a warm smile on his face.

"So, what looks good?" I ask, skirting around how that look makes me feel and all the tension radiating between us.

"It's tapas, so I figured we'd get a little of everything."

"Right, of course, duh." I feel so off-kilter right now, I genuinely don't know how to bring myself out of it.

I can't tell if it's everything that happened in the hotel room, or if I'm so sexually starved it's officially affecting my social skills. Either way, I need to figure it out ASAP because Ledger has the capability to consume me if I let him.

"Hey." He pauses until I meet his eyes. "Just breathe. There's nothing to prove here, nothing to be embarrassed about. Be excited, geek out over the menu, order as much shit as you want to. I'm along for the ride, Ains."

My shoulders slump, and I let out a self-deprecating laughter. My heart? It beats so hard in my chest over him knowing exactly how I'm feeling. And it scares the hell out of me.

"I don't know what's going on with me. I think you make me a little nervous." This might be the most honest I've ever been with him. I need a tiny bit of control, though.

"Well, if it helps, you make me a little nervous too."

I snort. "Yeah, right. Look at you over there, cool as a cucumber."

"You want honesty?" he asks.

Nodding my head is all I can do because I feel desperate to hear what he has to say.

"I feel like I've been out of my depth with you since day one. I've been awkward, made all the wrong decisions, and jeopardized a lot more than the best assistant ever. The crush I had on you in high school feels like child's play now. I wanted to get your attention, and I did but in the wrong way. I know I did everything possible to not have your trust, but I want to go out on a limb here and lay all my cards on the table."

He waits until I nod again, telling him wordlessly I want to hear more.

"Everything I've learned about you, every word from your mouth, digs me a little deeper in the whirlpool that is uniquely you, Ainsley. I want nothing more than to prove I'm worth taking a chance on, but I will give you as much time as you need to feel comfortable with that too. And if you decide I'm not worth it ... then I will respect that one hundred percent." He reaches across the table, grabbing my hand as my breathing gets a little unsteady.

"But make no mistake, my goal here is to date you and see where this goes. I think it's pretty obvious how attracted I am to you, but I wanted you to know where I stood before anything else happens. This is more than sexual to me. I'm sorry for what happened in our room. I got carried away, and I needed a minute to get my head back on straight so I didn't say something impulsively stupid yet again."

His tone is so earnest, and his confidence is something I haven't really seen from him. It's wildly attractive, as if he needed to be more so. It seems I haven't been very clear on things either, so maybe it's time I change that. Fortune favors the brave, isn't that the saying?

"I-I..." I clear my throat again, trying to get my thoughts clear. "I'm really nervous about starting something with someone I work with, let alone my boss. If we were to do anything, I would want things to go really slow. I'm just starting over, and I don't want to be put in another situation where I need to leave everything behind and do it all again. Hell, I don't even know what I want to do with my life, and I'm thirty-five! I feel like I'm in this vast state of transition, and I don't really know what that looks like in terms of a potential relationship. I'm nervous about starting something if I'm not one-hundred-percent sold on staying in Bluebell Falls too."

"I'm more than okay with that. I'll go at whatever pace you want; you can control everything in that respect, and we can just see how things go. You know I would never threaten your job, right? If things don't work out and you need some space, we can have less contact. Hell, I can have Rina be your point of contact for work so you're able to keep the stability. I never want you to feel like you need to quit because of the potential we don't work out. And I'm willing to try this even if you don't want to stay. That's something we can figure out if the time comes."

I chew on my lip, really taking in his words. He's saying all the right things, but can I trust him?

"I promise, all I want to do it make sure you're happy, even if it's not with me, but I want the chance to see if we work."

I'm not sure where this version of Ledger has come from, but he's very convincing and charming.

"If I say yes, where do we go from here?" I ask.

The smile that spreads across his face is breathtaking as he squeezes the hand he's still holding.

"If you say yes, then this is officially a date if you want it to be."

"Then this is a date," I declare, feeling shockingly secure in this deci-sion.

Dinner was a fucking blast. I don't think I've ever had that much fun with anyone except Larkin.

The two drinks I had were enough to make me feel loose but not drunk. Thank God too, because I need to keep my head around the man who is currently walking me backwards into the elevator.

His hands on my hips send sparks all over my body, and our vow to go slowly is dangerously close to being broken.

"Ledger…"

"Ainsley." He smirks as he presses the number for our floor.

"You're a tease, you know that?" I say with a laugh.

"I just had the best night in far longer than I can remember. Sue me for wanting to be close to you for a minute," he whispers in my ear as he nuzzles into my neck gently.

"Well, when you put it like that…" I run my hands up his muscled arms.

The elevator dings, signaling we've reached our floor, and we step back from each other like we've just gotten caught in a classroom in high school.

Clearing my throat, I step around Ledger and head to our door, needing the space before we reach the point of no return right there in the elevator.

We're both silent as we walk into our room before Ledger finally breaks it.

"I think I'm going to grab a quick shower, unless you need the bathroom first." He's suddenly changed back to the shy, slightly awkward Ledger I'm used to, and I feel back to normal. It's a strange comfort, but I'm finding I like this side of him a lot.

"Go for it."

He nods and grabs some clothes from his bag before walking to the bathroom and shutting the door behind him.

I finally take a full breath and plop down onto the bed.

Holy shit, either he's extremely sexy right now, or I'm just horny as hell.

I can't tell, but I know that I'll need to do something about it tonight in order to keep my head on straight. Good thing I came prepared, even if I don't actually turn it on.

I realize I don't know what a quick shower is to Ledger, but I'd rather be changed before he struts out of the bathroom wearing God knows what. Jumping up, I find my tank top and shorts that I usually wear to bed and keep my eyes and ears on the bathroom, looking for any sign that he'll come out when I'm half-naked as I strip out of my dress and put on my pajamas.

Not that it would be an entirely bad thing if he did.

Apparently, my inner devil is a hussy for Ledger now, and I can't even blame her.

I look around the room, marveling at how nice it is yet again, and then walk to the windows that overlook the strip.

It's funny how your whole world can change in the matter of a few short months. In Austin, it felt like my world had imploded, and it left me without a sense of self. It's scary as hell to be this age and feel like you're starting over. And it's even more difficult to realize the life you thought you were building wasn't all that shiny when the sheen wore off. Hell, I didn't even really have friends. Everyone I considered a friend bailed the second I was fired.

Coming back to Bluebell Falls made something click into place. I'm not quite sure what it is exactly, but I know Ledger is a huge component in it. Romantic involvement aside, the job he gave me means so much more than he'll ever know. It gave me a chance to prove I was more than Austin, more than someone who got taken advantage of and never recovered.

My viewpoint of my life has been altered. And somewhere in the back of my mind, I know things with Ledger have some serious sticking power, but I'm scared shitless of that. I wasn't lying when I said us working together was problematic for me. I just need to make sure I reinforce my boundaries and protect myself in case things go downhill.

"Hey." Ledger's voice startles me since I didn't hear the bathroom door open.

"Hey yourself." I don't turn around, too caught up in my thoughts still.

"What has you thinking so hard over here?" he whispers.

I try to think quickly on my feet because I don't want to dump my whole existential crisis at his feet right now.

"Just wondering about the sleeping arrangements," I blurt out. Well, it's not like we didn't need to address it, anyway.

"Well, I was planning to take the couch and give you the bed, if that's okay with you," he says as he steps up to the window next to me.

Lights, as far as the eye can see, cover the street, and the reflection glows in his gaze.

"I think that's probably a smart idea," I whisper. I'm not sure if I really want him to sleep on the couch, but it definitely seems like the best option if I want us to stay on this slow path he suggested. Which I absolutely should want.

So why is it so disappointing to not be sleeping in the same bed?

"Well, I think I'm going to try to get some sleep since we have an early start tomorrow." I spin around clumsily and smack my elbow into the glass.

"*Son of a bitch!* That hurt," I hiss, grabbing my elbow.

"Oh shit, are you okay?" Ledger grabs my arm to try to look at it.

"I'm fine, I'm fine. It just hit that spot that hurts so damn bad."

We both look at each other silently before bursting out in laughter. We laugh so hard, tears are streaming down my face by the time we both calm down enough to talk.

"I'm so bad at this," I wheeze out.

"I think you're doing pretty great, Ains," he says softly.

We stare at each other for a long moment.

"I should probably get some sleep," I mutter.

"Right, sleep. We definitely need sleep," he says as he takes a step backwards.

I walk to bed, climbing under the sheets as he stands by the window, watching me. Once I'm settled, he walks about the room, grabbing the extra linens that got sent up at our request earlier and shutting off all the lights. I hear him shuffling around, setting everything up, and finally lying down on the couch.

The silence is both soothing and has me waiting for the other shoe to drop. The dichotomy of feelings has me on edge as I wait for his breathing to even out. I need to let out this tension that's been building since that kiss, but I need to make sure he's asleep first because I don't need any more embarrassment in my life right now.

Five ... ten minutes pass. Who knows at this point, but I finally hear the telltale signs of Ledger's deep breathing.

An image of Ledger in nothing but a towel pops into my head, and I slide my hand down my stomach slowly until I find the waistband of my shorts. My fingers sneak underneath, trying to stay as quiet as possible. I slide my finger through the growing wetness there and move it back up to my clit, circling it as I remember the slightly curly hair that runs along his pecs and down his stomach to a delicious happy trail my mind is dying to explore.

I shift slightly, trying to give myself a little more room to work, as I dip back down to my arousal.

I start breathing heavier when I hear a low, gravelly voice.
"Move the sheet, Ains."

CHAPTER TWENTY-ONE
LEDGER 

Sleeping was impossible. I was so hyper-focused on every move, every little shift Ainsley made in the bed in that skimpy little outfit she called pajamas.

My dick was rock-hard the moment I saw her in them.

But then I heard the sheets start to shift, and I sat up quietly, trying to make sure she was okay. What I saw sealed my fate.

When she lets out a breathy whimper? A Norse God couldn't stop me from going to her. Silently walking over to the bed, I see a vision in front of me. Lit up by the lights on the strip, the sheet is draped just over her stomach, and I see one arm is underneath the sheet while the other is fisting her pillow.

"Move the sheet, Ains." I barely recognize my voice, and I feel bad when she startles and rips her hand away from the pleasure she was giving herself.

"Ledger," she whispers shakily.

"Move the sheet and keep going. Show me what you like. Show me what gets you off." I feel possessed almost, but I know that I need to see this. I need to know I'm the reason she absolutely had to take the chance and pleasure herself with me only feet away.

We stare at each other, neither making a move. And then Ainsley lets a sly smirk spread over her face, and I know I'm fucked in the best possible way.

She wordlessly sits up and leans over the side of the bed to grab something out of her luggage. The sheet pools around her waist, and I'm seconds away from ripping it off of her completely.

Sitting back up, she has something in her hand and when I realize what it is, my eyes pop open with intrigue.

"You want to see what I like?"

I slowly nod, watching her hand slide the sheet off her body. I look back up to her face, and we lock eyes as she hooks her thumbs into her shorts and possibly panties. I don't dare break the connection we have to look down. She shifts a little before settling back down on the bed, and I see her legs spread in my periphery.

My hand unconsciously moves to grab myself through my shorts in a punishing grip to help stave off the release that is entirely too close to the surface.

I'm weak.

That's my only excuse. My eyes flicker down and watch as her hand slowly travels down the sexiest sight I've ever seen. A trimmed thatch of hair frames the most beautiful, pink pussy. I can visibly see how wet she is, and a groan escapes me unwillingly.

"Show me," I growl, and I don't even know who I am right now.

The mischievous smirk is back, and damnit if it doesn't make me harder. I squeeze the tip of my cock, praying I don't blow my load into my pants.

She picks up a vibrator, and it takes every ounce of strength I have not strip her and take her, going slow be damned.

Turning it on so a faint, buzzing sound permeates the air, she draws a path, first circling her breasts one by one, and then moves it down her stomach toward her clit. She arches off the bed, and I take a shaky breath.

"I need to learn what you like, baby. Show me." I sound desperate, but I don't care because I feel fucking desperate.

She doesn't hesitate for a second. The vibrator circles her clit, and she moans out a heady sound. She reaches her other hand down, spreading herself open and getting the vibrator just where she needs it.

I tilt my head back, trying to catch my breath, but it's a lost cause.

"Your turn. Show me, Ledger. Show me what you like." Her breathy voice reaches my ears, and I follow her directions like a good man should.

I hook my thumbs into my basketball shorts—that aren't hiding shit since I'm not wearing boxers—and slide them down just enough to let my cock spring free.

"Holy fuck, you're gorgeous," she murmurs, eyes locked onto my dick.

You couldn't pay me to hide my smirk at her comment.

"Don't get distracted, baby. Keep going. Show me how to get you off. Teach me what does it for you."

"Touch yourself. I want to see what I do to you," she counters as she slides the vibrator to her opening and slides the tip in.

I grip my cock and start a lazy rhythm so I don't come too quickly.

She keeps the vibrator gently rocking back and forth inside of her, and her other hand starts circling her clit. I move from the foot of the bed, gradually making my way to the side of the bed closest to her.

I want to touch her so fucking badly, but I don't want to push too hard.

She licks her lips as she watches my movements. "Fuck, Ledger. I'm so close."

My gaze travels back down to her ministrations, and I take notes of exactly how she's circling her clit right now. I make sure I memorize the exact thing that will get her off in minutes. At the same time, my leisurely strokes quicken as I get caught up in her impending orgasm.

"Come, Ains. Come for me please," I plead.

"You have to come with me. Please, Ledger, come with me." She arches off the bed again, and I know she's so close.

"Tell me where, baby. Where do you want me to come?"

She doesn't miss a beat, and this, more dominant version of Ainsley is sexy as hell.

"Right here. Come on me please," she pants, and she rips her shirt up, exposing her stomach.

Her words alone send a shockwave down my spine as my balls draw up, but I refuse to come without her. Anything she asks of me, she'll get.

She plants her feet on the bed as I lean in closer to her, catching the scent of her arousal, and starts fucking the vibrator as her clit stimulation gets more unrestrained.

"Ledg, I'm coming," she breathes out as her whole body seizes up with her orgasm, and it's like my body subconsciously knows her orgasm is my permission to come. Rope after rope leaves my tip and paints her pretty body with my cum. I feel like a caveman, like I'm marking her as mine, and it makes me positively feral over her.

I sag when I finally stop coming and look at the gorgeous picture that is Ainsley, lying on the bed, satiated and covered in me.

"God, you're beautiful," I murmur.

Her giggle is a soothing balm I never knew I needed to hear.

"I did not expect that to happen," she says with a sigh.

"Me either, but I can't say I'm sad about it. Give me a second so I can clean you up." I pull my shorts back up over my still semi-hard cock and head to the bathroom to run a washcloth under warm water.

When I make my way back out, Ainsley has the most content smile on her face as she watches my movements. I carefully clean her up and grab her vibrator to clean in the bathroom as well.

"Oh god, you don't have to do that." She starts to get up, but I stop her with a hard look.

"I don't have to, but I want to. Let me take care of things, okay?" I say softly as I lean down and press a gentle kiss to the spot on her stomach I just came on.

She nods but has a confused look on her face, and I choose to not address that right now. She'll learn the kind of man I am, the kind of man I want to be with her, soon enough.

I give the vibrator a quick clean and then walk back out to the main room.

"Do you want this back in your bag? Or should I just leave it on the nightstand for later?" I ask with laughter in my voice.

"Shut up. You didn't seem to mind." Her face heats as she covers it with her hands.

I gently pull them away. "Oh, I absolutely didn't mind. I'll probably daydream about the possibilities for later." I smile.

I stare at her for an extended moment, wondering how I got so lucky to be in this situation, before realizing we really do need to get some sleep tonight.

"Get some sleep, Ains. We've got a busy day tomorrow." I lean down again, pressing a chaste kiss to her forehead before heading back to the couch.

Sleep came quickly for me, and judging by the well-rested, radiant look on Ainsley's face, it did for her too. Today we have our presentation, so the plan is to go grab a quick breakfast and head to our room, set things up, and run through everything one more time.

We both ignore the elephant in the room that is last night's escapades, but it feels like we were in another world. Like last night was us letting out the tension that's been holding us hostage, and now we can move on with this hesitant dating plan. With her completely in control. Not that she wasn't last night, but it feels more like we got it out of our system for the time being.

Ainsley is currently taking a shower and getting "dolled up"—her words, not mine—for the presentation today. I'm twiddling my thumbs and getting more and more stressed out by the minute, realizing how close the presentation is. This is something I've worked so damn hard for, and now that it's finally here, I'm scared I'm going to fuck it up.

This entire weekend has the potential to boost business, evolve it, and jump Bluebell Landscaping into a different tier of company. A lot rides on this, and it's making me nervous as hell.

"Hey, you doing okay?" Ainsley's voice pulls me out of my spiraling thoughts.

"Hey. Yeah, totally fine. Just presentation-day jitters." I give her what I hope is a reassuring smile, but she seems to see right through it.

"Everything is going to go perfectly. You know this inside and out, backwards to forwards, and full circle. And if you stumble, I'll be there to pick it up. I swear, you are over-prepared for this."

Her imploring look does very little to assuage my nerves, but the fact that she is here fully supporting me means more than she'll ever know.

I decide taking the attention off of me right now is the only way I'll hold myself together.

"You ready for some breakfast?" I say with more enthusiasm than I feel.

She stares at me a little too hard, seeing a little too much.

"Sure, let's go."

It's then that I fully take her in, and I nearly groan at the vision she is.

An emerald-green pantsuit makes her strawberry blonde hair pop, which is curled loosely around her shoulders. A cream button-up shirt and white heels complete the look, and if we didn't take the edge off last night, I might have just tackled her to the floor right now. This sexy-businesswoman look of hers is doing all sorts of good things for me.

She clears her throat, making my eyes snap up to hers, and I see the mischievous smirk on her face at catching me eye-fucking her.

"I'm not apologizing. You look amazing," I tell her plainly.

"I am representing the company, after all," she says as she spins around, showing off her delectable ass.

"So, breakfast. You ready?" I change the subject so that I'm able to stay on task, otherwise we wouldn't be leaving our room today.

"Definitely. I need some coffee, like, now." She walks toward the door, picking up her briefcase in the process. It has all our notes and copies of the presentation, so I'm thankful she's on top of things today.

Breakfast is a quick affair; we both grab the largest coffees we can and a breakfast sandwich, which we demolish the minute we get to the meeting room.

Setup is simple. We plug in the USB to the main computer and make sure all our slides work, and Ainsley listens to me run through it one more time.

"You know you've got this memorized. There's nothing to worry about," she says after the last run-through.

Logically, I know she's right, but somehow my nervous system and my brain aren't getting the message. I'm jittery and starting to feel nauseous. Maybe the breakfast sandwich wasn't such a great idea.

"Ledg," Ainsley whispers, and I turn around to see her cock her head to the door, where people are entering for the session.

I plaster on a smile, greeting people as they come in. Ainsley does the same, stepping in when she truly doesn't have to.

Once the room is full, I head up to the podium and Ainsley finds a chair in the front row, on the end.

I clear my throat, take a deep breath, and hope that I don't fuck this up.

"Good-Good morning, everyone," I stumble, and my eyes shoot over to Ainsley.

She gives me a bright smile as she nods and gives me an exaggerated thumbs-up. I know if I really need her to, she'd jump in and take over, but I feel like I need to prove that I can do this. I can take this next step in my career.

"Hope everyone isn't too hung over to learn about some innovations in sustainable landscaping," I continue as loud laughter breaks out through the group. I take another peek at Ainsley and see her hands clasped together in her lap, with a proud look on her face.

Yeah, I think I can do this.

CHAPTER TWENTY-TWO
AINSLEY

My heart is beating out of my chest.

I don't think I realized just how much I'm invested in this. Not just the presentation, but Ledger's company.

When he looks at me after a small stumble in his introduction, I do the first thing I can think of and give him a huge smile with a thumbs-up. I'm sure I'll overthink the fuck out of that later, but right now, I'm desperate for this to go well. He knows I'll step in whenever he needs me, but I know he can do this. I understand him more now. I understand his anxiety and how it pops up at the most inopportune moments.

He makes a joke, and that out-of-control heartbeat turns into a flutter and draws my mind to what happened last night.

It was ridiculous to think I could attempt to get off in the same damn room as Ledger, only separated by a few feet. What I wasn't expecting was the mutual show we put on together. It's by far one of the hottest sexual experiences I've ever had, and we didn't even actually have sex. I think that says a lot about my sex life, honestly.

My mind pings between last night and the phenomenal presentation this surprising man is putting on. Looking around the audience, Ledger enraptures everyone. Turning my attention back to him, his strong and confident voice permeates the surrounding air, making my breath catch in my throat.

The overwhelming feeling of being utterly proud of this man makes pressure pop up behind my eyes. I won't cry, but this entire morning made me realize how much I like my job, and like working for Ledger. And that's a scary thought because is this really how I envision my future?

I quickly realize this is something I need to spend some real time thinking about. Which means I need to talk to Larkin sooner rather than later. If anyone can help me gain some clarity, it's her.

I hear deafening applause and look back up at Ledger, who locks eyes with me. The smile on his face is stunning and infectious as I match it. The sound in the room fades away as we stare at each other. I don't know what he's thinking, but all I can think about is how much I really do *like* him. And how much I don't want to go slow, even if it's a smart move. Even if it's what we should be doing.

People start standing and making their way up to the podium to talk to Ledger, and I move off to the side of the room, taking it all in.

I feel proud to be a part of this. To say I contributed to such an over-whelmingly positive response is unlike anything I've ever been involved with professionally. The realization is jarring. I knew my finance career wasn't a feel-good job, but I was good at it. But this? Changing the way people think about landscaping and sustainability, of all things, makes me recognize I don't want to go back to the stiff, unfeeling job I used to have.

The room eventually clears out, and Ledger slowly makes his way to me on the edge of the room.

"Your presentation was fucking amazing, Ains." He leans his shoulder on the wall next to me, hands in his pockets.

"Technically, it's your presentation." I smirk, deflecting because of the sheer number of emotions running through me.

"Okay, stubborn. It's our presentation. How about that?" he asks with an easy smile on his face. He looks gorgeous like this—at ease and so comfortable with himself.

"I guess I have to agree, huh, boss?" I tilt my head.

"And now you have to agree to dinner with me tonight." His tone changes. He sounds slightly unsure of himself, and I both love and hate it. I love that he's still his shy self, but I want him to feel more comfortable around me. If we are going to make a go of this thing between us, I want to know I'm the one who makes him relaxed, that he doesn't need to shut any part of himself away.

"I think I can manage dinner."

"Did you pack anything fancy outside of business clothes?" he asks.

I lift an eyebrow at his question.

"A fancy dinner?"

"We don't have to if you'd rather do something different," he says quickly.

"Ledger… I have a dress that I can wear, and I would love to go out for a fancy dinner with you."

His shoulder sag with relief, and I act on impulse.

Gripping his cheeks in my hands, I whisper against his lips, "You were incredible up there. You completely blew me away." Then I press my lips against his.

He barely hesitates before I feel his hand gently fall on my hip and take control of the kiss.

In a matter of seconds, the kiss deepens into something highly inappropriate for a landscaping conference. His tongue parts my lips, barely teasing the tip of mine, drawing a moan out of me.

He abruptly pulls back, and I almost fall forward, following him for more kisses.

"You make me lose my head, Ains. We should probably go out to the main space and make the rounds," he murmurs before pressing one last kiss to my lips before stepping fully away and adjusting his suit jacket to cover the front of his pants.

I have a very hard time holding in my laughter as he adjusts the crotch of his pants too.

"This situation is your fault, you know." He chuckles as he leads me out of the room.

"Yeah, I'm mentally giving myself a high five right now." I smirk over at him as he shakes his head with mirth.

We're instantly bombarded when we leave the room by people wanting to talk more with Ledger. I try to move to the side to let him work, but he softly places his hand on my back, silently holding me in place. When I look up at him, the subtle shake of his head tells me he wants me to stay. And right now? After the kiss we just shared? I'll do anything he wants.

It takes the better part of an hour for the constant string of people to finally slow down. When we're completely alone, Ledger's shoulders slump with exhaustion and I can see how the past couple of hours have worn on him. I know there is a little more of the conference we were planning to attend, but all I want to do is take him to our room and let him unwind, whatever that looks like.

"We can skip the rest of the day if you want to," I offer.

He gives me a small smile. "I'd love to take that offer, but I need to network as much as possible. I don't want all the incredible work you put into that presentation to go to waste because I slacked off."

I'm about to rebuke him, but he grabs my hand and squeezes it.

"Take the compliment, Ains," he says with a little rumble in his voice, sparking a trail of goosebumps where he touches my hand.

Fuck, I don't know if I've ever been as affected by a man as I am by Ledger.

"Well, I'll follow your lead."

We stayed at the conference for most of the day, and I'm wiped out. Who knew a group of landscapers could put on such an intensive conference?

When we finally make it to our room, I collapse on the bed and let out an exaggerated sigh.

"We can rain-check dinner." Ledger's deep voice pierces through my tired haze.

"Nope, just give me five minutes," I mumble into the bed.

His chuckle sends goosebumps down my arms.

"I'm going to jump in the shower really quickly, but we've got plenty of time before dinner, so there's no rush to get ready." His soothing voice gets closer and closer as he talks, and before I realize it, I feel his lips on my temple as he whispers, "Thank you for today."

And then he's gone.

I lie there for far too long, or maybe it's only a couple of minutes. I've completely lost track of time at this point. But what I do know is Ledger just turned the shower on and my libido has suddenly kicked into high gear, imagining him stripping out of his suit that he looks far too good in.

I roll over onto my back and contemplate my next move. I know we talked about going slow and really getting to know each other before jumping into the physical stuff, but fuck if I don't want to throw that all out the window right now.

Hearing a soft groan from behind the bathroom door practically makes the decision for me.

I get up and make my way to the bathroom, stripping out of my favorite suit as I go. I crack the door open in only my bra and panties and see Ledger's head thrown back under the spray of the shower. His hand is running up and down his torso as the other hand rests on his thigh, forcing my eyes to wander to the erection he's sporting.

"Are you just going to stand there, or did you want to join me?" His gravelly voice jolts me out of my dick stupor.

"Umm..."

"I promise nothing will happen if you don't want it to. We can just shower together and save water." His smirk is devious, and I'm absolutely sunk for this man in this moment.

Fuck it.

"And what if I want something to happen?"

I open the door fully as I walk in and unhook my bra. The straps trail down my arms before falling to the floor in front of the shower. Ledger's gaze travels the path my fingers take, watching them hook into my panties as they slip down my legs. His hand casually grips his cock as he moves further back in the shower so I can come in.

The shower is huge. There's a bench along the backside and two shower heads on each side of it, making it easy to keep this to just a shower.

But I don't want to keep it to just a shower.

My eyes move back up to his as I climb in next to him.

I walk right up to him, tilting my head up to keep eye contact.

"I don't know if this is the right thing to do, but I want it. I want you." Raising up on my tiptoes, I press a light kiss to his lips.

"Be very sure right now, Ains," he whispers against my lips.

I answer him without words. Gripping his dick, I give it one long stroke and watch as his eyes roll back a little.

"Fuck," Ledger mutters.

The smirk taking over my face only grows, knowing how much I'm affecting him.

"I know we said we would slow down and take our time, but I don't think I want to," I whisper.

"I'll do anything you want to," he breathes out, and my heart jumps in my chest. Somehow, I don't think he just means sexually.

I keep stroking him, wanting nothing more than to see this man come unraveled for me, but he takes me by surprise.

His hands grab the side of my face, pulling me up into a fierce kiss before sliding his hands down my arms to my hips and around to my ass. With no effort at all, he lifts me up and presses me against the shower wall.

I let out a squeak, unprepared for the show of strength and finding it ridiculously hot.

"Jesus, you are sexy today," I say.

"Glad you think so," he says as he presses kisses on my neck and grinds against me.

"How much time do we have before dinner?"

"Plenty for what I have in mind." He slides his cock against my clit with emphasis, and I damn near lose my head.

"And what did you have in mind, Mr. Hutton?"

CHAPTER TWENTY-THREE
LEDGER

insley's a fucking wildcat, and I really should have seen it coming. But watching as she slowly walks towards me in the shower while stripping is by far the sexiest thing I've ever witnessed.

"I want to show you what I learned from last night," I tell her as I continue grinding against her.

"You're awfully confident, aren't you?" she says with mischief in her voice.

"I've made it a personal goal of mine to learn every single thing that turns you on, everything that makes you whimper, so yeah, I feel pretty confident." My voice is so low, I barely recognize it.

Her smirk tells me she thinks I'm joking, but I studied every little thing she did last night in that bed, took note of every change in tempo, every swirl of her fingers against her clit. And I plan to show her exactly how studious I am.

I slide my dick against her again, and the realization that I don't have a condom slams into me like a freight train.

"Shit."

Her eyes refocus on me with a question on her face.

"I don't have a condom with me. I didn't think this was even remotely in the realm of happening."

How the fuck do I not have a condom? Fucking amateur.

"Umm..."

"I can run down to the little store in the lobby," I tell her frantically as I start to pull back.

"Don't you dare leave this shower," she growls, then she pulls me down for a kiss.

"Yes, ma'am." I smile as I push her against the wall harder with my hips.

Her hand moves down my chest as her legs lock around my hips and draw me closer still.

"We can still play," she pants out as she tilts her hips to get a better angle, and a visible shiver travels down my spine.

"Absolutely," I mutter mindlessly. I think I would go along with anything she says right now because she feels too damn good.

She unravels her legs from me. I grip her tighter so she doesn't fall, but she drops her legs down, forcing me to let her go. When I step back, I'm unprepared for the sight that greets me.

Ainsley on her knees, legs spread so I can see her gorgeous pussy. She places her hand gently on my thigh as if asking if this is okay. I don't know how to tell her I'd let her do anything to my body, so I just nod my head, probably a little too enthusiastically.

Leaning forward, she confidently grabs my dick and licks the tip like a damn lollipop. I suck in a breath, hoping to God I can last a respectable amount of time.

My hand automatically goes to the shower wall in an attempt to distract myself with how fucking good her mouth feels on me. A second later, she has me fully in her mouth, pressing against the back of her throat, and I almost lose it.

"Shit, Ains," I pant out.

She looks up at me through her lashes, and the sight is so sexy I'm already thinking of ways to see her like this again while simultaneously thinking of plant species so I don't blow.

She grabs the hand that's not against the wall and puts it on the back of her head. I look down at her, making sure this is actually what she wants and when she nods as much as she can with her mouth full of my cock, my fingers tighten in her hair.

The moan from her nearly sends me to my knees. My hips thrust in time with her motion and before I know it, I'm right on the edge.

"Baby, I'm so fucking close," I grit out. "Let me pull out now if you don't want me coming in your mouth."

She reaches her other hand behind her head and grips my wrist, encouraging me to take what I want, and I lose it. Head tipping back, I groan out my release as I empty myself for this beautiful woman on her knees for me.

I loosen my grip on her hair and slump back into the shower wall.

"Jesus, Ains," I breathe out.

"That was your reward for such an incredible presentation." She smirks as she climbs back to her feet.

"I feel like the wrong person got rewarded then." I chuckle and bring her close to my chest.

"Nope. You were phenomenal, and you one-thousand-percent deserved that." She winks.

"Considering it was your presentation, I think maybe I need to reciprocate." I run my hand up and down her back soothingly. I don't feel like I owe her, but I do not want to be the man that leaves her wanting for anything. And it's no hardship to make her come by any means possible.

"Nope. This is not tit for tat. It never will be, so learn that now," she says, looking up at me with a serious expression.

Damn, I don't think I could love this woman more.

Love... Shit... Am I already that far gone?

"We'll see. You ready for dinner?" I change the subject, feeling very much the awkward teen I always was. Maybe I didn't grow out of it;

maybe this confidence is just a face I put on because just thinking the word "love" has me freaking out a little.

"Yeah, let's get dressed," she whispers.

Did getting dressed take almost an hour because I couldn't keep my hands off of Ainsley? Yes. Am I apologizing for it? Hell no. I feel like things have shifted between us, and I want to keep the progress going. I know my feelings have very quickly come to the surface, no matter how much I don't want to analyze them fully right now.

We're currently walking up the strip to the MGM Grand, and I can hardly take my eyes off the gorgeous woman beside me. A deep blue, silk dress is draped perfectly over her body, showing off every dip and curve I long to explore. Her arms are bare, and her strawberry blonde hair is flowing down her shoulders. The heels she's wearing make her a few inches taller, and all it does is make me want to kiss her. I'm utterly captivated.

"So, you really aren't going to tell me where we're going?" she asks as we walk side by side.

"Nope. It's a surprise for a job well done today." At least, I hope it will be. If I fucked up and picked the wrong restaurant for my little foodie, she might throw me to the curb before we even sit down.

When we walk into the MGM, Ainsley looks around in awe.

"We have a little bit farther to walk if that's okay." I can hear the uncertainty in my voice, and I hate it. I need to channel confident Ledger.

"Yep! Let's go." She practically drags me along when she sees the sign for the restaurants.

We get to the area that houses most of the restaurants and I take over, grabbing her hand and leading her to Craft Steakhouse.

Ainsley stops in her tracks, and I tense up.

I fucked up. This was the wrong place to take her.

"We can—"

"Shut up."

I slam my mouth closed and start to panic. Her voice is shaky, and I think I might have just lost all the headway I was making.

Turning towards me, I see her glossy eyes and it's like a gut punch.

"I have stalked this place and Tom Colicchio for so long, I can't even begin to tell you how much I know about him. It's borderline creepy level. This is, by far, the only place I wanted to go to while we were here."

"So, I didn't mess up?" I ask hesitantly.

"God no!" She raises up on her toes and grabs my cheeks, pulling me in for one hell of a kiss.

My shoulders finally loosen up, and then tension rolls off of me like a wave.

"Okay, good," I say breathlessly.

She grabs my hand again and pulls me toward the hostess stand.

Getting seated allows me to get back on my footing again. Having time to look at the menu lets me refocus on my reason for taking her out in the first place.

"You absolutely killed that presentation. I couldn't have done it without you," I tell her quietly.

"You managed it just fine on your own," she deflects.

I clear my throat. "You have blown me away with just how good at this job you are. I know it's not exactly where you saw your life going, but I'm very grateful to have you."

What I don't tell her is how thankful I am to have her in my life, period. I don't think she's ready for that, even if she's pushing us past the "slow" barrier.

"You know, when I took this job, it was because it was convenient. Sorry." She looks up at me sheepishly, but I nod my head to continue. I know why she accepted this job, but I want to hear where she's going with this.

"How much do you know about my old job?" she asks.

"Only what you've told me, which admittedly, isn't much."

"Okay, so I was climbing the ladder at the financial firm I was at, advising the shit out of clients. Bringing them in and making money for everyone. The money was good, I won't deny that, but I had bigger goals. I wanted to climb to the top. A management position was opening up, and I put my hat in the ring. The problem was a coworker who liked to make everything a competition. I didn't think much of it, honestly, because my numbers were better and I was the obvious choice.

"Joke's on me, though, because I not only didn't get the position, but they moved me to a different division, which made him my direct supervisor. That's when the harassment started."

I tense, not knowing how to react.

"It started as little things. Hanging out at my desk and telling inappropriate jokes. Nothing I thought much about, honestly. Then it moved to stealing my clients and taking credit for some of my more lucrative jobs. I started taking notes and documenting when things were happening.

"The sexual harassment started not long after that. He treated me more like a nineteen-fifties housewife than an employee, and it got really rough. He would make me get his coffee daily, then spit it on the floor when it wasn't right. Mind you, I was not an assistant—I was an actual financial advisor. His little, petty shit started taking up a ton of my time, and I started losing clients.

"I finally felt like I had enough to bring to the owners after he got a little too friendly in my office one time."

"Shit," I mutter.

"Yep. I won't go into the details, but I took my evidence to the owners and, low and behold, Dickface was already in their office. He claimed I was the one sexually harassing him and that I was using my sexual prowess—he actually said that. Can you believe it?" She shakes her head, but continues, "I was using my sexual prowess to tempt him and take his job. When I presented my actual evidence to the owners, they didn't even look at it. It was like a slap in the face. I knew I was in a male-dominated field, but I didn't expect to be taken advantage of like that."

"Jesus, I had no idea." It feels wholly inadequate, but I don't have an intelligent response right now. All I'm thinking about is that Ainsley was sexually harassed and no one believed her. How fucking messed up is that? I can't even imagine if that was Willow or Rina. I think I would burn the whole world down if I found out that happened to them. Hell, I want to burn the whole world down for Ainsley.

"You hear about it, you know? The discrimination in the workplace. But I had never directly dealt with it. I'll admit, I didn't respond great, and that probably contributed to me being fired."

"Absolutely not. There is no excuse, no reason for this situation to be okay. I don't care how you acted, the fact that they just blew you off is unacceptable." I can feel my face getting redder by the second, and I know I need to calm down.

"I appreciate that, but I didn't tell you so that you could go and play hero. I told you so you understand where my mind is with this job, and with us, honestly."

Everything clicks into place. This is why she's so leery of dating within the workplace. This is why she goes above and beyond at work but keeps her distance. Now, I feel like an asshole for ever pushing her for anything.

"Nope, get that look off your face right now, Ledger Hutton." Her stern tone makes my eyes lift up to hers.

"You did not know. Honestly, you couldn't have known. And I'm a big girl. If I really didn't want to continue things with you, I would have said so. You have not pushed me into anything."

Apparently, I'm wearing all my emotions on my face tonight.

"I don't want you to ever feel like that again, especially with me," I murmur.

"I know. Trust me, I know. If I felt like that again, you can bet I would run far, far away." She huffs out a laugh.

"All that to say, this job wasn't what I was expecting. I expected being your assistant would be boring as hell and I would be constantly looking for a new job, and it's been the exact opposite. I'm not sure if this is where I see myself in five years, but I'm not hating it either. I've learned a lot about myself over the last few months, and I feel like I'm starting to figure out who I really am if that makes sense."

"It makes perfect sense." I won't tell her that she's made me start to figure out who I am, who I want to be for her. I won't tell her that before her, my only focus was being a makeshift father figure and running my business. Eventually, I'll tell her how much of an impact she's had in my life in such a short amount of time, but that time is not now.

Now, it's time to make sure she knows exactly how thankful I am to have her in my life and eat some amazing fucking steak.

CHAPTER TWENTY-FOUR
AINSLEY

This trip has been nothing like I thought it would be. The presentation was incredible. The fun times in between all the work with Ledger were mind-blowing, and spilling some of my past at dinner was extremely cathartic, even if that wasn't my intention.

And dinner ... might be one of the best highlights of my life. Never did I think I would get the opportunity to eat at the restaurant of one of my favorite chefs, and it did not disappoint. I think I gained ten pounds during that meal, and I'm not remotely sad about it.

Now, we're on the plane home and I'm more than a little sad. This trip was everything I didn't know I needed. *Ledger* is everything I didn't know I wanted. And that's a scary thing to realize.

My head is stuck on the logistics of how we can make this work in the real world. The fact that we live in a small town makes me leery to be out in the open with our relationship. I don't want everyone in our business while I'm just trying to figure out how to be in a functional relationship. And although I'm leaning towards staying here for the foreseeable future, I'm not certain that staying in Bluebell Falls is the endgame for me.

"So, I think it would be smart to set some ground rules before we land." Ledger's voice pulls me out of my thoughts.

Even though I was thinking the same thing, his words send a jolt of unease through my body.

Is he already over this? Am I not worth the trouble?

"What I mean is, I don't think you would feel comfortable with this," —he gestures between the two of us— "being broadcasted in town."

My shoulders slump in relief, and it makes me realize how into Ledger I really am.

"You read my mind," I say, decidedly not focusing on the fact that I might be in too deep with this man already.

"I also think it's a good idea to keep things at work separate. I don't ever want you to question things between the two of us, and I don't want you to feel like you did at your old job either. Questioning if something we do outside of work will affect your job will never be on the table."

I turn completely to look at him, and the earnestness I see there makes my heart thump hard in my chest.

"I'll be honest. All of that has crossed my mind. And I'd be lying if I said the small-town aspect doesn't scare the shit out of me. I don't love the idea of having everyone knowing everything about our business. Hell, my dad is by far the worst offender. I don't want to say I want things to be a secret, but I am definitely leaning toward keeping this on the downlow for the time being." I hold eye contact the entire time because I want him to know this isn't about keeping us a secret. At the moment, I want to scream to the world that I'm with *the* Ledger Hutton and tell everyone just how damn amazing he is.

But I also know I'm not ready to share with the world what we've just barely developed. Call it selfish, but I want this to have a chance.

"I get it, I really do. I haven't dated in years, despite Rina and Willow pestering me constantly, so I know, without a doubt, we would be the talk of the town." He grabs my hand before continuing. "I want to keep you to myself a little while longer," he whispers.

"I like the sound of that." I lean into him and press a kiss to his lips. He deepens it quickly, but I shift away before we get carried away.

Pressing my forehead to his as best as I can on the plane, I take a breath before telling him what else is on my mind.

"Thank you for being considerate of my past with work. I honestly don't know how to attack all of this, but I do know that I need to be careful. Not because I think you'll screw me over, but because I feel like I need to figure out where I go from here, you know? What do I want to do with my life in the future? I know that all sounds existential, but it does feel like I haven't really stepped back and thought about where I'm going professionally."

"That makes sense. You've gone from one job to the next in a hurry out of necessity, and although I will say you are phenomenal at this job, I understand wanting more."

God, his understanding is too much. Outside of my family, have I ever had this kind of support in my life? In my job? I thought I had a successful career in finance, and look how that turned out. The lack of support is blinding now, but would I have ever noticed it if I had stayed in Austin?

Who knows, but I do know I don't really want to dive into all of that right now. Figuring things out with Ledger is top priority because, for once in who knows how long, I'm happy. And all I want to do is make sure I keep this feeling for as long as I can.

"So, we keep this quiet for the time being, and we keep work to work," I surmise.

"I'm good with that. It's not like it'll be all that difficult, what with us being neighbors and all." He grins as he leans in again, and I feel the smile overtaking my entire face.

"You drive a hard bargain," I whisper as we both lean in further.

When our lips touch, it just feels right. Like this is exactly where I should be, and whom I should be with.

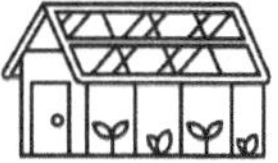

Shortly after our conversation on the plane, we land. The drive back home, on the other hand, feels like it takes forever.

We can't keep our hands to ourselves.

It started as little touches—holding hands, putting a hand on a thigh—but it's quickly turned a little more salacious.

Currently, Ledger's hand is creeping up my inner thigh because my hand is resting gently on the swell of his erection. Sound tame? What's coming out of this man's mouth is anything but.

"How bad do you want it? Do you want me to pull over here and take you in the bed of my truck?" His gravelly voice makes me close my legs and squeeze them together with his hand in between, to try to get a little relief.

"And what exactly would you do to me in the bed of your truck, Mr. Hutton?" I egg him on. Hell, if the dirty talk doesn't get me off, I know he will once we get home.

"First, I rip these fucking leggings off of you." He gives them a little tug before he continues. "Then I'd get down on my knees for you and worship every spot that makes you crazy. Every obvious area and all the tiny ones that you think are forgotten, and some that I'll find along the way. I'd kiss them and lick them, and make you so insane with need you'd melt before me, so compliant and wet for me."

"Jesus fuck, Ledg," I breathe out.

"Oh, that's just the beginning, baby. That's just the foreplay."

"You know, you're so fucking stealthy. You act so shy and unsure sometimes, but your mouth is so fucking filthy." I let out a whimper as his hand brushes against my clit.

"It's not about being stealthy. It's about learning exactly what turns you on, gets you to the best orgasm of your life, and doing it again and again. It's my current life goal to keep giving you the best orgasms you've ever had."

"And here I thought your life goal was to grow your company." I chuckle.

"Smartass," he growls.

"You like me this way," I counter.

"I absolutely love you this way," he whispers.

My heart pounds in my chest, and it has nothing to do with the hand that's grazing my clit. *He loves me this way? That's just a general statement, right? I totally shouldn't read into it.*

Except I'm kind of reading into it, and it's only scaring me a little.

I'm pulled out of my train of thought when I see Bluebell Falls in the distance.

"Home, sweet home," I mutter.

"It's not so bad," Ledger says as he applies more pressure to my clit. I slide down further in my seat in an attempt to get more friction where I need it.

"God, you're such a tease," I grit out.

"A tease? You think this is teasing?" I can hear the humor in his voice, and I'm almost scared to see what his version of teasing is. But the curiosity of it is far too tempting.

"What's your idea of teasing?"

"Oh, Ains, be very sure you want the answer to that question," he growls.

Holy shit. I think I definitely want the answer now.

I don't get time to answer him at the moment because his truck pulls into a driveway I realize is his.

I take a quick peek at his house, but what I see stops me in my tracks. His house is fucking gorgeous. It's a cottage-style house with a full wrap-around porch in the most perfect light blue color. The landscaping is gorgeous and everything I think of when I picture my dream yard. What has to be hundreds of blooms greet the eye, and it feels like it should be in a magazine. But I should have expected this, considering what he does for a living.

"Holy shit, Ledger, this is gorgeous."

"Thanks," he says shyly. "It was our parent's house, but I've kept up maintenance and updated where I could."

He doesn't say anything else, just gets out of the truck and walks around to help me out. I barely get my feet on the ground before he lifts me up, my legs wrapping around his waist. I vaguely see headlights in the distance, but it doesn't register in my brain because Ledger picks me up like I weigh nothing.

"Shit! You're going to hurt yourself!" I scramble to gain stability.

"Shut up, Ainsley."

"You did not just tell me to shut up."

"I think I did," he snarks back with humor in his voice.

"Ledger *Dean* Hutton, do not tell me to shut up!" I put up faux indignation, making sure to emphasize his middle name.

He makes his way up to the front door, still carrying me. He shifts me a little to unlock the door and then heaves it open.

"Would you rather I make you shut up?" he whispers in my ear before biting the lobe.

"Yes, please," I whimper involuntarily.

Slamming my back against the door as he shuts it, I let out a gasp of surprise. He takes advantage of my surprise and goes in for the attack. He starts with passionate kisses, his tongue tangling with mine. It's not a battle for dominance like it usually is for me, but it's a dance of intimacy that has me completely captivated by this man.

He gently pulls away, his eyes a little dazed, before he refocuses and shocks the shit out of me. He drops my legs to the ground, trailing his hands down my sides and hooking into my leggings and panties. Yanking them both down, I step out the best I can as he pulls them off completely. When he tosses them to the side, he smooths his hands up my thighs until he reaches my shirt, grips it, and pulls it up and over my head.

I stand there, completely frozen at the quick skill he just displayed and beyond turned on for him.

He stands back up, prowling toward me like a damn predator, and I'm practically dripping for him.

His hand palms my ass, lifting me up as I wrap my legs around him again.

"This seems a little unfair. How come I'm almost naked and you aren't?" I pout.

"Because I have something in mind for you, and it won't matter what I'm wearing."

I'm about to ask him what he's talking about when he uses both hands on my ass to push up my entire body. He literally pushes me up the wall until my pussy is at the height of his head, then he wraps my legs around his shoulders.

"Wha—" I don't even complete my question when he kisses my clit. It's gentle at first, easing me into it, but when I whimper? He doesn't hold back.

"Holy fuck, Ledg," I pant out.

He sticks to a steady pattern, and it's exactly where I want it. When he said he was paying attention and studying what I like, he wasn't lying because at the moment he's hitting the spot just to the left that gets me close every. Single. Time.

I throw my head back, thumping it on the wall, but he doesn't stop. *Thank God he doesn't stop.*

"I need more. I need your fingers," I whisper to him. "I'm so close, but I need to feel full."

He doesn't break stride, just takes one of his arms that's wrapped around my leg and moves it below me. When I feel the gentle touch of his finger, I nearly shoot off the wall.

"Yessss," I hiss out.

He adds another finger, and that's all it takes.

My entire body tenses up as I grind against the rhythm Ledger is using. I vaguely hear a scream, and somewhere in the back of my mind I know it's me, but the only thing I can focus on is just how fucking sensitive I am.

"Shit," I squeak and try to push Ledger's head away, but he resists.

"Ledger, I'm so fucking sensitive," I whimper.

"I know, baby, but let me try something. If you hate it, I'll stop immediately, but I think I can get you to come back-to-back." He pulls back just enough for me to hear him.

I nod, but I've never done that before and I honestly don't know if I can handle it, but I sure as hell want to try.

"Perfect. You're doing so good, baby," he murmurs before he goes back to work.

It takes him less than two minutes to get me to come again, and it's somehow even more intense than the last one. I've heard about this concept of a sort of never-ending orgasm or consecutive orgasms, but never in my life did I believe they could happen to me.

Ledger cautiously brings me back down but just enough to be at eye level.

"You are the sexiest woman I've ever seen in my life. And getting to feel you? See you like this? I'm a changed man, Ainsley," he whispers before kissing me softly.

I feel the pressure behind my eyes that's the telltale sign of tears approaching, but I won't let the tears fall. I'm just so overwhelmed by this man. I feel so fucking cherished that it drowns my soul in pure happiness.

He pulls out of the kiss with a wicked smile on his face.

"You ready for round two, baby?"

I smirk back at him. "I might die from orgasms, but it sounds like the best way to go, honestly."

He spins me off the wall and heads to what I assume is his bedroom.

CHAPTER TWENTY-FIVE
AINSLEY

Getting tossed onto the bed makes me feel as light as a feather. Lifting all that landscaping material has done good things for this man, that's for sure.

"This still seems pretty lopsided," I point to my nearly naked self and then to his fully clothed self.

"What would be the fun in making it easy for you, Ains?" The wicked smirk on his face has my legs rubbing together to help ease the tension I'm feeling.

Well, if he wants to play, I'm more than happy to oblige.

I sit up on my knees and drag my hands down his hard, muscled chest. *He's so fucking sexy.* Once they're down by his waist, I grip the hem of his shirt and drag it over his torso. I keep my eyes on the skin that's slowly getting revealed until I shift my eyes to his. He doesn't help me as I pull it over his head, standing still to let me play.

He looks ready to pounce, but I'm not quite ready to let him have all the fun. I smirk as my fingertips trail over his pecs, then down to his abs. He visibly shivers, and it makes me feel powerful in a way I never have before. Finally, making my way to the button on his jeans, I don't hesitate. Popping the button then sliding the zipper down over this pronounced bulge proves a little harder than I thought it would be, but it just makes me all the more eager.

"Ains, you've got three minutes before I lose all sense of being a gentleman."

"I can do a lot in three minutes," I say cheekily before shoving his jeans and boxers over his ass and down his legs.

"Jesus, woman," Ledger mutters.

I don't respond, too busy drooling over his perfect dick. I know this isn't the first time I'm seeing it, but damn, it's just so pretty. I know most of the time you could take or leave a dick, but this one? This one is genuinely pretty. The perfect size to feel a little bit of stretch and the slightest curve upward to hit all the right spots.

I shove his jeans a little further down his legs, and he takes the hint to take them off completely. Once he kicks them to the side, I grip his cock and start long, smooth strokes.

"One minute, baby."

His self-imposed countdown has my heart rate doubling, so I lean forward to lick the little pearly drop at the tip. Groaning at the taste, I waste no time sucking him as far into my mouth as I can. His hips thrust forward involuntarily, and he curses under his breath.

Swirling my tongue on his underside, I feel his hand reach behind my back and unhook my bra. I totally forgot I still had it on, but he's wasting no time making sure we're both naked and ready. Before I can do anything more, he pulls completely out of my mouth and gently pushes me back down on the bed.

He walks around the bed to the nightstand and grabs a condom, tossing it on the bed before getting on his knees and literally crawling up to me.

This man is crawling for me. Holy shit, I don't think there is anything sexier.

He shoves my legs open before kneeling in-between them and a whimper escapes me.

I don't know if I'll survive this man, but if this is the way I go, I'll be a damn happy woman.

"You have no idea what you do to me, Ains," he whispers so reverently, my eyes spring with tears. "You are a fucking goddess, and I'm wholly unworthy of you."

My mouth pops open to tell him he's wrong, that between the two of us, I'm the unworthy one, but nothing comes out. I *want* to be worthy of him, be strong enough to be by his side and help him thrive. I'm just not sure I'm there yet, and now is not the time to contemplate it all.

He leans down, kissing my chest right where my heart is before moving down my sternum to my little pooch of a belly.

I feel his fingers put pressure against my clit before they move down, testing my readiness. My hips shift of their own accord, practically begging for more, when he grabs the condom and rips it open.

I could tell him I'm covered, but I like this sort of protectiveness from him. He doesn't ask, doesn't push, just makes sure we're both safe.

Leaning back on his heels, he wordlessly rolls the condom down his cock while keeping eye contact with me. The connection is intense, more powerful than anything I've ever felt with a man before, and all I want to do is drown in it. I wonder if it will always feel like this between us or if this is just because we've been building to this.

He positions himself at my opening and leans forward, gripping my jaw before giving me a soft kiss. He's all-consuming, a tidal wave of sensation. When he deepens the kiss, he pushes forward, completely seating himself inside of me.

If there is a heaven, a utopia, a perfect world, this is it.

My hands move to grip forearms in an attempt to ground myself through all this sensation. He gives me a second to get used to the feel of him, and I need it. I'm not sure if it's just been so long since I've had the real thing or what, but my vibrators have nothing on Ledger right now. I feel full, almost too full, but it's not painful. It just intensifies everything.

His kiss grows frantic, and I can tell he's struggling to give me time, but I don't want it. I want him to lose control with me, show me what he likes, and see him in absolute ecstasy. I tilt my hips, letting him sink a little more into me, and then rotate my hips as best I can. He gets the hint and pulls out before slamming back into me, my back arching in pleasure.

He breaks the kiss, pressing his forehead to mine. Panting, the blue of his eyes turns almost navy, and I'm captivated.

"You, Ainsley Mathews, are perfection," he whispers against my lips.

"I'm just me, Ledger," I refute because I don't feel perfect. I feel like a mess who doesn't have her life together, but somehow at this moment, I don't want to think about all of my worries. All I care about is how this man feels inside of me and how to keep this feeling for as long as I possibly can.

He shakes his head at me but doesn't say anything else. Instead, he starts a punishing pace that hits a spot in me that sends me flying in minutes.

"Holy shit," I whimper, closing my eyes at the sheer passion of it all.

"Open your eyes, baby. I need to see your eyes."

My eyes pop open and find his, and when that smirk of his returns, I know I'm in trouble.

The hand that's cupping my jaw moves down to my nipple. When he lightly pinches it, I gasp for breath.

"Shit, you respond to everything," he grits out.

"Never," I try to pant out. "Never have before."

His head tilts back, and his hips slow. "You can't say things like that. This will be over before I want it to be."

I can't help it, and I laugh. Big, obnoxious, kill-the-mood laughter.

But apparently, I don't kill the mood.

Ledger pushes in deeper and groans. "That's not helping."

"Sorry! Sorry! I'll stop," I tell him as I continue to laugh. I can't control it. It feels like something inside of me has snapped, and my laughter is the result.

He lifts up on his arm a little, staying deep, and trails the hand that was exploring my breasts lower. When he breezes right over my stomach and straight for my clit, my laughing stops abruptly.

"Well, now I know one way to get you to stop," he rasps.

He's once again rendered me speechless, and I'm so close to the edge.

His hips start his rhythm again, and I see stars within minutes.

"Oh God," I whisper.

"Yes. Come, baby." His voice is hushed and gravelly, sending sparks down my entire body.

And my body obeys. I come harder than I ever thought was possible. My entire body feels like a live wire. He lessens the pressure on my clit but keeps his finger there as he wrings every ounce of pleasure out of me.

Once I collapse back on the bed, he pulls out and I look at him, confused.

"Flip over, Ains." His voice is tight and raspy, and somehow my libido wakes right back up. The complete exhaustion I was just feeling mere seconds ago is wiped away.

I flip over, but before I can get myself adjusted, I feel Ledger's arm wrap around my middle and yank my ass back to meet his hips. I brace myself with my hands and feel him thrust back inside of me.

"Fuck, Ains, you feel too fucking good." I can hear the strain in his voice, so I rock back with my hips, meeting him thrust for thrust.

I jolt when I feel his hand grip the back of my neck then melt into possessiveness.

"Shit, I'm close. Finger your clit for me, baby," he says as he picks up his pace slightly.

Adjusting my position, I reach one hand underneath me and circle my clit. I can feel his cock with my fingers as he thrusts, and it's so fucking sexy.

It takes me no time at all to feel the familiar pressure.

"I'm—" I barely get it out before I'm screaming into the mattress. If I thought the last orgasm took it out of me, it has nothing on this one.

I barely hear Ledger moan behind me, but his grip on my neck tightens ever so slightly and starts to pull me up. I follow his lead and start lifting up on my hands. His other hand wraps around my stomach and pulls me up so my back is to his front. His panting in my ear and my heavy breathing are all I can hear.

I rest my head back on his shoulder and melt into him, letting him take all my weight.

We wordlessly kneel there on the bed, just taking in the moment.

And for the first time in far too long, I feel like I'm in the right place in my life. Exactly where I want to be.

"Who knew sweet Ledger has a dirty-talking side?" I huff out a laugh.

"Who knew badass Ainsley could melt beneath me?" he counters with a chuckle.

"I'd call that a pretty excellent combination."

"The best," he whispers before kissing the side of my neck. "Stay with me tonight."

"Okay," I say quietly, scared to break the moment. Of course, I'll stay. The only thing I want to do right now is keep this feeling. Keep feeling like I'm special and wanted.

Leger presses one more kiss to my neck before slowly pulling out of me. I whimper at the lost contact, and it frightens me how attached I already am to him. I shouldn't be this attached already. We need time to know each other, right?

Time doesn't matter when the connection is this strong, the devil on my shoulder chimes in.

It's too much to think about at the moment. For once, I want my brain to shut up so I can enjoy the rest of my night with Ledger.

I collapse onto the bed when he gets up to get rid of the condom. I'm shocked as shit when he comes back with a warm washcloth and cleans me up too.

It's all very domesticated, and all I want to do is find a way to keep it forever.

CHAPTER TWENTY-SIX
LEDGER

The past three weeks have been incredible.

Ainsley and I have gotten into a decent routine. We don't see each other every day, but we do talk every day, whether it's at work or on the phone after work. She's even talked me into doing some video chats, which is something I won't even do for my siblings, much to Willow's chagrin.

It's been good. Hell, it's been more than good. Things have been *easy*, and it's beyond refreshing. And the only complaint I have right now is that I want more time—more time together, more time doing things like going on dates. Just ... more time.

But Ainsley is dead set against keeping this thing between us a secret for now, and I don't want to do anything to push her away.

The good news is we have an actual date tonight. The first one since coming back from Vegas, and I'm itching for some real quality time together that isn't sneaking into her house when it gets dark. Almost a month since our last proper date is too long for me.

We're driving almost forty-five minutes away to the neighboring town of Rosedale, which has some nicer restaurants and where no one knows us.

I don't care what it entails, as long as I can take Ainsley on an actual date. I want her to know that I'm in this for real, and that means treating her how she should be treated. Dates are just a tiny aspect of that, but it's a start.

I'm picking her up in fifteen minutes, and by picking her up, I mean I'm slowly driving by her house so she can jump in and make sure no one sees us.

I've been staring at my closet for entirely too long, trying to figure out the best thing to wear. We're going to an Italian place, and although it's not terribly fancy, I do want to impress Ainsley. I would love nothing more than to ask Rina or Willow, but then they would ask too many questions. And I honestly don't know how well I would lie to them, either. I've never needed to before.

Finally deciding on my best dress pants and a nice polo, I take one last look in the mirror before heading out to my truck.

When I'm close to Ainsley's house, I take a quick look around and don't see anyone, but still slow down to a crawl before I see her pop out the front door and jog to the truck. I hate this. I hate feeling like we're in high school, sneaking around, when all I want to do is show her off.

She looks gorgeous. The green tank top dress she's wearing makes her hair come alive. She has light make-up on, and her hair is pulled up into a sleek ponytail.

"Hey, beautiful," I say as she climbs in.

"Hey, let's go before someone drives by," she hurries out.

My chest aches at her words. I know this is the best thing right now and it's what she wants, but I don't want to hide. I don't want to omit this huge part of my life from my family, and most of all, I want to yell to the world that I finally got the girl.

But I know she needs more time, and I need to be patient. I can do this for a few more weeks. No problem. If I keep telling myself that, maybe I'll believe it eventually.

I speed away, tires squealing, causing Ainsley to giggle in her seat, and it soothes my uncertain soul for the moment.

Giggling Ainsley is one of my favorite Ainsleys.

"So, where are we going?" She asks once we're finally out of town five minutes later.

"We're going to Rosedale."

"Huh, I think the last time I went to Rosedale, I was maybe sixteen. And it was only because Larkin was being a little rebel." She snickers at the memory.

"I've done a few jobs out here, a lot more recently, actually. It's a good area," I muse. I'm not sure why I'm having a hard time with conversation right now, but I feel stilted as I respond. Maybe it's because she bewitched me with that damn giggle or I'm feeling trepidation about all this secrecy, but what I need to do is figure my shit out fast because I need to make this date count.

Who knows when the next one will be.

Okay, so maybe the secrecy is wearing on me more than I realize.

"Would you ever move out of Bluebell Falls if it made sense for the company to grow?" she asks so calmly.

But her question blows my little world apart. I've never once considered moving after my parents died. My place was always here, to take care of my siblings. I know they're grown now, but I can't imagine moving even a half an hour away from them at this point in my life. Small-town life grew on me quickly once I was forced back home, and the company is growing exponentially without even considering relocation.

"No," I say, my voice gruff and hard. I clear my throat, hoping to lessen the harshness I'm not intending to take out on her. "No. I mean, when I went away for college, I fully assumed I wouldn't be back here. But then my parents died, and I took over as guardian for Willow and Lennox. I accepted this is where I would stay to make sure they were always okay.

Now, the company is doing extremely well, and I don't see a need to change that." I shrug like this whole topic of conversation isn't making me itch with how uncomfortable I am. I'm not trying to be defensive, but I do need Ainsley to understand this is my home and I don't foresee that changing.

"I get that. I always thought I would never come back here, but when my … situation imploded, this was the first place I thought to come to lick my wounds. That's probably more telling than I realize." She huffs out a laugh and looks over at me. My shoulder tension instantly drops as I take in the direction of our conversation. She isn't accusing or wanting to take me away from here; she was just curious. She's trying to evaluate her own life and wanted another point of view. *Does this mean she's thinking of not staying?*

We fill the rest of the drive with conversations about our time in college, what grandiose thoughts we had that are laughable now. Like I always thought I could come up with the next big app idea and become an instant success, I just needed to wait for the idea to come to me. It's laughable now because I'm not the most tech-savvy person at all, but I really thought I was going somewhere with that plan.

When I pull up to the restaurant, we're both laughing so hard, there are tears in our eyes.

"I can't believe you tried to smuggle in your own cooking to the campus kitchen so you could prove you were better than they were," I gasp out in between laughs.

"I was such a cocky little shit." She giggles.

I put the truck in the park and hop out while she's still laughing, feeling more like myself now. I walk around the hood and open her door, holding my hand out to help her step down.

"And who says chivalry is dead?" She smiles shyly at me.

I lead her with my hand on her lower back to the front door.

"Good evening. Table for two?" the hostess asks once we're inside.

"We have reservations, for Hutton," I tell her.

She leads us to the table, and I pull out the chair for Ainsley. It feels weird that this is technically our second date, and it makes me feel like shit that it's been almost a month and I haven't done more.

I need to do better. I need to show Ainsley I see a real future with her. Dating, spending time together, and really becoming a part of her life need to be my priority.

"So, what's good here?" Ainsley asks once we're alone.

"I've honestly never been here, but Rina has been raving about it for months, so I figured it was worth trying. They make all their pasta fresh, so I don't think you can go wrong."

She hums while opening up the menu, and I can't take my eyes off of her. I want more of this, more domestication, more dinners, more dressing up and then going home and stripping her bare.

I never considered any of this before Ainsley. My past experience with relationships is limited to Jenna and a broken heart I'm not sure I ever really had time to focus on.

"I think I'm going to get the primavera." Ainsley's voice draws me out of my head.

My eyes skim down the page, snagging on the one thing that looks familiar. "I think I'm doing the lasagna." It's a panic pick, but you can't really go wrong with a classic, right?

"I was debating that one," she says with a sly smirk that tells me we'll be sharing our meals tonight.

I'll share every single meal from here until she drops me to the curb if it keeps that smile on her face.

"So, tell me what Ledger's grand plan for his life is." She sits back and takes a sip of her wine we ordered.

Grand plan.

My grand plan is to keep Ainsley. Work hasn't factored into those plans for weeks, though we're busier than ever since the conference. I've been wracking my brain trying to figure out how to utilize Ainsley better, create a bigger role for her, but I've been coming up blank. This is usually when I bounce ideas off of Rina and come up with something, but I can't do that now. I'll end up spilling my guts about us dating and just how far gone I am for this woman.

"Umm, I kind of feel like I'm living it." I skirt the truth. I do feel like I'm living it, but I know that Ainsley is not one-hundred-percent happy. That she needs more from her life than being a landscaper's assistant.

She narrows her eyes at me. "Liar."

I let out a sigh, debating how much to share.

"We aren't supposed to be talking about work," I remind her.

"This is my life's goals, though. It's not our work on a daily basis or talking about upcoming contracts."

"Okay, my goal is to keep growing the company, although I'm not sure how much growth we can logically handle at the moment."

"And what are your goals outside of work?" she digs.

Telling her the truth scares me, but I remind myself I need to. Being honest is a huge thing for us after my earlier fuck-up with lying.

"My goals outside of work are figuring out how to keep you. How to keep you happy and in my life, however that looks."

Her eyes widen. I don't think she was expecting that kind of honesty, but I promised her no more lies.

"What about you? Where do you see your life in five years?"

Her shoulders slump in defeat, and I instantly regret asking. I know she's struggling with her career and what she wants to do. I shouldn't have pushed, knowing how much she's struggling with things.

"I see... I don't know what I see. I feel like I've been thinking about this nonstop, and I'm not any closer to answers than I was months ago."

My heart crumbles in my chest a little. *I know* this is how she feels. We've talked about it before, but I was hoping I would start factoring in at some point.

"But I do know I like having you in it. I have no idea where my life is going, but I know I want you in it," she whispers so quietly, I almost don't hear the last part. But I do, and my very fragile heart feels stronger. Bandaged up with her words pounding in my chest.

"We can figure it out together. I'm here for support in whatever way you need, even if that means you no longer work with me." I smirk, letting her know whatever she decides is more than okay with me as long as we're together.

I love you.

That's what I hope my words convey without scaring her away. Because I do love her. I think in some convoluted way, it was always supposed to be Ainsley, it just took us a while to get here.

We stare at each other for a moment before the server interrupts, and we order our food. The rest of dinner is far lighter on topic. I think we both want to pull back from the heavy feelings and just enjoy our second official date.

When we finish, Ainsley leans back in her chair with her hands on her stomach.

"Oh my God, I ate too much. You may have to wheel me out to the truck," she groans.

I laugh. "I'll carry you anywhere baby, you know that."

The smile that spreads over her face is worth every second of sneaking around.

"You ready to go home?" I ask. After all, I have plans for her and that dress.

"Definitely."

I help her stand and lead her out to the truck, both of us lost in the magic of our date. After getting her settled, I walk around the hood of the truck and feel my phone vibrate, so I pull it out to make sure nothing happened with my siblings.

Rina:

Fancy date you've got there.

My heart sinks and I frantically look around, but I can't find her.
Shit, this is exactly what Ainsley didn't want.

Rina:

Call me later, big bro.

I stare at the screen for a minute longer and then decide to handle her later. This doesn't need to be a big deal—she knows how to keep a secret. I just need to tell her to keep it to herself before she blabs to Willow and Lennox.

I hop into the truck, flustered as hell.

"Everything okay?" Ainsley's voice makes me jump, and I realize how on edge I am.

"Everything is perfect," I lie.

I lie because I don't want to break the spell. I lie because Rina won't be a problem if I talk to her. I lie because I can't stand the thought of losing Ainsley because of a freak coincidence. And I can't lose her.

CHAPTER TWENTY-SEVEN
AINSLEY

Remembering the conversation at dinner a few nights ago is making me itchy.

It's stupid, really. I asked Ledger first what his life goals were. It made complete sense that he would reciprocate. I just didn't realize I had absolutely no answer for him. Or for me, for that matter.

Where the fuck do I see myself in five years?

I wasn't any closer to an answer than I was when I'd moved here, and I fucking hated it.

The other thing bugging me was Ledger's demeanor when we left the restaurant after our date. He looked like he had seen a ghost, and it sent me into a panic that we had been spotted.

But he didn't say anything, and I trust him.

What I don't trust is me to actually figure my shit out.

I know what I want to do before I even pick up my phone.

"Hey, Ains. Everything okay?"

"Hey. Yeah, everything's fine. I was just calling to see if I could leave work a little early today so I could go drive to see Larkin." It is weird asking your boyfriend for time off, especially when we don't acknowledge we are dating at work. Admittedly, it is by my doing, but it is starting to feel weirder and weirder as time goes on.

"Absolutely, and if you need more time than just the weekend, let me know."

God, he is so understanding. Here I am, having a third-life crisis, and he's doing everything in his power to help me, in true Ledger style. And maybe that's why I'm so conflicted. Why my chest is seizing up tighter and tighter as I think about my future.

"Thanks, Ledg," I whisper, incapable of forming more words at the moment.

He stays on the phone in silence, and I try to say something—anything—to reassure him. I feel like he can tell I'm losing it a little, but I don't know how to communicate it.

"I'll keep you updated if I'm going to be late on Monday." And I hang up. Business and straight to the point. It feels wrong, and I know with more clarity than ever that I need my sister. I need a sounding board for this entire situation, and who better than someone who married their office rival?

A text comes through almost immediately.

Ledger:

> Please call me if you need anything. I'll drive
> down there if I need to, whatever you need.

Tears cloud my vision, and I know taking a couple of days away is the right move. I'm genuinely falling for Ledger, but it also feels like I'm leading him on because I have no clue where my life is heading.

It makes me feel like shit because he is a damn good man. Initial meeting aside, he's proven time and time again that I'm a priority to him. And I want—no, need—to do the same for him. He deserves that and so much more.

Me:

> I will. Thank you for giving me this time. I feel like
> I need to get a hold of where my life is going, and
> I think I need my sister's help to do that.

Honesty. I need it as much as he does, and I don't want to worry him more than I probably already am.

Ledger:

I understand. Take as much time as you need.

I sink down into my couch and pull up Larkin's number.

"Hey, stranger!"

"I literally talked to you last night," I deadpan.

"Whatever. Talking on the phone is not the same as seeing you face to face, so it still counts."

"Speaking of seeing you face to face, you up for some company this weekend?" I suddenly realize it's very presumptuous of me to just barge in on her family on my own schedule. I should have made sure it was okay before talking to Ledger.

The sound of her squealing makes me pull the phone from my ear.

"Jesus," I mutter.

"Theo! We gotta make sure the guest room is cleaned when we get home. Ainsley's coming down for the weekend!" I hear her muddled voice as she, I assume, barges into Theo's office.

"I can sleep on the couch!" I interrupt her.

"Oh, shut up, you are not sleeping on the couch," she mumbles as I hear her shuffling around. "So, what time will you be here?"

"Umm, I can leave here after lunch? So that would put me there about the time you get off, maybe a little earlier. I could go pick up the munchkins," I offer.

"Gavin will lose his shit. Sold. Stop by the office, and I'll give you Maddie's car seat."

"Done." My heart feels ten pounds lighter with how easy our relationship is. She has the whole life—a husband, kids—yet they are all dropping everything because I want to come down and visit.

"See you in a bit, Ains. I'm so fucking excited to see you," she whispers, probably because she's still at work.

"Same. Love you."

Hanging up the phone, I look around my house. I've been here a few months, and the house is nice, but outside of the garden, I haven't really made a *home* here. I've never really noticed that until now. The conversation over our date has me thinking about not just existing but thriving. And it's scary.

The drive down is uneventful and beyond boring, but now I'm waiting in the school pick-up line for Maddie and I couldn't be happier. Weekly dinners with my mom and dad are great, but they aren't Larkin. We've always been super close, and I've always been a little closed off with my parents, purely because I hated the gossip and attention on me.

It's been wonderful forging a better relationship with my parents, but nothing beats our sisterly bond.

Picking up Maddie consists of screams that hit a decibel meant to break an eardrum and the biggest hug I've ever gotten from her. Next up is Gavin, and my heart is bursting with excitement. Listen, I love my niece. She's amazing and funny as hell, but Gavin will always be my soft spot. I would literally drop anything for that boy.

We pull up in my usual spot I used to pick him up on occasion and see him looking around, confused. Before I get the chance to do something fun, Maddie rolls down the back window and screams his name. *Jesus, it's no wonder Lark has a headache at the end of the day with this one.*

The sheer excitement on Gavin's face when he realizes who's picking him up makes me want to ugly-cry. I've missed him so damn much, and no amount of long-distance game nights will make up for actually seeing him.

He jumps in the car and bear-hugs me as best as he can with a center console between us.

"How long are you here for? Are you staying at the house? How's Bluebell Falls?" His rapid-fire questions make me laugh.

"I'm staying at the house through the weekend, and Bluebell Falls is fine." I smile at him.

He narrows his eyes, and I forget just how much he sees. His childhood wasn't a good one until Larkin and Theo came along. He grew up faster than any kid should, and he's far wiser than his years. It's easy to forget all of that until he sees past a canned answer like the one I just gave.

I let out a sigh. "It's good. There's just a lot going on in my head right now, I promise."

"Okay, well, let's go home. I have so much to show you."

Oh, my heart, I love this boy more than words can say. Hanging out with Larkin is definitely the right move. I realize that I'm homesick. I didn't realize you could be homesick for people, but my heart is so damn happy being here right now.

We get home in no time, and we spend the next hour going back and forth between Maddie and Gavin showing me all the new things they've gotten since I've moved.

"You know, you look a lot happier now," Gavin says out of nowhere.

"Oh, yeah?"

"Yeah. I know you weren't happy about moving to Bluebell Falls, but whatever you're doing there, keep doing it. It's nice to see my favorite aunt so content."

"I'm your only aunt," I rebuke, but his words stick with me.

"Doesn't matter. You're still my favorite." He gives me a huge smile.

The door slams open, scaring the shit out of the three of us but revealing Larkin and Theo holding a mountain of food. I stand up and help them lay it all out on the kitchen island.

Larkin bear-hugs me when she finally has her arms free.

"I've missed you so much."

"I've missed you too," I tearfully reply.

She leans back, scrutinizing my hazy eyes. She sees me starting to crumble and gives me another tight squeeze before pulling back and turning her focus to dinner. She knows once the kids go to bed; I'm unloading everything. The unspoken bond we have will never get old.

"Good to see you, Ainsley," Theo says, giving me a hug as well. He's the perfect man for Larkin, and I can't help the flair of jealousy I have when thinking about how out of control my life feels right now.

Dinner is full of laughter and the kids speaking at unreasonable volumes, but God, I missed them.

When it's finally bedtime, I tuck Maddie in and give Gavin a hug good night because he's too big to be tucked in now—his words, not mine.

I find Larkin on the couch with a bottle of wine and two glasses, and Theo nowhere to be seen.

"Theo is doing a little work to give us some girl time," she answers my unspoken question.

Collapsing back on the couch, I sigh in relief.

"Spill. What's going on?" The concern in her tone is comforting and exactly what I need.

"I'm dating Ledger but in secret, and I love it but I don't think I like the secrecy. I know he doesn't. And we work together, and we set a boundary where we don't talk about dating at work or work while we're outside of work, and it's so fucking hard. I have no idea what I want to do with my life, no clue what kind of career I want for myself, and I'm no closer to figuring that out than when I moved. And Ledger is this huge complication to it all." I blow out a breath after I word-vomit everything weighing on my chest.

"Holy shit, you're dating Ledger! And you didn't fucking tell me!" The hurt I see makes me feel guilty as hell.

"I know, but we work together, and I wanted to keep it quiet because that fucking town is nothing but a gossip mill."

"I don't live there! You think I would tell anyone?"

I sigh. "No, but the whole situation freaks me out. I mean, how did you do it? How do you still do it?"

"Do what?"

"Work with Theo? How do you separate everything?"

"Umm, we don't." She laughs. "Is that what you think? That we keep our home life separate from our work life? You remember how we got Gavin, right? We've never separated the two. I'm not honestly sure how that would work."

"But how do you make sure neither of you gets screwed at work?" Maybe it's my old boss, maybe it's the shitty finance world rearing its ugly head again, but it can't be that simple, right?

"Mutual respect? Obviously, at first it wasn't that way." She smirks. "But now we help each other when we can, bounce ideas off of each other, step up if one of us needs to get the kids. My mind doesn't go to, 'What if he screws me over?'. Even when we first got together, I thought about it for a half a second but realized we have too much respect for each other. Combining our work and home life just flowed naturally for us."

I stare at her in disbelief.

"Have I been making this harder than it needs to be?" I whisper.

"No. Maybe. Our situations are different. Ledger is your boss, so that adds another layer to it all. And after what your old boss did, you have every right to be cautious. Now, what about your job? You're having a hard time figuring out where to go from here?" she asks in a motherly tone that I have to smile at.

"I have no idea where I go from here. This job was supposed to be temporary," I remind her.

"But it doesn't have to stay temporary."

"But is this what I'm destined to do? Be an assistant forever?"

"Not if you don't want to. You can always bring it up to Ledger and see if there is another option within the company for you."

"I can't ask him that," I huff.

"Why not?"

"Because he hired me to be an assistant. And what do I know about landscaping?"

"You know enough to create an impressive presentation that stole the show at the conference." I called her when we got home from Vegas, so dang excited about that presentation.

"What if I look into a new finance job that's not in this area?" I ask, even though just saying it cracks a fissure into my heart.

Larkin shrugs like it's no big deal. "If that's what you want to do, then go for it."

"Well, that's not helpful at all," I mutter.

"You want helpful?" she asks, and I nod.

"You are happier in the last couple of months than I've seen you in a decade. You've always been amazing with numbers, so I think finance was a natural fit for you, but you didn't love it. I don't know what you really love in terms of an actual career path, but I do know that you've smiled more, been more excited about this job than I've ever seen you before. Who cares what the job title is."

I take a big gulp of wine and stew on her words.

She's not wrong. As much of a throwaway job as this was supposed to be, I've been a lot happier than I ever was at my old job.

Because of Ledger.

I want to believe he isn't the sole reason I love this job, but I know he's a huge cause of it.

"What if I look at job listings in finance and others like the one I currently have, but maybe with more responsibility and see if anything jumps out at me? I'm not saying I want to leave, but I can't help feeling like I want to do more."

"I still say you talk to Ledger," she says into her wine glass.

"But what if an assistant is all he wants?" I whisper, scared to voice my fears.

"Then you know for a fact. If you don't ask him, you'll never know. Besides, it's not like you have a solid plan for what you would ask for. What is higher than an assistant?" She ponders.

"Literally everything." I laugh.

"Can I be super blunt right now?" she asks.

"Of course."

"You're shitting on your assistant job purely because of the job title. You feel like you should be 'higher up' which is why you feel this need to look for a job elsewhere. Do you like what you do?"

"Yes," I say hesitantly.

"Do you want a different job?"

"Not really. I mean, I would like more responsibility, I guess. I really enjoyed putting that presentation together." Her words permeate my brain. I'm not sure I agree with her, but it is something to think about.

Am I having a hard time because of just being an assistant?

"And you solve that by talking to Ledger." She shrugs.

I take another sip of my wine as we sit in silence.

"Well, I think I'm going to call it a night. I'm exhausted after that long drive." Standing up, I deflect instead of looking internally at something I'm not sure I'm ready to face yet.

"Sounds good. Do you want to do brunch with the girls tomorrow?" Larkin asks.

Her and her three best friends have been thick as thieves since college and still do almost-weekly brunches. They're an amazing group of women that I admire a lot, both because of their professions and their personalities.

"I'd love to."

I give her another hug before I go crash in the guest room.

CHAPTER TWENTY-EIGHT
LEDGER

I've been texting Rina on and off all day. It's family dinner tonight, and I've begged her more times than I can count to keep what she saw between us. I fucking hate everything about this, but I don't want to jeopardize my very new relationship with Ainsley. It feels like I'm picking between my family and Ainsley.

I spent most of yesterday just twiddling my thumbs because Ainsley is in Austin. My life is utterly boring without her here.

Rina:

> I'm just confused about why this all needs to be a secret. You know the entire town would be fucking ecstatic about this, right?

Me:

> And that's the problem. Ainsley doesn't want everyone in our business, and I agree.

Rina:

> So, you're acting like teenagers and sneaking around… Yeah, that sounds like a much better option.

I don't want to admit I agree. Don't want to admit that the secrecy is wearing on me, or admit that I'm fully in love with a woman who wants to hide everything we're doing together.

Me:

Just keep it to yourself. Please, Rina.

Rina:

Whatever, big bro.

She's exacerbating, but I know she'll keep it to herself even if it kills her.

Tonight's dinner is Willow's favorite: fajitas. I already have the meat marinating, and I've cut up all the fixings so we can just cook and assemble when everyone gets here.

The door flies open, and I cringe that Lennox probably put another damn hole in my wall.

"I didn't dent it this time!" he yells triumphantly from the front door.

"Good job, Lenny." I smirk as he narrows his eyes at me when I use his nickname. Some days, he's too easy to mess with.

"What's for dinner?" Willow asks as she walks through the door.

"Good to see you too, sis." I lean in and side-hug her.

"Yeah, yeah, good to see you. I'm starving."

"Well, you're in luck because it's fajitas tonight."

"Fuck yes." She bounds to the kitchen, and I know she'll start cooking all the veggies.

Rina walks in silently and gives me the side-eye.

"Rina..."

"I know the rules, Dad, don't worry." She rolls her eyes, and her words make me cringe. I don't want to make any of them feel like I'm telling them what to do. But this is different. This involves someone who isn't here and has said she isn't okay with people knowing.

By the time everything is cooked, I feel a little less high-strung. Until Lennox opens his mouth.

"So, when were you going to tell everyone about you and Ainsley?"

I nearly spit out the sip of beer I just drank. I look over at Rina, and her pale face tells me this wasn't her doing.

"Umm…"

"Yeah, it's like you actually think you're being sneaky," Willow says with a smirk.

"Fuck."

"Don't stress it, big bro. I think we're the only ones who have figured it out. You know the entire town would be talking if they knew." He takes a huge bite of his overfilled taco.

I wipe the sweat off my brow and push my plate away. *Fuck, fuck, fuck.*

"Hey." Rina puts her hand on my forearm. "It's okay. You know he's right. If everyone knew, it would be the talk of the town. We can keep it between the family, I promise."

She looks around at Lennox and Willow, who both have their brows furrowed.

"Why are we keeping this a secret?" Willow asks gently.

"Because Ainsley is nervous and doesn't want everyone in our business. She's been burned before, and I'm her boss. She doesn't want the repercussions that can have. Not that I blame her, even if I would never screw her over."

"Shit, I didn't even think of that," Willow mutters.

"Please keep this to yourselves," I beg.

Rina and Willow nod so hard their messy buns flop everywhere.

Lennox is looking at me weirdly, though.

"And how do you feel about keeping this all on the down-low?"

"No one says on the down-low anymore, Lenny," Willow adds.

"Whatever. You know I'll keep this between the four of us, but how do you feel about it all, Ledg?"

This is the most serious I've seen Lennox in a long time, and it unnerves me.

"Honestly?" The three of them nod again. "I hate it. Or rather, I hate that I have to hide my affection. That I'm planning dates forty-five minutes away just to have some semblance of normal. Everything else is fucking perfect. She's fucking perfect. But the sneaking around? I'm too old for this shit, even if I understand her concerns."

What a clusterfuck. This is not how I imagined family dinner going.

"Downside to a small town." Rina says it so quietly as if she knows firsthand what this feels like. I tilt my head at her, wondering what she could be talking about. As far as I know, she hasn't had a boyfriend since maybe college, and even then, I'm not so sure.

"So, how are you going to change that?" Rina asks.

"How am I supposed to change it when it's the one thing she's asked of me? And hell, who can blame her after what happened to her at her old job?" Willow and Lennox look at me curiously, and I realize my fuck-up. It seems Ainsley told Rina a little about her job, so at least she understands a little more.

"I can't tell you about that. Shit, it's not my story to tell." I bury my head in my hands. "I'm really fucking this up."

"You are not fucking this up, Ledger Dean Hutton. You are the sweetest, most caring man, and she's lucky to have you being so damn thoughtful," Willow says with major conviction.

"Do you want to talk about how things are going? Leave out all the extra personal stuff?" Lennox asks with his mouth half full.

Gross.

"Things are going well. Vegas really changed our whole dynamic. It felt like we both were a little freer than we usually are here. It was easier." *God, it was easier.* "We just had a blast. It's been fun since we've been back, but..."

"Oh shit, you love her," Rina whispers.

"I'm not letting you be the first one I say that to," I say without thinking. It's then I realize I essentially said yes, but the first person I say those words to will be Ainsley. When she's ready. *If she's ever ready.* Fuck, my head is a mess.

"Aww, big bro," Willow swoons.

"Okay, get it out." The girls talk a little more before I clear my throat.

"We need to go around the table."

"Shit, totally forgot. I'll go first," Rina says. "My favorite part of the week was finally getting that huge-ass cabinet out of my workshop."

"No shit? You finally sold it?" That thing was massive and had been sitting in her store for almost a year.

"I did indeed, to a lovely widower who will apparently be keeping her dead husband's clothes in it."

"Oh! Let me write that down. That would be good for a story." Willow pulls out her phone and types up some notes.

I chuckle at the two of them.

"Okay, I'll go next," Willow says. "My favorite part of the week is finishing this damn story!"

"No shit? You finished it?" I ask.

"Fucking finally. This one took, like, three times as long as it normally does. But whatever. It's done and in the hands of my editor." She claps her hands together excitedly. "Proud of you, Will," I say. And I really am. It's incredible to me that she writes the stories she does.

"I'll go next. I think my favorite part of the week was taking Ainsley out on a proper date." I figure since they all know, I'm safe to at least talk about it.

"Was the Italian place not the best ever?" Rina asks.

"So fucking good. Maybe we should have family dinner there sometime," I muse.

Silverware clatters to the table.

"No," all three of them say.

"Okaayyy…"

"Family dinner means we cook for each other. It's just how it is," Willow says.

"That's fine. Just throwing out the option that I promise I will never do again."

Willow and Rina nod their heads, and I almost laugh. I never knew we relegated family dinner to only cooking for each other. I love it, but now I know not to mess with the tradition at all.

"Okay, my favorite part of the week is seeing Ledger, our fearless leader, finally take steps to being happy." The seriousness in Lennox's tone and on his face stops me in my tracks.

"You know, I may be the baby of the family, but I still remember when you went off to college. How excited you were about the future. When Mom and Dad died, you lost that excitement. I know grief is a fickle bitch, but you've literally never put yourself first since. I know that chick in college had a lot to do with it, but it's nice to finally see you just being happy."

I'm speechless.

"Lenny, I didn't know you had it in you."

"Oh, fuck off, Rina." He huffs out a laugh.

"He's right, though. I've never seen you this happy before. It's noticeable just having a normal conversation with you. You're a little easier-going, a little looser if that makes sense," Willow adds.

"Did you know you haven't been micromanaging the nursery at all in the last three weeks?" Rina smirks.

"Umm, no? I didn't realize I was micromanaging to begin with." I feel attacked, loved, and very embarrassed by my siblings' observations. I had no clue they saw so much.

"We're proud of you, big bro," Lennox says softly.

Clearing my throat, I nod at them in acknowledgment. I don't think I can talk right now with the lump in my throat. I feel less like a father figure and more like a friend to my siblings than I ever have before.

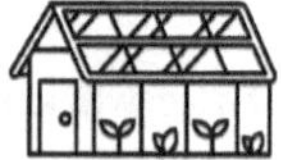

She called in sick.

Not just she'll be a few hours late or taking the day off, no. Ainsley called in sick, and I'm officially in panic mode.

Is she actually sick? Or is she avoiding me and trying to let me down easy? I know I'm overreacting, but I feel like if something happened, she would just call and tell me, not call in sick. It feels like she could be using this as an out because she doesn't want to tell me the real reason she's not working today. Illogical, I know, but my anxiety is running my brain right now.

I haven't even gone into work today. Haven't checked out any of the jobs that are in progress, stopped by the nursery, none of it.

I'm pacing in my house, trying to figure out what to do.

We're still so new. I don't want to barge over there if this is her way of telling me she needs a breather. Although, I think that would kill me, honestly. If she felt like she couldn't just tell me that, it would kill me.

Rina... They're friends, right?

I realize how fucked up it is to text my sister to ask my girlfriend if she's okay, but my anxiety is at an all-time high, so I don't care. Logic has no place here.

Me:

Can you text Ainsley and check on her? She called in sick, and I just want to make sure she's okay.

Rina:

And as her boyfriend, why aren't you doing that?

Me:

Because if she called in sick because she needs some space, I want to give that to her, but I want to make sure she's okay.

Rina:

Jesus, you're worse than a high school girl.

Me:

I realize that.

She doesn't respond for five minutes, and I'm really starting to panic. When my phone pings, I fumble with the keypad until I finally get it unlocked.

Rina:

She's really sick. Apparently, kids have lots of germs and she is now infected. She told me she's fine and not to come over.

Me:

Thanks, Rina.

Rina:

Make her your chicken noodle soup and take it over there.

I smile at my sister's response. She plays hard-ass all day, but she probably cares more about people than most.

Me:

Yes, Ma'am. Can you call the nursery and tell them they're on their own for a few days? I have enough people scheduled. They should be fine.

Rina:

Done.

I walk back to my kitchen and grab everything for the soup. I'll just make it at Ainsley's house so she can have it fresh.

Bags in hand, I load up everything I can think of that could help. I handled a lot of sick days when Lennox and Willow were younger, so I'm trying to remember everything that helped them.

The drive is quick. Being down the road from each other comes in handy for times like these, apparently.

I load my arms with bags as I walk up to her front door and knock a little harder than I need to.

It takes her close to five minutes to open the door—I know, I timed it—and when she does, she has a blanket wrapped around her, her hair is in shambles, and her nose is bright red.

"Can I come in and take care of you? I brought stuff to make soup."

CHAPTER TWENTY-NINE
AINSLEY

hose fucking kids are cesspools. I spend one weekend with them, and my body revolts and I get sicker than I have in years.

I know that's not how sickness works, but that's what it feels like, so I'm blaming them. It was probably Maddie's fault. That attitude alone has to mean she's carrying more germs than Gavin.

I'm currently curled up on my couch, surrounded by blankets and tissues, watching whatever food shows I can find. My head hurts, my nose is stuffed, and I'm freezing.

A knock sounds at my door, and I figure Larkin called my parents and they're just checking up on me. I don't really want to get out of my gross-ass cocoon, but they'll freak out if I don't answer. Shuffling to the door slowly, I yank open the door and am horrified to see it's not my parents but my sweet boyfriend—*is that what I'm calling him?*—overloaded with bags.

"Can I come in and take care of you? I brought stuff to make soup."

If that's not the cutest thing in the world, I don't know what is.

"I don't want to get you sick," I whine because I really want the soup, but getting him sick is a dick move.

He doesn't respond, just gently pushes his way in and leads me to the couch.

"Sit. I'm going to get you some tea, and then I'll start the soup."

My eyes flood with tears as he walks to my kitchen.

Have I ever had someone take care of me that isn't related to me?

The answer is never, and the thought causes big crocodile tears to spill over my lashes. I hate being emotional, hate crying. I learned to hide my emotions pretty early in my career, and I became very good at it.

But right now, I don't feel good. Everything hurts, and the sweetest man I've ever met came over to take care of me without me asking. It's too much for my very fragile heart.

Ledger comes back out with a steaming mug of tea and a big smile on his face. It instantly drops when he sees me crying.

"Shit, what did I do?" he asks, rushing over and putting the tea on the coffee table.

"N-n-n-nothing. It's just s-s-s-so sweet, a-a-and I've n-n-never had anyone t-t-take care of m-m-me before." I can barely get the words out with how much I'm ugly-crying right now. My shoulders are shaking, my nose is running, and I'm sure I look like absolute hell.

"You're crying because I'm being nice?" he asks with his brows furrowed in confusion.

It's beyond adorable, and if I wasn't losing my shit right now and sick, I would kiss the confusion off of his face.

"I'm just a mess. Ignore me." I huddle further into my blanket nest to hide the shitshow that is me right now.

Wordlessly, Ledger scoots closer to me on the couch and picks me up like I weigh nothing, setting me on his lap.

"I'm going to get you sick," I whisper.

"Don't care," he murmurs, putting his forehead against mine.

"Ledg…"

"Shh, let me take care of you. Let me love you," he whispers as he tucks my head against his shoulder. His scent, wood and a slight spice, soothes me more than any cold medicine has, and before I know it, I fall asleep.

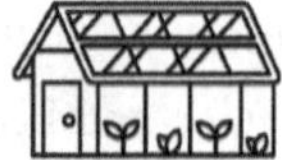

I wake up with a start and hear Ledger's voice.

"I was covering for you, and you shot me!" he says in outrage. "Nope, not cool man," he chuckles.

What the hell?

Did I take too much cold medicine, and now I'm hallucinating?

I sit up a little and see Ledger on the other side of the couch with the headset I use to play games with Gavin on and a controller in his hands.

"She's doing okay, bud, I promise. She just needs to sleep to kick the cold she has." Pause. "I'm taking great care of her. I even made homemade chicken noodle soup while she's been sleeping." Pause. "Yes, I cook." He chuckles again. "You don't? Well, we're going to need to change that so you can help your mom out occasionally." Pause. "Yeah, I can teach you, no problem." Pause. "Well, I could come there the next time Ainsley does, or you could come visit us. We can pick you up for the weekend." Pause.

His burst of laughter startles me, but I calm myself quickly because he's playing a video game with Gavin and I'm greedy for this interaction.

"You act more like a big brother than her nephew, but I appreciate that about you. My intensions are... I'm not sure I should be telling you this." I hear his sigh this time before he continues. "My intentions are that I just want to love her. I want her to be happy, and I'm trying my best to make sure that's with me, but I'll take her happy even if it's not with me."

Here come the damn tears again. *This fucking man.*

"You're a wise man, Gavin. That's good advice." Pause. "I had a blast today too, even if you shot me in the back." Pause. "We can definitely play again. I might need to get another controller, though, so Ainsley can play with us." Pause. "Sounds good. I'll make sure Ainsley texts you when she up."

He puts the controller down on the table and chuckles to himself.

"He's a good kid," I grate out, realizing my voice is almost gone.

His head lifts up, and a small smile tilts the corner of his lips up.

"He's the best. Sorry, I didn't mean to take over. I went to turn on the TV and the game popped up with Gavin typing very frantically to come play with him. My intention was to just tell him you were sick, but he suckered me into playing."

"He's good at that." I try to clear my throat as I laugh, but it turns into a nasty cough.

"Here." He hands me some tea that's somehow still warm, and I take a large sip. It instantly soothes my throat, and I moan at how good it tastes.

"I used to make that for Willow when she got sick. She always lost her voice no matter what, and that helped get it back faster," he reminisces.

"You're a good man, Ledger." I mean it more than just making me tea. I mean it in the way he played with Gavin when he didn't need to, when he came over when he found out I was sick and proceeded to take care of me, when he told the boy who has such a huge part of my heart that all he wanted to do was love me.

And I want to love him too.

I'm not sure how we get to that point. I don't think it'll be easy, but I know I want to try. He makes me want to try. The sudden clarity is like a wave of silence in my brain. My nonstop thoughts are finally quiet.

"How are you feeling?" he asks while not acknowledging my words.

"About the same, honestly. I'm not very good at being sick. I'm sorry for getting emotional all the time."

"Don't apologize. I just wanted to make sure you were okay. I got a little worried when you called in sick after visiting Austin." He has the grace to look a little sheepish, and I very slowly put two and two together.

"You thought something happened, and I called in sick to what? Avoid you?"

"Umm..." He grabs the back of his neck with one hand, his cheeks turning a super cute shade of pink.

"Hey." I clear my throat again and make sure that he really hears me. "I'm committed to being with you. If things change for me, you will be the first to know, but I honestly don't see that happening. I don't want you to feel like you're waiting for the other shoe to drop every day." The way he's feeling is entirely my doing. But if I'm able to give him some of the clarity I just found, maybe it'll help.

The look in his eyes is pure affection and love, and my heart pounds in my chest because, for the first time, I feel the exact same way.

"My turn to apologize for jumping to conclusions and not taking you at your word."

"No apology needed, Ledg. I am eternally grateful you came over, even if I still think you'll end up sick. And I'll feel guilty as hell about it when it happens." I cuddle into his side as he wraps his arm around me. I feel him press a kiss to the crown of my head, and I sink further into his warmth.

"Do you want some soup?"

"In a minute," I murmur as my eyes get heavier.

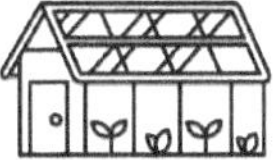

I don't even remember falling asleep, but when I wake up again, I'm in my bed surrounded by blankets and damn near dripping sweat.

Flinging the blankets off of me, I stumble out of bed and start stripping off my clothes, trying to get out of the grossness breaking a fever leaves behind.

"Well, it's good to see you up, baby," I hear from behind.

I cringe, realizing how much he's seen and dealt with over the last day or so.

God, I don't even know what day it is.

"You didn't need to stay," I tell him, feeling very insecure right now.

He doesn't acknowledge my words, just walks past me and turns the shower on. He ducks down and picks up my sweat-laden clothes, and I flinch. Reaching out, I attempt to grab them from him because that's a level of closeness I'm not sure I'll ever be ready for, but he turns around and heads back out of the bathroom.

"I'm going to run a load of laundry and get all of your bedding clean. I have dinner in the oven, and it'll be ready when you're done with your shower."

Dumbfounded. I'm completely dumbfounded.

"Umm..."

He turns back around. "I had to grow up at a young age. Being the sole guardian for Willow and Lennox wasn't a walk in the park. I had to handle more sick days than I care to admit. I promise this is nothing, and I promise I wouldn't be here if I didn't want to be."

We lock eyes for an extended second, and I feel like I see all the way to his soul and it's beautiful.

"I need to take care of you, Ains. Just try to let me, okay?" He says it so softly like he's scared I'm going to push him away. But pushing him away right now is that last thing I want to do.

But I really do need to take a damn shower and get some actual food in my system.

I slowly walk up to him as he tilts his head. Lifting up on my top toes, I press a soft kiss to his lips before pulling back.

"I think I like you taking care of me." I step back with a smirk before turning around and stepping into my shower.

CHAPTER THIRTY
LEDGER

Apparently, when the woman I love is sick, I lose all sense of rational within my brain. Freaking out when she called in sick felt like child's play to how I feel not being able to do a lot to make her feel better.

I did what I could—cooking and cleaning, making sure she was hydrated—but it still doesn't feel like enough. The fact that she is currently in the shower and requesting actual food has me calming down a little.

I pull out the enchiladas when she comes out of her room. Dressed in some lounge shorts and an oversized T-shirt, I see my entire future before my eyes.

Sunday mornings, cooking brunch for her while she relaxes. Cooking dinner together, laughing and dancing to whatever music she puts on. Random date nights, just enjoying the life we've created. Creating a business we're both proud of.

I really need to find a bigger role for her within the company.

"Hey," she says shyly.

"Hey, beautiful. You ready for some food?" I ask instead of spilling my inner thoughts to her.

"God yes. I'm starving." She plops down into a chair in the small dining room.

I serve up plates overflowing with cheesy goodness and set one down in front of her.

"You know, you might give me a run for my money in the cooking department, and I don't know how I feel about that."

"If we combine our powers in the kitchen, we won't have to fight about it." I smirk as I place my plate on the table and sit down to eat.

She stares at me for a moment, and I see the impact of my words in her eyes. Something has changed with her. She looks less hesitant, less closed off, and all I see is a complete openness to this relationship of ours.

The rest of dinner is quiet. I think both of us felt the shift and didn't want to voice it. Too worried it would break the spell.

We're now lying in her bed, cuddled together under her blankets.

"Relationships are hard for me," she whispers.

"I don't think anyone is good at them. I think we just learn to adapt if the person is really worth it."

"Maybe. I wouldn't really know. I was too focused on school in college, too focused on climbing the corporate ladder after that, and I never really dated. Hell, outside of Larkin, I never even really had friends. I couldn't trust the people I worked with because I had seen them back-stabbing people far too often."

"It must have taken a toll on you to always have to be on and not really have people you could let loose with," I say.

"I never thought that until I moved back here. I felt like I could do everything on my own, and if I needed a sounding board, I had Larkin." She sounds sad, like she's realizing it's not the way she wants to live her life anymore.

"Shifting the way you want to live your life isn't a bad thing, Ains. It's good. It means you're taking a step back and prioritizing yourself for once."

"Huh, I've never thought of it that way," she says as she brushes her fingertips along my jaw. "You've been through a lot in your life too. How have you stayed so ... humble? No... Self-aware, maybe?"

I bark out a laugh at her question.

"Oh, I am far from self-aware. I think it's easier to see things when you're looking in from the outside. When it's not you going through all the shit. When I was in college, I was dating a woman named Jenna. I was convinced she was the one. Maybe that's not true. I thought it was the natural progression of things if that makes sense. I proposed, and three days later, I caught her cheating on me in our bed. It was a shock to the system, but the timing of it all made it so I couldn't focus on it. My parents died the day before I caught her, and I was a fucking mess. I barely remember anything about the whole situation other than breaking it off with her."

"Holy shit, Ledg," Ainsley whispers.

I huff out a sad laugh. "Yeah, it was a messed-up time, and I didn't really handle things well. I didn't have time to cope, to mourn a relationship while I was mourning my parents and trying to figure out how to be a guardian at the same time. I haven't spoken to Jenna since I kicked her out of our apartment. That's strange, right? To just cut someone out of your life and act like they never happened?" I muse out loud.

"I don't think it's strange, considering the circumstances. Your focus turned to your family, and there's nothing wrong with that. Honestly, it's admirable that you didn't even second-guess your decision."

Looking up at the ceiling, I really think about it. I'm completely over Jenna, have been for a long time, but have I ever really gotten closure with the whole situation? I don't think brushing shit under the rug counts in this case.

"You might be right, but I still feel like I could have handled things differently."

She leans forward and presses her forehead to mine.

"You, Ledger Dean Hutton, are a phenomenal man. Many people wouldn't have taken on what you did, let alone at your age. Many people would have crumbled for less. Hell, I've crumbled for less." She lets out self-deprecating laughter.

"Hey, I'm not telling you this to compare. I just want you to know more of my history, more of why I am the way I am."

"You make that sound like the way you are is something bad, but I happen to think you are the best kind of man, Ledg." She presses a soft kiss to my lips.

"I honestly think you've made me a good man," I admit in a whisper.

"And I think you've made me realize there is more to life than what I relegated myself to."

She presses her lips to mine again, and I just feel whole. For the first time in my life, I feel like all my hard work, all of my sacrifices, have led me to this woman. Lead me to this life I want so desperately for us. I know we have things to work through still, but I have never felt surer about something in my life than I am of Ainsley and me.

She pulls away and settles herself on my shoulder as I trace patterns on her exposed shoulder.

"I think I've had two boyfriends total in my life. And they were both in high school." She chuckles. "God, that sounds ridiculous. I don't know why I gave up on this idea of finding a person for me, but by the time I got into the workforce, I didn't care enough to try to date. Hell, I didn't really have time. There were weeks I was working seventy to eighty hours. My job made it so I couldn't even think of anything outside of making clients more money. I don't think I realized how messed up it all was until Larkin got with Theo and they adopted Gavin."

She takes a deep breath, and I pull her a little closer to me. She's opening up to me in a way she never has before, and I don't want to do anything to interrupt that, but I need her to know I'm here for her.

"Gavin changed everything for me. I wanted to spend as much time as I could with him. I would pick him up from school, make time to have dinner with him. He changed my entire priority system. But then that promotion came up, and I knew I would probably only have one to two chances at it. The firm I worked at was very unforgiving and rarely gave second chances. So I applied, worked my ass off, and saw Gavin less. I hated every second of it, but I knew this was the only way to get ahead. The promise of more money and better hours was too tempting.

"Not getting the position was one thing, but being taken advantage of? Having the guy that got the position treat me like his assistant and start being sexually suggestive was my last straw."

I squeeze her a little tighter, not for her but for me. My anger takes over, hearing the shit that guy put her through, and I want nothing more than to find him and pound his face into the pavement.

"It's fine, I promise," she placates me. "I'm not telling you this to get you worked up." She already knows me so well, and she doesn't even realize it.

"I know, but I swear if you ever run into that man, ever get a phone call, anything... I will not hesitate to show what the pieces of shit deserves."

She looks up at me with a giant smile on her face.

"You're quite sexy when you get all alpha and protective."

"I'm only this way with you, Ains."

"I know. I love it." She smirks. "Anyway, I started writing things down, documenting the shit he was doing. I thought I was getting ahead, but he was devious and beat me to the punch. My already lacking trust in men was obliterated.

"I had every intention of hiding out here, only interacting when it came to my parents and getting food. I didn't trust anyone, and I wanted to lick my wounds in peace. Feeling like I had failed at everything took over. Honestly, I still kind of feel that way," she admits.

"Ains..."

"I know, I know. We did wonderful things at the conference, and I'm actually loving this job, but is this what I truly want to do with the rest of my life?"

I know she's not asking to diminish her role with my company. But I also know she's right. I need to figure out how to restructure the company to give her more responsibility, more ownership. Something to keep her happy and feeling like she's making a difference.

"I still have a lot to figure out in my life, and I need you to understand I might be bad at this."

"Bad at what, baby?" I ask because she's good at everything she puts her mind to from what I've seen.

"Relationships, being open with you, and communicating what I need. I've been a loner for too long, and I don't know how to shift that way of thinking."

"I think you're doing a hell of a job right now," I offer.

"We'll see if I can stick to it. I just need you to know trust comes very slowly from me."

More things click in my brain, and I start to realize why she was hesitant for so long.

"And lying to you about who I was made you doubt everything again. I'm so sorry, Ains. "

"I will admit, the whole situation threw me for a huge loop. But you know what helped?" she asks.

"What?"

"The fact that your heart was in the right place. After I heard your explanation and talked to Rina, I understood it better. It also helped that you have a little nervousness, anxiety if you will, that comes out sometimes and it made me realize I made you nervous. You didn't intentionally want to hurt me, you just panicked." She shrugs.

"Yeah, but that doesn't excuse my actions."

"Forgiving you might be the best thing I've done in my very lackluster life so far," she murmurs.

I slide down the headboard and readjust us so we're side by side in bed.

"I'm very thankful you saw fit to give me another chance," I whisper as I press a kiss to her cheek, her forehead, and finally her lips. Feeling her melt into me and slide her hands under my shirt sends shivers down my spine.

Subtle touches and kisses last well into the night. A lot has happened in the last day, and I think both of us opening up to each other made us closer than ever. But we're still fragile, still figuring out things as we go. And it's going to take time.

I know that I'll do anything in my power to make sure she always feels like she can open up to me. That she can have the life she never thought she could have.

CHAPTER THIRTY-ONE
LEDGER

The past couple of weeks since Ainsley was sick have been amazing. We're closer than ever, and I've been brainstorming how to restructure the company to give her an actual place within it, not just as a virtual assistant. I've had to consult a lawyer in a neighboring town so I can make sure the paperwork is correct, but at least it's in progress. Ainsley doesn't know about it yet, but I plan to surprise her with it when it's closer to completion.

We still haven't gone out in town and been openly together, but I understand her reasoning for the secrecy a lot more now and it bothers me a lot less. All I need to give her is time, and I'm willing to do that for as long as she needs.

Today, I'm working at the nursery while Ainsley holds down the fort with all the landscaping projects we've got in progress. I'm rearranging some trees in the back when I hear a voice call out.

"Hello?"

"I'll be right there!" I yell out.

Finishing up this row of trees, I head out front when I'm done.

"How can I he—" I stop dead in my tracks when the woman turns around."Long time no see." She smiles softly.

Jenna.

"Umm..." I'm speechless and have no idea how to react to this.

"Sorry to barge in unannounced. I heard your name through the grapevine after you did a presentation and wanted to come and see you." She still has a small smile on her face, but I'm at a loss. Why is Jenna here? Why now? Right when things are finally going well with Ainsley.

She must see the sheer confusion on my face because she continues talking like I'm not gobsmacked she's here.

"Do you have a few minutes to talk?"

I nod slowly and then finally find some words. "We can head back to my office." My blunt tone doesn't get missed, but there is no reason for her to be here right now.

"That sounds perfect. Lead the way."

It's surreal having Jenna in my space again, and I can't say I'm not curious about why she's here. The thing that's hitting me hard is how much I *don't* feel for her. I haven't seen her since I left college to come back here, and it's not that I expected lingering feelings if I ever saw her again, but I thought I would feel *something*. Instead, it feels like I'm walking a stranger back to my office for a meeting. I may be shocked, but that's all it is. There's zero attraction, no what-ifs, and the only thing on my mind is Ainsley.

We both sit down at the little table I have here, and I wait patiently for her to talk.

She doesn't look all that different from over a decade ago, but what is different is the giant rock on her ring finger.

"You've become quite the talk of my neighborhood. Apparently, the landscaper who does a lot of work in the area was talking up your sustainable approach after he heard you present at a conference. I took a business card, not thinking anything of it until I looked up the company and saw your name."

"And you decided the best plan was to come all the way out here? I don't even know where you live," I muse out loud, realizing how snarky I'm being. None of this makes sense.

"I actually live in Vegas now," she says, undeterred by my attitude.

"So, you flew all the way out here for what, exactly?"

"Mostly to apologize. I never got the chance to do that—my fault." She holds up her hand when I open up my mouth to interrupt her.

"I was young, and although that wasn't an excuse, I was only thinking of myself and not how my actions would affect others, specifically you. When you … found me, my head was on what it would mean if you needed to come back here permanently after your parents died. I probably self-sabotaged because I wasn't ready for the kind of responsibility you needed to take on."

Her words are what I needed to hear for so many years, and yet… Right now? At this point in my life? It means less than I hoped it would. It's nice to hear where her head was at, but none of it matters anymore. Things happened the way they did and if they happened differently, I may never have had Ainsley in my life now, and that's not something I can accept anymore. What I've always thought was the worst point in my life has developed over the last six months. I no longer think of it as a dark point. I think of it as what I needed to do to be the man that Ainsley deserved. The man that would do anything for his family, and I wouldn't change that for anything. Seeing Jenna now makes me realize my path was never with her.

"I am truly sorry for everything, Ledger," Jenna says so softly I almost miss it because I'm so lost in my head.

"I appreciate the apology, although it's not needed." I don't want to dwell on the past, and this entire interaction has made it so blatantly obvious to me. All I want to do now is get her out of my office as fast as possible.

"Is there anything else I can help you with?" I'm not mad, not angry. I'm not even remotely upset. I'm just ... done with this interaction.

"Umm..." I've thrown her off, but all I want to do right now is call Ainsley and hear her voice.

"Umm," she continues. "I was actually going to see if you could help my husband and me with some landscaping at the house."

It's my turn to be thrown for a loop. But if her ring is anything to go by, this may not be something I want to turn away. The goal has been growing the business, after all.

"Sure. If you want to send an email to me, Ainsley will get you on the schedule for a consult. We usually do out-of-state jobs remotely and use local contractors for you, but we monitor everything closely." I give her the usual script. She's just another client now, and I plan to treat her as such until our job with her is done.

It's strange... A year ago, this conversation—hell, just seeing Jenna—would have sent me into a spiral. I feel a little rude since she flew all the way here, but she's had many years to give me this apology and only did so when I had something to give her in return. She may act like she's turned a page, but her actions say otherwise. Good thing it doesn't affect me anymore.

"Oh, okay. That sounds like a plan. Thanks, Ledger." She stands up and pauses before saying one last thing. "I am truly sorry for how I handled things. I really hope you're happy." She gives me a sad smile before walking out the door.

I sit back in my chair and exhale in relief as I watch her walk out of my office.

I never thought I'd see Jenna again, and I certainly didn't expect to feel the way I do right now. All I want to do right now is call Ainsley to come down here, but I know I need to make sure my head is completely clear first. Because what I want to tell her can't be misconstrued in any way.

I pick up my phone and send a message to the family group text.

Me:

Guess who showed up at the nursery?

Willow:

A bear.

Me:

?? What are you talking about?

Willow:

Sorry. I just wrote a scene where a bear tore apart a camper, so apparently my mind is still on it.

Rina:

And people are scared of me… You're the real one they need to be scared of.

Willow:

That might be the nicest thing you've ever said to me.

Lennox:

Was it food delivery?

Me:

You guys really suck, you know that?

Rina:

Oh, big bro, you know we love you. Who showed up at the nursery?

I feel the silence through the group chat. Everyone is radio silent for a long minute.

I chuckle at how different their personalities are, but beyond that, I feel an overwhelming amount of love for them. Rina was right all those months ago. They just want me to be happy. And now that we're all grown, it's time for me to finally take some time for me and go after what I really want in my life.

Me:

I'm good, you guys, I promise. I'm going to call Ainsley to come over here, and I'll be good.

Lennox:

I would call you pussy-whipped, but Ainsley is the shit. Have you invited her over for family dinner yet?

Rina:

Yeah, what the hell? Are you scared to bring her around us?

Willow:

I'm not going to lie… I would be scared if I were him. It's not like any of us will go easy on her.

A smile so big stretches across my face, my muscles start to hurt. Not because they're giving me shit, but because I know with every ounce of my being that Ainsley will fit into our dysfunctional group like she's always been there and absolutely give as much as she gets.

Me:

I will ask her soon.

You do that. Are you seriously good, Ledg? I know you haven't seen her since everything went down.

Shockingly, I'm great. It was nice to get the closure, honestly, but I don't think there was ever anything really there between us. Not like there is with Ainsley and me.

And that big truth hits me in my chest. I was prepared to marry Jenna because it was expected, not necessarily because I wanted to. But I *want* to marry Ainsley. I want everything with her, and I know she needs more time, but just knowing I'm fully committed eases any worry I have. I'll wait a lifetime for that woman.

Well, that's good to hear. Go call your woman, and text us all later so we know you're okay.

Lennox is such a conundrum some days. He's a goofball and immature, but his soft little heart makes me want to always protect him. He tends to make sure everyone else is okay but never himself. A lot like Ainsley, actually.

I shake my head and exit the group chat, then pull up Ainsley's number.

"Well, hello there, boss man."

A smile spreads across my face.

"Hey baby," I say softly.

"Is everything okay?" Her tone instantly shifts.

"Everything's great. Do you want to come down to the nursery right now? I have some things I want to talk to you about."

"Yeah, of course. Give me five minutes." I hear her shuffling around.

"See you soon," I say before hanging up.

Five minutes later, Ainsley is walking through the office doors.

"Hey, what's going on? Are you okay?" She looks concerned, and God does it make me love her even more if that's possible.

"Come here." I pat my leg and hold my arm out for her.

She sits on my lap with her eyebrows furrowed. I take the opportunity to smooth them out with my fingertips before leaning forward and pressing a kiss to her lips.

"What's going on, Ledg?" she whispers.

"So much. Jenna was just here."

She reels back, eyes wide. "What?"

I fill her in on everything Jenna told me and wait for her reaction.

"There is so much to unpack here," she says.

"I know." I smile.

"Are you okay? You look okay. In fact, you look too okay," she rambles, scrutinizing my face.

I laugh at her words. I'm sure I look certifiable right now, but I feel nothing but content.

"I'm more than okay. She apologized for the entire college situation, and I accepted it. Then told her if she wants to hire us to send me an email and you would get back to her to get on the schedule."

Ainsley bursts out laughing. "Damn! You shut her down quickly."

I chuckle along with her. "Yeah, I don't really know if she had an ulterior motive, but I didn't want to hear it at all."

"So, she's in Vegas and heard about us?" she asks once she stops laughing.

"Yeah. Apparently, a landscaper in her neighborhood went to the conference and was super impressed, so he's been recommending us for sustainable landscaping whenever it comes up. I probably need to figure out who he is so we can use him as a contractor," I muse out loud.

"I can do that," she says, already mentally adding it to her workload.

I look at her and ask the first thing that pops into my head.

"Are you happy, Ainsley?

CHAPTER THIRTY-TWO
AINSLEY

For the first time in far too long, I don't have to think about the answer to his question.

"Very happy."

He gets a devilish smirk on his face before saying, "Wanna play hooky?"

I burst out laughing. "Hell no! I have shit to do to keep the business running, boss man." I start climbing out of his lap, but he holds me tight to him.

Kissing my shoulder before he leans his cheek on it, I feel a deep sense of devotion radiating from him. Three months ago, a conversation like this would have sent me off the deep end. I would have been jealous, scared, and fearful things were coming to an end. But right now? I feel nothing but peace. Do I still have things to figure out? Yes, but the way forward is much clearer now.

I don't feel this crushing weight to figure out what direction my life is going to go immediately. I have a good job and enough time to really think about my career. And I have Ledger.

I quickly peck his forehead before climbing off his lap.

"I really do have a lot that needs to get done today, but dinner later?" As much as I want to stay with him and play hooky, he's running a business and someone needs to keep the wheels running. I smirk at the thought of having such an integral part in this company when I started with the intention of this being a throwaway job.

Who knew things would change so drastically? Larkin was right that my mindset about the job title needed to change. No longer looking at it as a shitty job and instead taking pride in it. And trying to make sure to lessen the load on Ledger's shoulders at the same time.

"Dinner sounds great. I'll see you at my place later?"

I nod and head for the door, counting down the minutes until dinner. Cooking with Ledger most nights is something I never knew I wanted. Never knew would fill me with so much happiness that I just want to scream from the rooftop.

And yet, I'm still forcing him to keep us a secret.

It feels like if I let the town in on our new coupledom, it'll pop this bubble we're living in. The outside influence still scares me more than I want to admit, and I worry I won't be able to handle the attention all the time. I've come a long way since moving here, but I still feel like things are fragile.

I definitely need to work on that. Ledger deserves better than hiding.

The quick trip home gives me time to wrap my head around the gossip mill learning about us. I'm nowhere near ready, but just having it in the back of my mind feels like progress.

Plopping down in my office chair, I jump back into emails. I wasn't lying when I said I had work to do. We've gotten an influx of emails for consults, and I need to get a handle on them. If we played hooky, the entire company would be behind on things, and I don't want that to happen.

It's nearing five o'clock, and I'm close to a stopping point when my phone rings.

"Ainsley Mathews," I answer absentmindedly.

"Ms. Mathews, this is Craig Sutter from Sutter and Philipsen Financial Advisors." He pauses as I register what he said.

"Umm, hello." *What the hell? Why is my old company calling me?*

"We're currently conducting an investigation, and your name came up. We'd like to have you come in and discuss things if you're able to."

"Am I in trouble?" It's the first thing that comes to mind because I don't understand why they would call me in six months after they fired me.

"No, ma'am, nothing like that. We've had some complaints about an employee, and your name came up during some interviews. We were told that you might have some information on said employee, possibly more proof of his wrongdoings."

He's being vague as shit, and it's only making me more nervous. But the only thing I can think of is Lance and how he behaved while I was still there.

"Is this about Lance Lafay?" I ask, needing some hint.

"I'm not at liberty to discuss this over the phone, but if it helps make the decision for you to come in, I will say you have the right hunch."

His overcomplicated language reminds me of how fucking political the entire profession is and how much I don't miss it.

"Is there a particular day that works better to come in?"

"The sooner, the better. If you're able to come in this week, that would be ideal," he concedes, but he already sounds done with this conversation. I've taken up too much of his time, and his attempt at being polite is translucent.

"Okay, I need to move things around. Can I call you back and let you know?"

"That's fine," he clips, then gives me his direct number. We hang up without preamble, and I sit back in my chair, confused as hell.

Why now? Why is Lance getting investigated now and not six months ago when I had an abundance of shit against him? Why wasn't I taken seriously?

My anger starts to spike, and the pressure of frustrated tears makes its presence known in the back of my eyes. Right this second, I don't even know if I want to go in there and give them all the information I still have.

I don't know how long I sit here for, just thinking about how unfair the entire situation is. I know this was my opportunity to clear my name and show people who Lance truly is, but does it even matter anymore? Do I even care?

I want to be the bigger person. I want to say I don't need this closure and that it doesn't bother me anymore, but that would be a lie. It still bothers me that I was fired the way I was. And maybe if I'm able to fight this battle, prove that I wasn't the fuck-up, I can really move forward with the life I'm becoming quite fond of. My life with Ledger.

My phone interrupts my thought process, and I answer without looking again.

"Hello." I can hear how my voice is a little shaky, and I clear my throat.

"Ainsley? Are you okay?" *Ledger.*

"Umm, yeah. I think so. What's up?" I'll tell him, deciding to tell him over dinner when I ask for the time off.

"I was expecting you to be at the house when I came home, and you're not here." He sounds a little unsure, a little of his anxiety drifting into his voice.

I look down at the clock on my computer and realize it's well past when I would normally be over at his house.

"Shit, sorry. I got a phone call and lost track of time. I'm on my way now." I don't give him a chance to ask questions because I need the added five minutes to get my head on straight before I talk to him about all of this.

The drive over is short, but I come to a huge realization. I want to go and do this, but I also need Ledger's support. I need him to tell me it will all be okay, even if this isn't the closure I thought it would be. Even if it's not the moment of clarity I've been waiting for.

Walking up to his front porch, I don't even get the chance to knock before Ledger yanks the door open.

"What's going on, baby?" Concern is etched on every inch of his face.

I grab his hand and lead him inside.

"I got a phone call that I wasn't expecting," I say as I sit down on his plush couch.

"Okay... Was it a client? Did they mistreat you?"

"No, no, nothing like that. Sit," I tell him before continuing.

He gingerly sits down while not taking his eyes off of me.

"My old boss called me. Well, technically, the owner of the firm called me." His eyes widen as I keep talking. "Apparently, the douchebag that was my boss is under investigation and somewhere along the way my name came up, so they want me to come in and talk."

I hold my breath, unsure of what his thoughts on this will be.

"Okay, what do you need from me?" he asks.

"Umm, I need a day off to drive down there, most likely Friday since we're usually less busy. And I can spend the weekend with Larkin too."

"Done. What else?"

His complete willingness to do whatever I need is something I've never had before. He isn't obligated to do anything, yet here he is, not worried about his bottom line for the company but for his girlfriend who needs support.

Girlfriend.

"Am I your girlfriend?" I ask impulsively. I consider him my boyfriend, but we haven't really had that talk outside of saying we're dating.

"I was just thinking, and we haven't really put a title to this, so I'm just wondering what your thoughts are on that." Great, I'm starting to sound like him when he gets nervous now.

"Do you want me to call you my girlfriend?" he asks instead of answering outright.

"I think I do," I tell him honestly. I've been thinking a lot about what I want lately, and the one thing that is clear is I want Ledger to be a mainstay in my life.

"Then I will call you my girlfriend." The grin on his face is infectious and I join him, feeling like a giddy schoolgirl.

"So, just to recap. You're taking Friday off to deal with the asshole and then staying the weekend with Larkin?"

"Correct. I'm sorry I'm ditching you again, but I think I need to do this. I need to shut the door on that job once and for all. I'll check emails when I can and try to stay on top of things," I offer.

"Stop. You're not going to work at all." He shakes his head in exasperation.

"But I can. It's not a big deal to check in," I say.

"It is a big deal. I'll hold your laptop hostage if I need to. Listen, take the long weekend. Do what you need to do and then spend time with your family. There is nothing so important here that it can't wait. And shockingly, I'm more than capable of checking my own email while you're gone."

"Are you ,though?" I laugh at him as he tackles me to the couch.

"I'm capable of a lot of things," he murmurs against my neck.

Goosebumps trail down my arms as I embrace him.

"Thank you for letting me go down to Austin," I whisper, wanting him to know how I see him and how it's a huge deal that he supports me.

"Never thank me for that, Ains. If you ever need to do anything, all I want to do is support you." He cups my jaw in both hands, looking intensely into my eyes.

"Don't you realize I'll do anything for you?"

"Ledg—"

"Just let me say this, please. I don't want a response. I don't need anything reciprocated, but I don't think I can go another minute without telling you so you understand how much you mean to me. I love you, Ainsley. I will do anything to make you happy, to help create the life you want. If you need a weekend in Austin, I'll make it happen."

My heart stutters in my chest, and I know he means every word.

"I had such a crush on you in high school, but it pales in comparison to how I feel now. Never in a million years did I expect to see you again, let alone fall in love with you, but I wouldn't change it for the world." He leans down and kisses me, then does a push up to get off the couch.

"I'm going to go start dinner," he says softly, leaving me to stew in the mess of emotions he just caused.

He loves me.

He was right. I'm not ready to reciprocate, but I feel the stirring of those feelings deep in my chest.

Now, more than ever, I know I need this Austin trip. Going down the last time was helpful, but now? I need to put the past behind me and be one-hundred-percent ready to move forward with Ledger.

CHAPTER THIRTY-THREE
LEDGER

I wasn't planning on spilling my heart to Ainsley, but it just felt right. I needed her to know that I supported her through everything. Hearing her thank me for "letting" her do something broke my heart a little and made me realize I needed to show her we're equal partners.

In more ways than one.

I have some work to do in the next couple of days to make this idea a reality, though.

Currently, I'm cooking a simple dinner of chicken stir fry and completely lost in my thoughts. I'm not freaked out by my confession; it feels more like relief. Relief that Ainsley now knows exactly how I feel for her, no more hiding it, no more pushing it deep down inside so I don't scare her away.

The one thing I'm nervous about is this Austin trip. Not because I'm worried about Ainsley, but because I'm worry she won't feel like I supported her enough.

"What's got you thinking so hard?" Ainsley says as she takes the spatula from my hands and stirs dinner.

Sighing, I decide to focus on something other than my anxiety over her Austin trip. "I think I want to restructure the company a little. If what Jenna said was true, then word is getting out in areas we know nothing about, and I think we need to take advantage of the word of mouth, no matter what city it's in."

"I agree, but how do we even make that happen? It's not like you can landscape remotely." She chuckles, but all I can hear is the use of "we". How do *we* make it happen?

"I have no idea, and that's the problem." I've never seen something like this done, but it could revolutionize the company and expand the business to a level I never even thought possible.

"Then let's brainstorm," Ainsley says.

"No, baby, let's eat. Work can wait." And I mean that. I don't want our time outside of work to be consumed with more work. I want our time to be just that—time together to lose ourselves in each other and think of nothing else except the way we make each other feel. I may not want to stay hidden, but her thought on keeping work and our personal life separated was a good one.

Ainsley plates up our dinner and sets them down on the table as I grab our drinks. Plopping down in my chair, I look at the woman who has changed every aspect of my life without even knowing.

I live for her now.

I live for her happiness, for growing our business together, for ensuring that she is living life the way she truly wants to.

Shit, what if she doesn't want to stay in Bluebell Falls?

The thought is like a lightning bolt to my heart, but I keep my face neutral. We haven't talked specifically about this, and for all I know, she may still not want to stay here permanently. But there's no need to jump to conclusions before I know any facts. Maybe I'll just come up with contingencies within the company for all the options.

"Ledger." Ainsley says my name like this isn't the first time she's said it.

"Yeah? Sorry, lost in my head."

"You okay?"

"I'm great, I promise. I just want to eat so I can take you to bed." I smirk.

Her eyes light up, and I have to laugh at her enthusiasm.

And take her to bed I do.

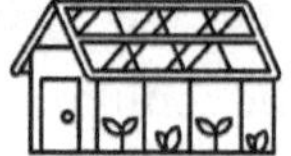

I'm antsy as I walk into the office an hour away from Bluebell Falls. I'm hoping what I want to do is doable, but I won't know until I talk to this lawyer. Ainsley heads to Austin tomorrow, and I want to get a jump on things.

"Ledger Hutton?" a man calls from the doorway.

"That's me. How are you doing today?" I ask, trying to get my jitters out.

"Pretty good. Come in and have a seat."

He walks around behind his desk and takes a seat as I take one of the visitor's chairs in front of him.

"So, what are we looking to do today?" he asks, turning his attention to a notepad.

"Two things, really. I want to adjust the structure of my landscaping company and potentially add someone as a co-owner. I'd also like to have a contingency like naming a CFO instead of a co-owner. And I need to see what I need to do legally in order to run my business in multiple states. If I'm running things remotely, using local contractors, how much needs to be done so all my bases are covered?"

"Interesting. Well, let's start with the easier of the two. Restructuring isn't all that complicated. I'll have to look at what you already have in place, but it would be a matter of an addendum and very easy to file. I can have a couple of options drawn up, and all you'll need to tell me is which one to run with."

"Okay, good. I can get you all the paperwork for that within the week."

"Good. As far as the other, I'll need to do some digging because I'm not sure if we would need to get you licensed in each state or if there is a loophole to all of this. So, give me some time, and I'll look into that one for you."

"Thank you."

"I have all your contact details, so when I get more information, you'll be the first to know." His tone is practiced, and I know that's all I'll get today. It's not a lot for the two-hour round-trip drive, but this is just the start. This is what I need to do to make sure Ainsley feels valued in her job, and turn it into something she really feels fulfilled with.

That's hoping she even likes this plan. You're really jumping all-in without consulting her.

The devil on my shoulder has a point, and I did mentally tell myself I would start thinking of ideas if that was the case.

My gut reaction is to give the whole damn thing up. If an opportunity came along and was perfect for Ainsley and it involved moving, I would give up my entire business and follow her.

I know it's drastic, and realistically, if I turn the business more remote, it won't come to that, but I'd do it in a heartbeat.

She needs to be fulfilled in her career, and I need her. It's as simple as that.

Since I drove all the way out here, I pull up to a restaurant to have lunch. My phone dings, and my heart skips a beat thinking it's Ainsley.

Rina:

> Bad news, big bro. Your secret is out.

Fuck. Ainsley wanted it to be on our terms.

Me:

> Who? When? Fuck, where did you hear it from?

Rina:

> I'm sitting in Sal's, and Alice was talking about you and Ainsley in the booth behind me. Said they saw you two on Ainsley's front porch together and then go into the house. Mabel chimed in, saying they say you two driving out of town not too long ago, and now the whole damn place is talking.

God fucking damnit! Things were going so well, and there is too much unknown right now for this shit to be popping up.

Me:

> How many people are there exactly?

I know it doesn't really matter. Whoever isn't at Sal's right now will know within minutes of everyone leaving.

Rina:

> Everyone except old man Walter.

Me:

Yeah… Sorry, Ledg.

Switching over to my text thread with Ainsley, I write out the words I know are going to do damage that I can't undo.

My phone rings immediately, and I answer it without preamble.

"How did anyone find out?" Her voice is boarding on hysterical.

"I don't know. Rina just texted me saying Alice and Mabel were talking about us, and it blew up from there. It appears we weren't always as sneaky as we thought we were."

"Oh God. My parents?"

I cringe. "Were in Sal's and heard everything."

"Shit, my dad's going to be so upset with me. How did this happen, Ledger? We were being careful!" she borderline yells.

"I don't know, baby."

"Don't call me 'baby' right now," she snaps.

"I'm sorry. I didn't want this to be out of our control." Nothing I say right now will help, I know that, but this is all coming at the worst possible time. Ainsley is already stressed about talking to her old bosses, and this isn't something she should have to worry about.

But deep down in my chest, I'm hurt. Hurt that she still feels the need to hide us, hurt that I don't seem to be worth the challenges.

I know I'm turning it into more than what it truly is. And I know her reasoning is good and letting our relationship develop outside of the nosey eyes of the entire town was smart. But when does that end?

"I'm sorry, I didn't mean that. This is just throwing me for a loop I wasn't prepared for," she murmurs.

"I know. It's okay." I don't say anymore, letting her have time to process all of this.

"Can I just... I don't know, head to Austin early? I don't want to deal with this right now. I just want to go talk to these people, see Larkin, Theo, Gavin, and Maddie, and when I come back, I can deal with all the small-town drama."

My heart drops. This feels like I'm not worth the trouble, the effort, of dealing with family and friends who are most likely just there to support us.

Instead, I let her go because it's the only thing I can do.

"Of course. Take all the time you need. Keep me updated on how the meeting goes." I can hear the despondency in my voice, and logically, I know I'm taking this harder than I should be. But after I've decided to restructure my company with her and turn it into something we both can be proud of, this is how she reacts to people who love us finding out about us being together.

But she doesn't know about the changes in the company.

That may be, but it doesn't change the gaping wound currently in my chest.

"Ledger..."

"It's fine, Ainsley. I completely understand. We can talk more when you get back home. Or when you get some time this weekend."

I don't wait for her response because I can't. I can't hear more excuses as to why letting the world know I'm in love with her is a bad idea.

The server delivers my food, but I have no appetite. "Can I actually get a to-go box and the check?"

"Absolutely."

It takes all of five minutes for me to head back out to my truck and hit the road. I don't know where I want to go from here, but I do know that I just want to go home and be alone.

CHAPTER THIRTY-FOUR
AINSLEY

I'm the worst person—the worst girlfriend—ever. I know that, but I can't stop the fear.

The second I read Ledger's text, it felt like this protective bubble around us popped. This safe space, where I could just be who I wanted to be just ... disintegrated.

And I panicked. My first instinct was to run, so that's exactly what I did.

Now, on the road to Austin, I feel like shit. I'm almost at my sister's house, and I'm miserable.

I ran away from someone who just confessed their love to me. Who has proven time and time again that he's willing to go at my pace, go along with my asinine rules, and never push me for more than I can handle.

And at the first sign of my precious control breaking, I treated him like shit.

It wasn't his fault our sleepy little town housed enough amateur sleuths to notice more than the average person. It was only a matter of time before someone saw something. Hell, I'm shocked it took this long, honestly.

And this whole freakout is fueled by fear.

I pull up to Larkin's house and sit in my car for a minute. I need to call Ledger back at some point, but hanging out with my sister will probably calm me down more than anything. My phone pings with a text from my dad, and I ignore it.

My passenger door opens, scaring me enough to let out a scream.

"It's just me, Aunt Ains," Gavin laughs, and I slap his arm.

"What the hell?! You're supposed to like me, not scare me!"

"I do like you. That's why when I saw you pull in and not come in, I came out here while Mom and Dad were distracted, so you could talk it out."

"And what wise wisdom are you throwing my way today, Gav?" I ask, amused.

"I just came to see if you wanted to talk. You look like you have a lot on your mind." He shrugs.

"There's just a lot changing, and it's a little hard to keep up with." I'm not going to unload my messed-up life on a thirteen-year-old, but maybe telling him some generic stuff will help me get in the front door.

"Is this about Ledger? Are you not with him anymore?"

"It's about a lot of stuff, but we're still together." *If I don't push him away altogether and he gets fed up with my shit.*

"Okay, so what other stuff?" he asks.

"Work stuff, mostly. I'm not really sure what job I want to do."

"Well, you've been a lot happier since you moved, even if it sucks not to see you all the time. And Ledger is your boss, right?" I tilt my head in question. "He told me when we were playing the video game together."

"Right. Yes, he's my boss."

"Well, then why not ask him? You're happy there, and if you want a different job, couldn't you just ask him for something different in the company? I'm not sure how all of that works," he adds shyly. "But I do know he's awesome and would probably do anything you ask."

He says it so matter-of-factly that a smile spreads across my face. He may not be Larkin's biological son, but you can't tell me they're not the exact same person. The fact that Gavin just gave me the same advice as my sister did speaks volumes.

Gavin's right—Ledger is awesome, and I need to figure out how to get over this crushing fear because I don't want to lose him.

"That's a great idea, Gav. Thanks."

"No problem. You ready to come in now? I see Mom peeking through the curtains." He says it like an annoyed teenager, and when I look up to the front of the house, sure enough, Larkin is sitting there with the curtains pulled to the side. She waves as I shake my head.

Time to stop hiding.

I climb out of the car and make my way around to the trunk, only to see Gavin has beaten me to it and has all the luggage in his hands.

Following him to the front door, where Larkin is waiting, she yanks the door open and wraps me in a warm, comforting hug. I embrace her, breathing her in and feeling a sense of calm I haven't since my phone call with Craig Sutter.

"Come in. I have a feeling we have a lot to talk about."

Following Larkin in, I see Theo cooking dinner in their kitchen. I throw him a wave as I walk into the living room and collapse on the couch. I watch Gavin climb the stairs with my luggage, taking it to the guest room.

"Okay, spill." Larkin sits next to me, handing me a glass of wine.

I chug half of it before word-vomiting everything that's happened in the last couple of days.

"Well, shit," Larkin says, then takes a sip of her wine.

"Yep. Too much is happening, and I feel like I'm drowning."

"Okay, let's start with something easy. Your old job and this 'investigation' they're doing. How do you feel about it?"

"I feel conflicted," I say honestly. "I mean, I'm glad karma is getting Lance, but why now? Why ruin my entire career before it's taken seriously?"

"I get that, and it is really shitty that they just now realize what a dick head he is."

"But then I think if all that wouldn't have had happened, I wouldn't have gone back to Bluebell Falls..." I trail off.

"And if you hadn't moved back, you wouldn't have met Ledger," she fills in.

"Exactly, and Ledger is ... everything," I sigh out. "But I fucked that up too."

"Okay, number one, you did not fuck up anything. Get over this pity party, thinking you fucked up all the things. Number two, how do you know you fucked things up with Ledger? Did you handle things well? I don't think so, but you're stressed and your knee-jerk reaction to finding out the gossip club figured you out was to lash out. Not the best approach, but from the little I know about that man, I don't think you fucked anything up."

"But I was so mean to him," I whisper.

"Yes, you were. And you'll probably need to grovel because he didn't deserve that. He wasn't responsible for any of it."

"I know."

"And why are you wanting to hide things, anyway? It's not like you can get in trouble for dating the boss. The rules are different for you than it was for Theo and me."

"I ..." *Why did I want to hide things so badly?*

It's only now that I'm truly thinking about it that I realize every decision I've made about my relationship with Ledger was made of fear.

And it makes me angry at myself.

Angry that "getting my life together" now feels like it was only on the surface level. Angry that the first thing I did when things didn't go the way I wanted them to was run.

This isn't who I want to be. This isn't who I *thought* I was. The burst of clarity is like a sunrise over the ocean. And I see my whole path clearly for the first time in far too long.

"Okay, I need to figure this out. I don't know why I wanted to hide things with Ledger, but I think I just realized everything I've done in the last six months is because of fear, and I don't want to live like that anymore."

Hello, third-life crisis, my name's Ainsley.

"Okay, that's good. Not the fear part but the realization part," Larkin says, taking another sip of wine.

"Since I moved home, my goal has been to figure out where I go from here, right?" She nods. "Okay, so the only thing I've figured out is that I don't want to be back in corporate America, and I don't want to go back to a financial firm. I want to pave my own way." The more I talk, the stronger I feel.

"That's good. So, let's start with the job. Any thoughts on what you *want* to do?" Larkin asks.

I take a moment to really think about my answer, even though a thought comes to my mind immediately. I don't want to just spew unfiltered thoughts. I want to give myself time to think about things, really make some decisions about my future so I don't lose the best part of it.

"My gut is that I want to stay with Ledger, with the company, and help him grow it. I'm not entirely sure what that role would be, but I've enjoyed being his assistant more than I ever enjoyed being a financial advisor."

"Perfect, let's talk that out then. I know a lot of it will be up to Ledger, but it doesn't hurt to have an end goal to work toward."

Nodding, I take her words to heart.

"I don't want to take advantage of my relationship with Ledger, though. I don't want to get a position within the company just because we're dating ... or I hope we still are."

"Agreed, but let's dream big and then do contingencies."

God, I love her. This is exactly why she's such a good social worker—because she genuinely cares.

"Well, I want to stay with the company, but I also want to help grow the company. The presentation Ledger did in Vegas made me see that there is a huge opportunity to grow, but at the moment, it's not set up that way."

"What do you mean?"

"Looking at it from a financial advisor perspective, he needs to set up the company so we could work around the country, or at least manage teams around the country. But right now, he's set up like a basic small business, and the nursery is basically added on and not making a ton of money. If I could set up the company to run more like a project management firm, only landscaping, we could start working on projects all over," I tell her, thinking out loud.

Nodding wordlessly, I'm getting excited about the prospect. I know Ledger and I have talked about this, but it was just this vague idea. I just figured out how to actually make it work.

"So, I could ... what?" I look up at Larkin, who has a huge smile on her face. "Run the setup? Take over the financials and logistics so he can continue doing what he's so damn good at?" It's all rhetorical, but it's exactly what I want to do.

And for the first time in way too long, I'm excited about the future. It feels tangible instead of this obscure idea that may never happen.

Then my smile drops as I think about Ledger and how I left things.

"What are you thinking about?" Larkin asks.

"That I need more wine because I think that was the easy part."

She laughs as she yells out to Theo to bring more wine. He happily comes to deliver and kisses her before whispering in her ear and leaving again. My sister's bright pink cheeks tell me Theo did not keep that PG, but I love seeing their dynamic.

"Okay, let's talk about Ledger," she says as she pours more wine.

"I messed up," I say simply. I know I did. I made a man who was nothing but sweet and caring hide our entire relationship. Made him think we weren't worth it, and my heart aches at the thought.

"I was scared after Vegas that the outside influence would take away from what we have. That if the whole town knew about us, we wouldn't be able to figure out if we were truly sustainable. I know that doesn't make a ton of sense, though."

"It makes sense. You may have taken it to a bit of an extreme, but I understand your thought process. New relationships are scary. Hell, look and Theo and me. We were a hot mess when we started, and there was so much going on that I was sure we would have to set us aside, and I was almost positive that would end with us no longer seeing each other. But you know the biggest lesson I learned?"

"What?"

"A relationship consists of two people, not one. You can feel however you feel, but you have to remember there is another person in this dynamic and you can't make decisions that affect both of you by yourself."

Rolling her words over in my head, I take a long draw of wine. I've never thought of things like that. Always been determined to figure things out on my own and that extended over to my relationship with Ledger. It felt like second nature, but hearing Larkin's thoughts is like the sky opening up and down-pouring when you aren't expecting it. A splash of cold water on your face, giving you all the clarity you needed.

"So, how do I fix this?" I ask in a whisper.

"Well... First, ask yourself if you're all-in with Ledger."

"Absolutely," I say with authority.

"Perfect." She smiles, but it drops with her next words. "Next, you prepare yourself for him not to be on the same page. You hurt him, and that may not be forgivable to him."

Her words are a dagger to the stomach, but I know she's right. I've been thinking about myself this whole time and not really considering Ledger until it was too late. I was focused on making sure *my* life was put together before turning my attention to us, and that was definitely the wrong move. I see that now. And although this gives me a ton of clarity, I also feel like the worst human being on the planet.

I hurt Ledger due to my inability to look past *myself*. It's selfish, and I need to figure out a way to get him to forgive me because I don't think I want to live my life without him in it.

No, I know I don't.

"He told me he loved me," I murmur into my wineglass.

Larkin's eyes widen with shock. "And how did you react?"

"I didn't. And then shortly after, I got the call for the meeting and decided coming here would be the best way to clear my head."

She bursts out laughing.

"Yeah, I see the error in my ways, thanks," I droll.

Her laughter dies down, and she gets serious. "Do you love him?"

I don't immediately answer her because I haven't had time to really think about it.

The first thought that pops into my head is absolutely yes, I love Ledger. But I also don't want Larkin to be the first one to hear that. If this conversation has taught me anything, it's that Ledger and I should be a team, and that starts with me talking to him about things like this first.

She smirks and tilts her head before taking her last sip.

"Good to know," she says after she puts her wineglass down.

I don't dignify her all seeing-ness with a response. Instead, I get up, give her a hug, and head to the guest room where I'm staying. My phone pings again with a text from my dad, and I continue to ignore him.

I have a lot of things I want to talk to Ledger about, but a good night's sleep before this meeting is necessary. I'll call him after my meeting and hope that he's willing to hear me out for all my foolishness. Then, I can deal with my dad and the gossip mill.

CHAPTER THIRTY-FIVE
LEDGER

My pity party lasted all of an hour. Sitting on my couch in the silence of my house made me realize I don't want to be alone. I just want Ainsley.

So, I did something I'm not proud of. I semi-broke into her house so I could get information.

I didn't really break in; I used the spare key she keeps hidden under a rock by the back door, but desperate times.

This was always going to be a long shot, but when I turn on her game system and see Gavin's screen name on, I don't hesitate to pull on the headphones and contact him.

"Who is this?" he asks hesitantly, and internally, I praise his caution because Ainsley is currently at his house.

"It's Ledger."

"Prove it." I smile at the caution in his voice.

"The last time we played together, you won four out of five rounds, and the only reason I won the last round was because your mom was talking to you and I took advantage of your distraction. A dirty move on my part but worth it." I chuckle.

"Why are you using Aunt Anis's login?"

"Because I technically snuck into her house, hoping I would catch you online." I'm not lying to him. He may be just thirteen, but he knows when I'm bullshitting him.

"Snuck in… I don't really like that, but I have a feeling you have a good reason for doing it."

"You would be right."

"So, what's the reason?" he says simply and starts playing a round of the game he absolutely kicked my ass in.

"I needed to see if I could get your address so that I can come and see Ainsley. We… we had a fight, and I don't want to leave things as they are." More information than he needs to know? Possibly, but I also need to tell him the truth or he won't let me within a mile of Ainsley. I love his protectiveness of her.

He shoots me in the game before I even have a chance to get my bearings, and I realize I might be shit-out of luck here.

"*Mom!*" Gavin yells suddenly in my ear, causing me to yank the headphones away. When I hear Larkin, I put them back on.

"Why are you yelling? Geez, what's up?"

"You have to stay quiet, okay?" he says like we're in some huge conspiracy, and I almost laugh.

"Umm, okay."

"I need you to check your phone in a couple of minutes."

"What kind of cryptic stuff is going on here?" I hear Larkin say, and I have to hide my laugh.

"I just need you to help me really quickly," Gavin says, avoiding every question she sends his way.

"You still there?" His voice becomes a little stronger, so I assume he's talking to me.

"Yep, still here, bud."

"Good. Text a picture of your license with your thumb at the top left corner."

"Who in the hell are you asking for their license? Do I need to take the whole damn console away?" Larkin says.

"No, but I need to give him your number to send it to. You'll see why when you see the picture," Gavin says like this is the most logical way to go about things. I have to give him credit, though. He's being extra cautious and not giving information out to just anyone. Pride for him beams through my chest as I pull my wallet out and take the exact picture he asked for.

"Okay, send it to this number." I do as he says, and within a minute, I hear Larkin taking the headphones from him.

"Sorry about my lovely son. He tends to go a little overboard when it comes to Ainsley. How can I help?"

"Umm." Her words catch me off guard, but I have to assume that Ainsley talked to her a little about what's going on.

"I, umm, I need your address if that's okay. I'd like to drive down tomorrow and see Ainsley."

She hums under her breath as I hold mine.

"This is interesting. Her meeting is at nine tomorrow morning. Either Theo or I can be here to let you in when you get here. Just text us when you're close."

I blow out my breath and hear her getting more distant, telling Gavin bed is in ten minutes. My phone dings with a text, and I see Larkin sent me her address with an "I'm rooting for you" GIF.

Relief surges through me. This was an asinine plan, but desperation will make a man do crazy things.

"See you tomorrow?" Gavin asks.

"If your aunt doesn't kick me out, definitely."

"Sweet. Night, Ledger."

"Night, Gavin." I exit out of the game and just sit there, in Ainsley's house, in silence.

I'm not sure what I'm going to say to Ainsley when I see her, but I know that regardless of how we left things, I need her to know that I'll be there for her. That we can work it out, talk things out, and really figure out how to make a real go of this, once and for all.

The drive is fairly boring, and I'm grateful to have Theo let me into the house right when I get there. We exchange basic pleasantries before he gives me a hard stare.

"Ainsley has had a lot going on in her life. She needs someone who is willing to work through the bumps while she irons everything out. If you are looking for the perfect relationship, turn around and go home."

"With all due respect, I'd deal with a hell of a lot more than bumps in the road for Ainsley," I tell him bluntly. We don't know each other, but if he feels the need to pull a big-brother act, I'll be sure to give him the overprotective-boyfriend act right back.

"Welcome to the family, Ledger," he smirks and walks away.

I feel like I have a serious case of whiplash, but I'll take the win.

Now, I'm sitting at the kitchen island, picking at my cuticles, and waiting for Ainsley to come back.

The garage door opens suddenly, and I jump in my chair.

Ainsley rounds the corner, a dazed look on her face, and I immediately wonder what happened at the meeting. When she looks up, she jolts and throws her hand on her chest.

"Holy shit, Ledger! You scared the shit out of me!"

I scramble out of the chair and walk over to her, hesitating to pull her to me.

"I'm sorry."

"No, no, it's fine. I just wasn't expecting anyone to be home. How did you even get here?" she asks, stunned, before shaking her head slightly and wrapping her arms around my neck.

"I just wanted to make sure you were okay after the meeting. I know it was stressing you out."

She pulls back, her eyes shifting between mine, before she startles me with a kiss. I sink into it, glad this is her reaction to seeing me and not turning me away.

She pulls away while I'm still dazzled by her kiss. "I can't believe you're here. How?"

"You want to come and sit?" I offer before sharing the story.

"Yes. Let me change, and then we can crash on the couch." She pulls my hand and drags me to what I assume is the guest room, and I sit on the bed as she strips out of the pantsuit she wore in Vegas.

Memories flood through me, and my cock hardens before I have any control. An article of clothing flies at my face and I reach up my hand to pull it down, and the smirk on Ainsley's face has me feeling playful.

My heart thunders in my chest because she looks happy. So fucking happy, and I just hope she brings me along for the ride. *God, I need her to bring me along.*

"It seems like the meeting went okay," I observe, needing to hear everything that happened.

"Nope, you first. Then, we'll talk about my day." She pulls on a pair of lounge shorts and a tank top, then bounces on the bed next to me.

I shift and scoot back so we're both sitting against the headboard.

"I broke into your house." I cringe at my lack of a filter or capability to tell a story correctly.

She bursts out laughing.

"Technically, I used your spare key and let myself in. Then I jumped onto your gaming system, hoping Gavin was online."

"That's very crafty of you."

"I was a desperate man," I concede. "I got lucky, because he was online, and managed to get the information out of him and Larkin." I'm not sure I want to get into the whole embarrassing saga of a thirteen-year-old treating me like a predatory online threat, even if I was proud of him for doing it.

"Oh, I'll be getting that full story out of you later. But first, tell me why you came."

The way we left things, I don't blame her for asking. I was nervous as hell the entire drive here that I was making a mistake and that she would push me away further, but I didn't care because deep in the recesses of my brain, I need to be here for her. I need to show her through better or worse, I will always be here for her.

"It's simple." I shrug. "I love you, and I need to support you. I knew this meeting wasn't going to be easy, no matter the outcome, and I didn't want you to feel forgotten and unimportant."

She stares at me with her eyes clouded with tears.

"I've had a lot of revelations in the last day, and I have a lot to tell you."

"Lucky for you, I have a lot of time." I wink.

"Lucky for you that you're the boss and make your own schedule," she counters.

I don't tell her I haven't taken a real day off for as long as I've created the company. I don't tell her that I've never once put anything other than my family ahead of my business.

"So, I was a bitch the last time we talked, and I need to apologize for that. My sister, and all her therapist insight, pointed out how much I haven't been considering your feelings in my decision-making. I've been very focused on where I go from here and not really realizing that I like this pit stop I've made. I like—no, I love—my job. I love what I do, and I have so many thoughts on how to grow the company. And it all came to a head when I thought about this not being my plan. This isn't what I intended when I moved home.

"It scared me that making the choice to stay in Bluebell Falls would be short-lived. I was scared that in a few months, a few years, I would feel trapped and break both our hearts, and I couldn't do that to you. Everything I've done lately is purely based on fear. Keeping us a secret was a protection of sorts. I didn't want everyone's opinions to infiltrate what we had created with each other. I didn't want them convincing you I wasn't worth it. I handled things fucking terribly." She lets out a self-deprecating laugh as she brushes a single tear from her eye.

"And now?" I ask softly, not wanting to break this confession.

She sits up and straddles my hips, looking deep into my eyes.

"Now, I want to make it up to you."

"Ains—"

"Let me finish. I want to show you that I don't care about the gossip mill. The only thing that matters is how we feel about each other."

"And how do we feel about each other?" I ask tentatively.

"Well, you told me you loved me, and I am hoping that still rings true because I love you too." She sucks in a breath, waiting for my response.

I sit completely still, shocked as hell at her words. Apparently, an extra night at her sister's gave her all the clarity she needed, and I'm running full-force ahead with it.

"I love you so fucking much," I breathe before gripping her hips and yanking her closer to me. Our lips clash in a mash of tongues and teeth.

Everything else can wait. All the details and plans can take a back seat. Right now, I need to feel my woman. I need to feel her love as I bleed mine into her.

CHAPTER THIRTY-SIX
AINSLEY

Relief like I've never felt before courses through me. Ledger got creative and found a way to be here for me, no matter what, and I couldn't be more thankful. His steadfast love for me is proving to be exactly what I need right now.

Although, grinding on him might be showing him a little of that gratitude.

"One day without you was too much. Let's not do that again," he says against my neck. "I'm sorry," I whisper, tears coming to my eyes because of how I've treated him. I need to show him I'm in this and probably need to grovel like Larkin said.

"Don't apologize, just be with me here. Now." He rocks my hips against his already hard cock, and a whimper breaks free from me.

Ledger has this power over me. He sneaks in behind my defenses and loves me even when I'm adamant I don't need it. Even when I haven't shown him the same.

That changes today.

"Thank you for being here," I say as drag my hands down his chest and abs. Reaching for the hem of his shirt, I start lifting it up and over his head. He reluctantly takes his hands off my hips and lets me strip him of his shirt.

I lean back and admire his muscles from the physical labor he does daily, the muscles that are hard-earned. The patch of hair on his chest trails down his stomach into his happy trail. It hits me hard that this man is all mine, and my favorite thing about him isn't his body or his job. It's his heart and just how hard he loves those he cares about.

"Hey," he murmurs, drawing me out of my thoughts. "You okay?"

"So good." I smile and then yank my tank top up and over my head before throwing it across the room.

Before he can say anything else, I slide off his legs and down to the floor, kneeling in front of him. I unbutton his shorts as he lifts his hips to let me pull those and his boxer briefs off too.

"Seems a little unfair that I'm naked and you still have bottoms on," he says.

"I think you'll find this very fair," I tell him before wrapping my hand around his cock and pumping him leisurely before leaning forward and licking the pearl of pre-cum off his tip.

"Jesus," he mutters.

I feel a surge of power in my veins, knowing I can reduce Ledger to a puddle of pleasure. I circle my tongue around his tip a few times before wrapping my lips around him and sliding down as far as I can. His hips arch up, pushing further into my mouth, and I groan at the feeling of him filling me.

Just when I set a good rhythm, I feel his hands under my arms as he pulls me up.

"Hey!"

"Get your ass up here, baby. It's my turn." He doesn't waste any more time, just tosses me on the bed and rips my shorts and panties off of me before burying his face in my pussy.

"Holy shit!" I yell. His tongue is alternating between my clit and thrusting inside of me, and I feel like I've died and gone to heaven. When he turns his attention to just my clit, I whine because I need more.

He either takes the hint or knows exactly what I need, and I'm guessing it's the latter because no sooner than I think it, he's thrusting two fingers into me. Arching off the bed, I feel on the verge of coming and I'm speaking nonsense at how good it feels. When he said he wanted to learn how to please me, he took it to heart, and I've never been so happy to have a studious boyfriend.

He pulls away suddenly, and I almost scream at my frustration. I was so fucking close.

When I look up at him, he has a cocky-as-hell smirk on his face that I just want to slap in frustration.

"We're going to have some fun," he mutters darkly.

"Who is having fun?! I was so close, Ledg," I whine.

"Oh, I know. But here's the thing." He crawls up the bed, caging me in with arms. "You ran and didn't talk to me about how you were feeling."

I go to open my mouth to respond, but he cuts me off.

"I know you needed and got some clarity, and for that I'm glad, but from here on out, I need to know that you'll come to me. Talk to me if something is bothering you. No more running." His stare is serious, and there is hurt lurking in the dark recesses. And who can blame him? Everything he's said is true.

"No more running," I whisper as my hips subconsciously lift up to get closer to him.

"You're not getting off that easily, baby. I need to make sure you remember. I need you to think of this moment every time you think of running and know what'll happen if you make decisions about us without me."

Where in the hell did this Ledger come from?

I nod frantically as I watch him sit up on his knees and grab his cock in one hand, the other dragging along sternum and down my soft belly, stopping just short of where I need him.

"Ledger, please…"

"Hearing you beg for me does wonders for my confidence. Keep going."

There's a glint in his eyes, and I'm wholly unprepared for any of this.

"Please fuck me. Please. I promise I'll always talk to you. I'll remember we're in this together."

He leans forward and circles his cock covered in pre-cum around my clit, making me jolt. I'm so sensitive already, it's not going to take long and I'll do anything he asks if it means I can get my orgasm.

"You forget I've spent a lot of time learning everything that gets you going, every little thing that turns you on. If I want you to come, I can certainly make it happen." He continues his leisure circles around my clit, but he knows it's not enough to get me off.

He dips it down, barely pressing the tip in before sliding it back up to my clit, and I growl in frustration.

"You're so fucking sexy like this."

"Like what? Frustrated beyond belief?!" I practically yell.

"No, baby, needy and so close to exploding. Knowing I'm the one who controls your pleasure right now is doing things to me. You, lying here at my mercy, is my new favorite place to be."

I'd be pissed if his words weren't an immense turn-on. I'll let him edge me all day if he keeps talking like this. Hell, his words alone might have the power to bring me to orgasm. *Maybe we should test that theory.*

"Please, Ledger," I whisper so quietly I don't even know if he can hear me.

I'm so needy, I can't stop squirming, just trying to find some relief.

He leans down on his forearm, the other hand still teasing me with his dick, as he looks down at me. He notches his cock and moves his fingers to my clit, swirling around hard and fast, getting me close within seconds.

"Oh God," I whimper.

"That's it, baby. Now, you can come." His words are like a trigger, and my pussy starts pulsing as I start to come.

But he shocks me yet again by thrusting fully to the hilt as I'm coming, and I scream out at the feeling. It's like my orgasm intensifies tenfold, and it brings tears to my eyes.

When I finally come down, I look up at Ledger.

His head is tilted toward the ceiling, and his jaw is clenched so tight I worry he'll break a tooth. The strain on his face makes me feel like the tables have turned, and I jump on the opportunity to tease him the way he just did to me.

I tilt my hips, sinking him into me a little more before pulling myself off of him completely.

"Ainsley..." The growl in Ledger's voice hits me hard.

"Lay down, Ledg." There's no room for argument in my voice. I just kneel off to the side and wait for him to follow my directions.

He blinks at me, maybe gauging if I'm serious, but I've never been more serious in my life.

He lies flat on his back, and I swing my leg over his hips, sinking down onto his cock at the same time.

"Holy shit!" His upper body flies up before I shove him back down.

Swiveling my hips, I'm still so sensitive, but I need to make him just as crazy as he's made me.

Planting my feet on either side of his hips, I lift until just his tip is inside of me, then slam back down hard. Ledger throws his head back and grips my ass in a punishing grip as he groans. I continue my movement until the veins in Ledger's neck are bulging.

Suddenly, Ledger bolts upright and tries to pull me off of him.

"What?" I ask, thinking I hurt him.

"I don't have a condom on. Holy shit, how did I forget a condom?" He's beginning to panic—it's written all over his face.

"Hey." I pull his head to mine. "I'm protected, have an IUD, and have tested clean within the last year."

His unfocused eyes lock onto mine as what I said registers.

"So, no condom?" he whispers.

"No condom," I echo.

Before I can take my next breath, he flips me around so I land on my back. He takes my right leg and puts it in between his while he takes my left and puts it on his shoulder. I've never been put in a position like this before, but it opens up my clit and my chest for stimulation. His hands wrap around the thigh of the leg that's on his shoulder, and he thrusts hard.

"Oh my God, that's deep," I breathe out.

I'm straddling one of his thighs, and it's putting constant pressure on my clit as he keeps driving inside of me.

I can barely breathe. It feels that good.

"Fuck, baby, I need you to get there. I'm too close," he grits out.

Matching his thrusts puts more friction on my clit, and it sends me within seconds. I'm incoherent, chanting Ledger's name while whimpering in pleasure.

I have never felt anything as intense as this. Our connection has never felt so strong, so deep.

And when I open my eyes in time to see Ledger straining with his orgasm? It sets me off again. He shouts and moans out his release, and it's the sexiest thing I've ever heard in my life.

We both collapse on the bed when we finally come down from our high.

When I catch my breath, Ledger gets up and heads to the bathroom, coming back with a damp washcloth to clean me up. He takes his time, making sure nothing is missed and using such a tender touch. My eyes burn with unshed tears.

When he comes to lie back down, I turn toward him.

"I love you. Thank you for finding a way here." I tell him simply. He probably knows how big of a deal it is to me, but that doesn't mean I shouldn't recognize it.

"I love you too." He presses a kiss to my forehead and draws me into his chest.

"So, tell me about the meeting," he says as his fingertips brush up and down my shoulder.

"Well, I'll start by saying it was nothing like I thought it would be."

"Oh, yeah?"

"I get there, expecting an interrogation of sorts, and both Sutter and Philipsen are sitting in the conference room waiting for me. My anxiety is off the charts by this time, but I sit and listen to what they have to say. They told me a group of women came forward about Lance and how he was taking advantage of his position. And started sexually harassing a couple of them and blackmailing them into dates—all the things he was doing to me, except they didn't get fired." I laugh, but it still really bothers me.

"The women came forward threatening a lawsuit, but the owners nipped it in the bud."

"What do you mean?" Ledger asks.

"The owners offered a settlement, a rather hefty one at that, as well as a recommendation for another job if they wanted to leave."

"So, why did they call you in?"

"Well, they heard I had evidence of Lance's bullshit, which I do, so they wanted to cover their asses. Since I wasn't under an employment contract with them, I could make their lives a living hell, I guess."

"That's shitty," he grumbles.

"Very. But the best part is they made me an offer. Sign off on a settlement and get paid."

"What the fuck?" Ledger being upset on my account is adorable, but he doesn't see it the way I do yet.

"I accepted, signed off on their bullshit that I wouldn't use any of the information I had to sue them at any point in the future. They accepted that Lance was a shithead and fired him without a recommendation, so he's blacklisted. And they give me two hundred and fifty grand."

I hold my breath, waiting for Ledger's reaction.

"Well, that's unexpected." He says it so calmly, it's almost disappointing, but he also doesn't know what I want to do with that money, so I may get the reaction I'm after either way.

"It was. I didn't even hesitate to take the money. Six months ago, I think I would have fought tooth and nail to do what I perceived as right, but now? What's right is what will make my life in the future the best. And that, my dearest love, is taking that money and putting it into Bluebell Landscaping and expanding the company."

CHAPTER THIRTY-SEVEN
LEDGER

Did I just hear her right?

It can't be that easy, can it?

"What?" Her question makes me realize I haven't said anything yet.

"I'm just shocked. Why would you want to put that money into Bluebell?" What I'm really asking is if this means she wants to stay with the company and in Bluebell Falls.

She shifts so that she's lying on her pillow, facing me, and I sink down to get on her level.

"When I took the job as your assistant, I took it as an in-between. I took it as a stepping stone to the next big thing I was going to do. The universe works in mysterious ways, though, because I'm happier being a lowly old assistant than I ever was at the financial firm."

"But you have so much more to offer than just being an assistant," I counter, not trying to push her away but trying to make her see she's capable of so much more. I want her to be so much more in the company.

"Well, that's where we agree. I want to put this money into the company, but I have some thoughts on how to grow the company and turn it into a nationwide thing."

Pride.

I feel an abundance of pride for this woman.

"While we both were apart, we seem to have had the same ideas."

She tilts her head in question, and I can't help myself. I brush a soft kiss against her lips before continuing.

"I met with a lawyer the other day. And I know I should have talked to you first, but I wanted to surprise you. I want to reformat the company to give you a larger role, more control over the entire thing, honestly."

"Oh my God, I have so many thoughts about this!" She sounds excited, but it's hard to tell until she sits up and claps her hands together.

I take it as my cue that we're no longer in a cuddling mood and join her, sitting up against the headboard.

She draws the sheet over her lap but leaves her breasts bare, and I almost cave and decide talking can wait for later. I don't, though, because she's too excited about her ideas and I want to hear them.

"So, I think we need to turn the business into a sort of project management setup."

"What does that mean?"

"Basically, that you have a core group that organizes more than they get their hands dirty. So, it would be us two and whoever else we could throw into the mix in Bluebell Falls that would keep track of different projects all over the country, making sure deadlines are met, contractors are doing what they need to, that kind of thing."

"And you think we can pull that off?" If she says we can, I believe her. She would absolutely be running the show, though, because I only know how to run things by getting my hands dirty and being involved in every single project. This is the shift I want, I just didn't really know how to go about it.

But Ainsley sees it all, and somehow even during the unknown, we were on the same page all along.

"Absolutely. It's going to take a little restructuring, but we can use a couple of projects as tests and iron out all the details."

I'm in awe of this woman in more ways than one. She's so fucking smart, it's amazing I haven't thought to bring her on in a bigger way before.

"Love it. You take the lead and tell me what you need from me. This is your baby now."

"What?" She startles.

"This entire project is yours. Tell me where you need me, what you need me to do, and I'll do it. You're the one in charge, baby."

She clammers over my lap and straddles me again with a giant smile spread across her face.

"You, Ledger Dean Hutton, are fucking amazing, you know that?" She leans down to kiss me as I grip her plump ass in my hands.

The front door slams, jolting us away from each other.

"*Aunt Ains!*" Gavin yells at the top of his lungs, and I'm sure the entire neighborhood hears him.

Ainsley and I scramble off the bed, grabbing whatever clothes we can find. I toss her tank top at her as she throws my underwear at me, as we attempt to get dressed.

"Just a second!" Ainsley yells back frantically, and I can't help the bark of laughter from my chest.

"Shut up. Oh my God, my freaking nephew is going to see something if he comes in here!"

I pull up my shorts and bend over, laughing so hard I have tears streaming down my face. Ainsley straightens herself out and walks over to me, pushing me over onto the bed before heading toward the door. "Get your shit together, then come join us." There's laughter in her voice, and it only makes me laugh harder.

I hear the voices of not only Gavin, but Theo and Larkin as well, and I pull myself together and toss my T-shirt on before heading out into the main living area.

"Are you Ledger?" the teenage boy standing straight in front of me asks in an accusing tone, and it's somehow endearing on him.

"I am, indeed. You must be Gavin," I say, holding my hand out to him.

He looks me up and down, and I look over his head at Ainsley and Larkin with my eyebrows raised. They're both hiding their giggle behind their hands, and I smirk before turning my attention back to Gavin.

He takes my hand in a firm handshake, and if I didn't already like the kid, that would have sealed it.

"Hi, I'm Maddie," a small voice to my right says. I look down and see a mini-Larkin with her red hair falling out of its ponytail and what I'm assuming is chocolate, smeared all over her shirt.

"Hi, Maddie. It's nice to meet you. I'm Ledger." I hold my hand out to her too, but she just stares at it like I have cooties.

"Mommy says you're Auntie Ains's boyfriend. Do you kiss her?"

My lips roll inward on themselves as I nod, unable to answer her without cracking up, and I'm not trying to offend a sassy toddler today.

"Eww." Her nose scrunches up in disgust, and my laughter breaks free.

"Maddison," Larkin scolds her.

"She's good, I promise," I say with a laugh.

"The two of you need to get cleaned up and ready for dinner," Theo says with a smirk as he comes in from the garage.

Gavin rolls his eyes but heads upstairs, and Maddie gives me a death-stare I'm honestly scared of before joining him.

"She's scary," I mutter.

"She's too smart for her own good," Larkin says. "You're staying for dinner, right? We got Thai from Ainsley's favorite restaurant."

I look at Ainsley, and she has a soft smile on her face as she nods at me.

"I'd love to stay, thank you."

Theo walks into the kitchen holding two giant bags of food, and I rush to help him, not noticing it before now.

"Thanks. Gavin eats, like, triple his weight in food right now, so I feel like we're feeding an army."

We both start unloading all the food on the kitchen island while the girls get all the serving wear together.

"He's a great kid," I tell Theo.

"He's the best," he says wistfully, and my mind wanders to what the future holds for Ainsley and me. I think I could go either way with kids, willing to go whatever direction she wants to. I've never really put much weight into having kids, but I would absolutely do it with her. What I do know is it would thrill me to have these kids as a niece and nephew.

I would marry that girl tomorrow if she let me.

The thought slams into my head, but it's not a lie. I would take her down to the courthouse anytime she wanted. She's stuck with me now.

"So, how'd the meeting go?" Larkin asks Ainsley.

"Great. Handed over all the shit I had on Lance and got a big fat check for two hundred and fifty grand." She says it so nonchalantly, I almost choke on the sip of water I just took.

"What the fuck?" Theo sounds outraged.

A sigh sounds from the doorway. "That's a dollar in the swear jar. I thought you guys were doing better," Gavin says, and I almost lose my composure entirely.

Wordlessly, Theo pulls out his wallet and hands Gavin the dollar as he continues to stare at Ainsley.

"I should probably pay for that one, sorry." Ainsley cringes. "But yeah, they offered me a settlement to not take further action against them, and I took it and ran."

"Why?" is all Larkin can ask.

"Because of everything we talked about last night. I want to stay in Bluebell Falls. I want to be a bigger part of Ledger's company, and this money was just gravy. I think this is how things would have worked out, anyway." She looks at me for reassurance, and I nod at her. "But now, we can throw some capital into the business to grow it."

"Or we could add on to my house, or yours," I offer. She doesn't know Bluebell Landscaping's financials yet, but we aren't hurting for money. The house idea pops into my head, but the more I think about it, the more perfect I think it is.

"What?" Ainsley sounds shocked, and who can blame her? So much change has happened in a couple of days, and I just threw this out there without really thinking about it. It's a gigantic step and not something we need to rush into.

"It's just a thought. No decisions need to be made anytime soon."

Her eyes hold mine, and I see the moment she starts taking my suggestion seriously. Her eyes light up, and I know I'm not the only making big plans for the two of us.

Maddie comes storming into the kitchen. "I'm so hungry! Can you hear it?"

Without missing a beat, Theo scoops her up. "There's an angry bear in your tummy, Mads. We should feed it."

"It's not a bear, it's me!" Her indignant tone is adorable, and I truly don't know how Larkin and Theo keep a straight face around her.

"Here you go." Ainsley saddles up next to me, handing me a plate. We dish out a little of everything on our plates and take a seat in the attached dining area. I watch Gavin fill his plate so high it's comical, and then he turns to the fridge and pulls out a container filled with fried chicken. He plops a couple of pieces on top of his plate and then joins us at the table.

"So, what's the plan? Are you both staying the weekend?" Larkin asks as she sits down.

"Umm." I hadn't planned that far. I just knew I needed to be here for Ains and didn't second guess it. I didn't come up with a plan.

"I think we'll probably stay tonight since it's already late, and then drive back tomorrow if that's okay with you?" Ainsley says before shoving a fork full of noodles in her mouth.

"Yeah, the guest room is yours until you want to leave. You know our house is your house."

The love in this family reminds me of mine. The fact that we both have families that love us, that support us and show up, is as incredible as it is rare.

"Thank you both for letting me invade family time," I say, suddenly feeling a little intrusive.

"You're never invading, Ledger. You're welcome anytime," Larkin says.

I smile, thankful for their hospitality. And when my eyes move over to Gavin's, about to say something to him about his fierce protection over Ainsley, I see him demolishing the cold chicken on his plate.

My eyebrows furrow as Ainsley leans in and whispers, "Long story, but he found cold chicken when they first took custody of him. He became obsessed and still won't eat it any other way."

A chuckle escapes me as everyone digs into their food. Their family dinner doesn't look much different from mine, and I'm eager for the day we can have everyone together for one big family dinner.

CHAPTER THIRTY-EIGHT
AINSLEY

Ledger and I have been busy as hell the past couple of months, restructuring Bluebell Landscaping and finally testing things on Jenna's yard. Shockingly, she's been a breeze to work with and there has been no awkwardness between any of us.

It helps that she pegged us as being together immediately, so the elephant was no longer parading around the room.

That's the other thing. Life with Ledger is fucking incredible. We spend our days turning Bluebell Landscaping into the next big thing and our nights wrapped up in each other, enjoying the hell out of not hiding anymore.

Once word got out about us, the entire town was in our business. It was something I dreaded so much. It caused a lot of hurt within our relationship. Now, I realize that yes, everyone is in our business, but it's because they care about us. They just want to see both of us happy, and it thrilled them that we're together.

It's been quite the change of pace for me, and I'm happy to say I love it.

To the shock of no one, when we came back from Larkin's house that fateful weekend, my parents were sitting on my porch, waiting for us. My dad immediately embraced Ledger and told him he was glad to have him join our family. Everyone's eyes were glassy, and I finally felt like this place was home. Like it was where I was always supposed to be.

Things have moved quickly since then. We decided my settlement money should go to creating a house both of us would feel comfortable in. The choice seemed obvious: turn Ledger's current house into our dream home and add an actual office to the nursery so we have a designated workspace to grow with. My house was always just going to be a rental, no matter how much I love that wildflower field in the backyard. Keeping the house that holds so many memories for the Huttons was the only thing I wanted.

So, after Jenna's yard is complete, we'll be drawing up plans for the house. It's overwhelming in the best kind of way.

A knock sounds at the door and I look over, confused. No one knocks here. They just burst in whenever they need something. That was a lesson that was learned the hard way, so maybe one of the Hutton siblings finally got the memo that Ledger isn't alone anymore.

I go to open the door and see Arlo on the porch.

"Good evening, Sherriff, what can I do for you?"

"There's been word about a new guy in town. Alice and Mabel were concerned that he seemed 'unsavory'—their words, not mine. So I'm just checking the outskirts, seeing if anyone has noticed anything. They said they overheard him asking Kelly about an assassin in these parts."

"I haven't heard anything, but I'll definitely keep an eye out," I tell him, seriously doubting Mabel and Alice's story.

He bows his head as he walks backward to his truck. "I'd appreciate that."

I watch as he pulls out of the driveway, making his way to the street. As he does, a car passes his and travels up the driveway.

"What did the asshole want?" Rina asks after she climbs out of her truck and up the porch.

My eyebrow raises at her question. I knew they didn't get along, but damn, I didn't realize it was that bad.

"He was asking about some new guy Mabel and Alice were worried about."

"Nosey ass," she mutters before walking around me and heading inside.

"Okay, then. Is everyone else on their way?" I ask, following her into the house.

"Who knows? I know Willow said she was on her way five minutes ago, but she was also writing. Lennox is in the wilderness. Who knows when he'll show up." She walks into the kitchen, opens the fridge, and pulls out the cheese plate I had set up in there.

This is my first official family dinner with the Huttons where I'm in charge of dinner. It feels like I'm legitimately part of the family now that I'm taking the lead on dinner.

"Help yourself." I motion to the tray.

"This is fancy as hell, girl. Whose favorite meal are you cooking tonight?"

"Ledger's, duh." I laugh at how oblivious she is right now as she shoves cheese and crackers into her mouth.

"I'll be honest. I don't know the last time we made his favorite meal. We should probably be better about that," she concedes.

"Honey, I'm home!" Ledger's voice calls from the garage door.

"Rina's here," I yell back, warning him to keep it PG without saying as much.

"Hey, sis," Ledger says as he walks in, wrapping an arm around my waist and kissing my cheek.

"So, what did you tell Ainsley your favorite meal was?" Rina snarks.

"Umm, I didn't. I told her to make one of your favorites." Poor thing looks confused as hell—it's really adorable.

"You didn't think you would leave me in charge of family dinner, and I wouldn't make your favorite?"

"Gah, this is fun," Rina says with her head propped up on her hands on the kitchen island.

Ledger side-eyes her and pulls me along with him to his bedroom. Slamming the door and pushing me up against it, he nuzzles my neck.

"What are you up to, baby?" he drawls, making me shiver.

"Treating you, for a change. When's the last time someone cooked your favorite for family meal?"

He pulls back in thought, and I see the second he realizes the truth. It's not that his siblings don't care about him, it's that he makes sure family dinners are still a thing. He takes the initiative and usually cooks everything too, so it's become the way of things unintentionally.

But tonight, I wanted to treat him.

"Have I told you how much I love you today?"

"You have," I say. "But do we ever stop at once?"

He sinks into me a little, wrapping his arms around my waist and holding me close. I love him like this, completely vulnerable and open to me.

"I love you, and I can't wait to show you just how much when the cretins leave."

His hands slide down to my ass and squeeze before he kisses me breathless. He steps back, making sure to hold me up as I melt to the floor.

"You're a tease, Mr. Hutton."

"You love it when I tease you. It only makes the orgasms that much stronger." He winks and moves me so he can sneak out the door.

Well, he's not wrong, but damn that man and the way he can render me useless with a few dirty words and a kiss.

I take a deep breath and head out the door to find the kitchen full of the Hutton family. The cheese plate is half gone already, but I stand in awe of this amazing family I, not too long ago, was hiding from.

"So, baby, what's for dinner?" Ledger smirks, letting me know he sees how frustrated I am. I want to flip him off so badly, but I refrain.

"I made homemade gnocchi earlier with a spicy tomato sauce that just needs heating up."

His eyes jolt up to meet mine, and I give him a knowing smile. I may have wanted to hide our relationship, but that didn't mean I wasn't committed. I paid attention to all the random shit we talked about and filed it away as facts about my favorite person.

"Damn, she's good," Willow whispers before taking a bite out of a piece of cheddar.

Lennox is pouring the wine I set out into glasses for everyone, and I look around, happier than ever.

I walk to the refrigerator, pulling out the gnocchi and sauce that I pre-made. Ledger walks up next to me.

"How did you know?" he murmurs into my ear.

"Vegas. You mentioned it briefly, and I tucked the information away."

He presses a kiss to my cheek, wrapping an arm around my middle before taking a deep breath. "You are so fucking incredible." I can hear the emotion in his voice. It's a little shaky with a crack at the end, so I lean back into him, giving him support through our connection so he can hide it from his siblings.

He still feels the need to be the father figure to them, and we've talked a lot about how they are all adults. It's okay to worry about them, but it's his turn to be a brother and focus on his own happiness instead of living through theirs.

"What can I do to help?" he asks.

"Just grab a couple of pans and put them on the stove. I've got the rest." I turn around in his arm and press a chaste kiss to his lips before ducking under his arm and heading to the stove.

Dinner takes no time at all to make, and before the first glasses of wine are drunk, we're sitting at the table, waiting to dig into our food.

"I think I'll go first if that's okay," I speak up.

Nods greet me, so I continue.

"My favorite thing this week has been starting on Jenna's landscaping and seeing the fruits of all our hard work over the past couple of months," I say.

"Mine is starting a new book. I'm excited about this one. It's going to have *Only Murderers in the Building* vibes, so it should be a little more lighthearted than I usually go for," Willow says.

"Oh, how fun!" I tell her. I've started going through her backlist, but some of her books are scary as hell, so it's slow going to finish them.

"Mine has been that it's been a quiet week. No animal births, no trapped animals, just peace and quiet in the forest," Lennox adds.

"Nice. Rina?" Ledger asks.

"Hmm, let's see. I got a new commission." She says it bluntly and does not sound happy about it at all.

My eyebrows shoot up to my hairline, but I don't say anything. If she wants to talk about it later, I know she'll come to me.

"Okay, then." Ledger moves on. "My favorite thing this week is watching Ainsley thrive in the business. You're absolutely killing it, and it's so fun to watch. I truly believe you were born for this job."

"You mean the job you created for me?" I give him a hard time.

"Doesn't make it any less true. Now, let's eat. I'm starving." He doesn't wait for a response, just digs into his gnocchi and moans as he takes a bite.

Pride fills my chest. We do a lot of cooking together, but somehow this feels different, more important.

Everyone else digs in, and it's silent for the next fifteen minutes while we eat.

Once we're done, leaning back against their chairs and sipping more wine, I speak up.

"So, Sheriff Arlo stopped by, asking if I had seen a new guy hanging around." Rina shoots me a dirty look, but I'm curious if anyone else knows anything. Whatever is going on between Rina and Arlo is not something I'm privy to.

"What exactly did he say?" Willow sits up and leans in closer. Her little, thriller author heart loves this, and I may have just inadvertently piqued her interest in a story I know nothing about.

I tell them all what he said, and Willow pulls out a notebook out of nowhere and starts taking notes. Rolling my lips inward, I use every ounce of control to not laugh.

"That can't be right. There's no way something like that is happening here. Bluebell Falls is boring, and there are too many nosey old folks to actually hide anything here," Lennox observes. He's not wrong, but Ledger and I hid our relationship for a hot minute, so it is possible.

"I'll have to talk to him tomorrow, see if he needs help," Ledger adds.

"He's fine. You should just let him go around in mindless circles by himself. It might help his personality a little," Rina says.

She's trying a little too hard to say bitchy things about Arlo, and it makes me think there is significantly more to this drama between them.

Everyone seems to ignore Rina and talk about what they've got upcoming in the week. Ledger talks about some projects we've got coming up, and it pulls my brain into work mode a little.

We have so much to get done. Jenna's project is just the start. We've got five other projects lined up in the next month, and that's not counting what we've taken on locally. I zone out. My head is mentally tallying up expenses and timelines, and I don't realize everyone is leaving until Rina and Willow bend down to give me a hug.

"Oh shit, let me walk you out!" I try to jump out of my chair, but Ledger stops me.

"I've got it. Relax, baby," he says, leaning down to press a kiss to my forehead.

I watch as he walks his siblings out, thinking about how lucky I am to be a part of this whacky group of people.

"Come on, let's head to bed," Ledger says as he joins me again.

Leading me to his bedroom, he shows me exactly how appreciative he is of this particular family dinner—all night long.

CHAPTER THIRTY-NINE
LEDGER

I have a surprise for Ainsley, and it's making me freak the fuck out, honestly. I haven't been this nervous since the first time we were face to face and I said my name was Dean.

For the past six months, the addition to my—now, our—house has been in progress. After the initial planning period, I made Ainsley promise to stay away so it could all be a surprise. With a little reluctance, she agreed, and I was thankful. Because I didn't give a shit if she saw the progress on the house. What I needed to surprise her with is what I'm currently looking at from the newly built back porch.

Wildflowers as far as the eyes can see stretch to the trees backing up to our backyard.

It was the one thing from the rental house she was sad to have to leave. The same house we've been living in until everything was done over here. Every morning, she sits on the back porch with her coffee and stares at the wildflowers. Every evening, she takes five minutes to decompress with the wildflowers.

I couldn't take it away from her. I knew as soon as we agreed we would permanently move into my house that I would turn our backyard into the wildflower field of her dreams. And I must say, it's better than I ever could have planned for.

"You ready for this?" Lennox steps up next to me.

"Yes and no. I'm not as nervous as I thought I'd be, but I'm hoping I did the right thing with the field."

"She's going to love it, and you know it. This field is, like, ten times better than the one at the rental."

"Yeah, well, the good news is I don't have to wait too long to get her reaction."

"Rina and Willow should be here with her in five minutes. Everything is good to go." He claps the back of my shoulder. It's a bizarre day when Lennox is the one supporting me. But a lot has changed recently.

He leaves me to my thoughts, and I take the five minutes to clear my head. Walking around the house to the front, I wait for the girls on the front porch. When they finally pull up, Ainsley hops out of the car as Lennox takes her spot, and they all leave as quickly as they came.

"I thought everyone was staying to have dinner." Ainsley's brows are furrowed as she watches them drive away.

"Change of plans," I say as I grab her hand and pull her around the side of the house. My initial plan was to tour the house and then land in the backyard, but I can't wait any longer.

"By all means, just drag me around. It's not like I can easily walk by—" Her snarky words stop the second the field comes into view.

"Ledg…"

"Every day, I see how much that field out back soothes you. How much it's turned into your happy place, and I couldn't take that away from you. This is the reason I wanted you to stay away while the addition was being built. I needed time for the flowers to grow."

A calm has settled over me. There's no anxiety, no nerves, no freak out.

I grab her hands, leading her to the perfect spot, just before the flowers start.

"Ains, baby, since I was seventeen, you've been my crush. When you came back to town, that crush seemed so small in comparison to how I already felt about you. You're everything I've ever dreamed of in a woman and so much more I never considered. All of it adding up to make you the most amazing woman I've ever met. We've been through a lot over the past year, lots of changes, lots of challenges, but being by your side made it all worth it. You've taught me how to grow, how to love, and how to live a life I never knew I could have."

I draw in a shaky breath as I watch tears fall from her eyes.

"You are everything to me. Our life together is everything to me, and I think it's time to make things more official."

I drop down to one knee, still holding her hands, not wanting to let go even if it's to get the ring in my pocket.

"I love you. I can't imagine living this life without you. Will you marry me?"

"Oh my God!" she hiccups before tackling me to the ground with a hug. Kisses rain all over my face as I wrap my arms around her.

She finally pulls away enough to look down at me. "How the fuck did you pull this off? How did you find the time to do all of this?"

"Well, the thing about wildflowers is they are wild. I didn't have to plan a lot, just scatter a ton of seeds onto the area and watch them grow." My technical side is coming out before I can help it.

"You are the best kind of human, the best kind of partner," she says.

"So, is that a yes?" I tease. My anxiety is still firmly in the back seat because I know with everything I am that this woman wants to marry me as much as I want to marry her.

"Yes! Of course, yes! I can't believe you did all of this." She leans back down and kisses me.

I lie back on the grass and pull her on top of me. Her head naturally rests on my chest, and I draw undiscovered shapes on her back.

I have no idea how much time passes, but when I hear the slam of a car door, I know our time for quiet is gone.

"Ready for the first family dinner in the new house?" I whisper against the curve of her ear.

"So ready. I wish we could just stay here all evening, but I'm excited to host in the new space."

We didn't only add to the house; we rearranged what was already there to make room for the extended family we have. We decided while we were making the plans for the house that we wanted to include both of our families in family dinner, so that meant making sure we had the room to do so.

She climbs off of me, holding her hand out to help me up, and I take it graciously, only so I can pull her to me when I'm finally on my feet and steal one more kiss.

"Y'all done out here?" Ainsley's dad calls from the giant sliding doors in the back.

"Yes, dad!" Ainsley tries to yell back, but it's muffled by burying her head in my chest.

Ainsley's shoulders are shaking with laughter as she pulls back, but the smile on her face is breathtaking. Something clicks in my brain, and I realize I still have the ring in my pocket.

"Wait." I pull her back to me. "I forgot the most important thing." Reaching into my pocket, I grab the ring box, opening it up and pulling out the large, green, moissanite, oval solitaire.

We had talked a lot about finances and our future, and the one thing Ainsley was adamant about was not spending a ton of money on a diamond ring or a wedding. So, this is what I found as a compromise.

"Holy shit, Ledg," she whispers in awe.

"It's a moissanite, the next closest thing to a diamond but wallet friendly," I reassure her. Her budget-conscious mind never quits, so I didn't want her to even think about it.

"It's absolutely gorgeous." She kisses me hard as I move my hands lower, sliding closer to her ass.

"Alright, you two, let's go. You've got one hell of an audience right now," Rina yells.

"Should have had everyone come later," I grumble as Ainsley giggles.

"Patience, Mr. Hutton. We'll have time later," she says as she drags me into the house.

She stops in her tracks as soon as she's through the door.

"You like it?" I ask as I step next to her.

"I know I helped pick out all the furniture and finishes, but seeing it all together is something else. It's so perfect." She turns to me with watery eyes.

"Wait until you see the rest of it."

"Do the tour later," Ainsley's dad says. "I thought you said you were proposing during dinner?"

Everyone in the room turns to us, and I know my face is beet-red. Yes, I had a different plan, but this felt perfect at the moment, and I don't regret it.

Ainsley slowly raises her left hand, showing off the ring I just put on her finger.

"So, an engagement party instead?" Willow asks from the kitchen.

"Happy engagement!" Rina and Lennox yell, and I have to laugh.

The group descends on us, giving hugs and checking out Ainsley's ring. Congratulations ring out as I sneak away to the kitchen. This is Ainsley's day, and I'll gladly let her soak up the attention. I'm just glad everything is finally in place. The house is done, we're officially engaged, the business is flourishing, and I already have thoughts about the wedding. I'm hoping Ainsley doesn't want a long engagement because I'm ready to be her husband.

Ainsley's dad walks up to me and pats me on the back.

"You did good, kid. I always thought if we could get Ainsley back to Bluebell Falls, that you two would end up together. I'm proud of you and everything you've done since your parents passed away. They would be so proud of the man you've become."

I drop my head down to attempt to hide the tears rushing to the surface. I couldn't talk right now, even if I wanted to. I've often wondered what my parents would think of how not only I've turned out but my siblings as well. If I did right by them. His words bring an acceptance I've always been desperate to hear, but never thought possible.

"Thank you," I choke out before turning to the refrigerator and pulling out all the food that I prepared earlier.

A huge charcuterie board should hold off the crowd until I can get the burgers and brats cooked. I went for ease instead of someone's favorite because I knew no one would care about the food. Today is the day to celebrate, and nothing is as important as making Ainsley feel loved and taken care of.

I sneak upstairs to get a moment of quiet after Mr. Mathew's speech. As much as I wish I could say I didn't need the words, it feels like all the emotions have unlocked in me. Between his words and getting engaged to Ainsley, my emotions are on a hair-trigger, and I just need a minute.

"Hey, you okay?" Ainsley's soft voice reaches my ears, and I turn to her.

"Yeah, your dad sure knows what to say to bring a grown man to his knees, though." I let out a watery chuckle.

"What did he say?" Her tone is worried, but she has nothing to worry about.

"That he was proud of me, of us. And that my parents would be too."

"Oh, Ledg," she whispers. She wraps me in her arms, and I let the tears fall for a minute until I can gather myself again.

"I was expecting a huge celebration not a gut-check from your dad." I chuckle.

"Yeah, he has great timing sometimes. You should be proud, though, Ledger. You've done so much in the face of heartache and somehow still managed to make sure those three hooligans turned into amazing humans. You built a business that has thrived and are living the life you want to not the life you have to."

"You do realize you're a large part in all of that, right? This has not been a solitary endeavor." I want her to see that almost all of that would not have happened without her. This life we're living, creating together, is because we came together and took a chance.

"Eh, I'm okay, I guess." She grins.

"Liar." I press a kiss to her lips. "You ready to head back down?" I say against her lips.

"No, I'd rather fuck you in that new tub I know is sitting in our bathroom." A laugh burst out of me at the abrupt change in subject.

"Later, baby. We can break in any room you want to ... later."

"I will absolutely be holding you to that."

"It will be my absolute pleasure, almost-Mrs. Hutton." I raise my eyebrows at her.

"God, I love the sound of that." She lifts up to her tiptoes and kisses me again. "Let's get back down there or they'll send a search party, and I definitely don't want anyone in our family catching us in a compromising position."

"You're making me really want to kick everyone out right now, you know," I tell her as I grab her hand and lead her out the door and to the stairs.

"Get to grilling, and we can kick them out immediately after everyone eats." She winks.

"Done."

I'd do anything this woman asks of me, and I wouldn't change that for the world.

EPILOGUE
AINSLEY

A *year and a half later...*

"You better not be wearing panties under that dress, baby. When we're done here, we're going up to our room because I can't wait any longer. You look too fucking amazing, and the way you just took charge of that presentation... Damn, Ains, you make me weak for you," Ledger murmurs in my ear as I watch another colleague walking toward me.

My knees almost give out, but I hold strong. He will be waiting until everyone has come to talk to me because our business is important to both of us. Even if he makes me want to ditch it all.

Last year, we just attended the conference, no presentation, and it was fun. But this year? They asked both of us to be the keynote speakers.

I was so fucking nervous, but Ledger calmed my nerves the whole time, and now apparently, he's done with the niceties.

"Thank you so much," he says to the man who just walked up. "We're on our way out for a bit, but we'll be back later for the luncheon." I don't even get a chance to protest before he drags me out of the conference room and over to the elevators.

Vegas does something to this man, and I'm fully here for it.

"Mr. Hutton, that was very rude," I tell him.

We've been married for a year now. Neither of us wanted to wait long after we got engaged. It was perfect and simple. I married the love of my life standing in the field of wildflowers he grew for me, surrounded by our little family—and most of Bluebell Falls, of course. It was romantic as hell and something I still think about daily.

"Well, Mrs. Hutton, if I don't fuck you in the next five minutes, I will not be held accountable for how rude I really get." He smirks, and I laugh at his desperation.

"I think I like you like this," I tell him as we step into the elevator.

He cages me in with a devious smile on his face. "Like what, baby?"

"Needy, impatient, sexy as hell," I say.

He leans in close, nose nuzzling just below my ear, and I shiver as goosebumps spread down my arms.

A whimper escapes me, and Ledger tips his head back on a groan, pushing his hips to mine, showing me just how ready he is.

"You, up on that stage, completely owning the room, was the sexiest thing ever. Knowing that you're mine and watching all those men so rapt with attention did things to my ego, baby," he says, head still tilted back with strain.

The elevator dings, informing us we're on our floor. Ledger shifts away from me and pulls me out of it so fast, I almost get whiplash.

We don't say a word. We just race down the hallway to our room like teenagers, too impatient to slow down and be civilized. By the time we reach our door, I'm giggling and trying to catch my breath.

He fumbles with the keycard, tapping it a couple of times before it registers, then he rips the door open.

Grabbing me by my waist, he spins me around and bends me over the table in the foyer of our suite. He wastes no time flipping up my dress and discovering he was, indeed, right about me not wearing panties. I had a sneaking suspicion that he was going to go caveman today, so I figured I'd help him out a little. Now, I'm thankful I had the forethought because

I'm so needy it feels like it would be impossible to wait long enough to rip panties off.

"Dirty girl. I didn't think you would do it," he growls as I hear the zipper of his pants.

He drags a hand down over my exposed ass, dipping a finger inside my pussy and moaning at how ready I already am.

It's always like this. In the two years we've been together, nothing has changed. If anything, things have gotten hotter, more intense.

"Fuck, Ains," he whispers as I feel him remove his finger and replace it with his cock.

Dragging it through my arousal, I whimper in need. He may be a caveman right now, but I'm not far behind him. His faith in me during that presentation was so sexy, and it made me feel like I was the queen of his world.

Without warning, he thrusts long and hard into me, and I melt into the table. *He always feels so damn good.*

I move my hands over my head and grip the opposite end of the table. I have a feeling this is going to be a rough ride, so holding on is really my only option—not that I'm sad about that.

"You were fucking amazing today, Ains." Thrust. "God, watching you up there was a fucking privilege." Thrust. "I'm so fucking proud of you." Thrust.

That's all it takes.

I'm coming; my knuckles turn white, and I don't even know what's coming out of my mouth. It's like I black out and come to with Ledger lying on top of my back.

I frown, disappointed that I missed his orgasm. It's always a sight to behold and one of the sexiest things I've ever seen.

"Sorry, shit, I'm sorry. That was so rough. Are you okay?" he asks through his panting, trying to catch his breath.

"So good," I reply wistfully.

He relaxes a little, reaching up to intertwine our hands.

"You make me lose my head. Damn, I had all these plans after the keynote. I was going to take you back to Craft, wine you and dine you. The hotel is decorating the room later with rose petals and whatever other fancy shit they find."

"That's sweet, Ledg. But I like this too." I sigh.

He tucks our hands, which are still connected, against my side and gently helps me up. We're still fully dressed, and when we stand up, he slips from me.

Pressing his forehead to mine, I breathe him in. He gently picks me up and sets me on the table, and I start to protest.

"We're going to make a mess on this table, Ledg."

"Don't care. I'll clean it," he says against my lips.

I wrap my arms around him as he does the same, and I rest my head on his chest, soothed by the rhythm of his heartbeat. Now that the highs from the keynote speech and the mind-blowing sex are gone, I just want to be held by him and do nothing.

"Can we just order room service?" I say softly.

"We can do whatever you want."

"I think I just want to be a homebody and keep you to myself tonight."

"I'm definitely okay with that," he says, stroking my back soothingly.

"We still need to go back to the luncheon."

"They can wait."

I don't know how long we stay there, but I do know that I needed the reset.

Ledger always seems to know what I need before I realize it. He's so attuned to my wants and desires that I feel like I'm never wanting for anything.

Every day, I aspire to do the same for him.

Bluebell Falls was supposed to be a pit stop in my life, a place to regroup and plan. Instead, I found my soulmate. I found a work-life balance that has Ledger in every aspect of my life, and I love it more than I can put into words. We've built a life we're both so proud of, and I wouldn't change it for the world.

THE END

ACKNOWLEDGEMENTS

There are so many people to thank for making this book, and this series the best it can be! Bear with me as I ramble out my gratitude.

Michelle- I swear nothing would get done without you! Our brainstorms, random talks, and friendship mean more to me than I could ever begin to tell you.

Emi- Thank you for your wonderful insights and edits!

Nina- Thank you for making me a better writer, I really can't thank you enough for going above and beyond.

Kate- You made the prettiest cover I could have ever imagined for this book and I'm so thankful for your friendship.

Dani, Joscelyn, and Kathryn- My betas!!! Y'all worked so hard and provided some incredible feedback! Thank you for taking this journey with me and making sure Ledger and Ainsley were the best they could be.

Kait- Girl... No words are enough to thank you for everything you do. You are an incredible friend and an awesome hype girl! You are officially stuck with me forever.

Husband- For the never-ending inspiration, the support, and banter that always ends up in my books in some way, I love you and thank you.

To you, wonderful reader- THANK YOU! Thank you for taking a chance on me, thank you for hopefully loving Ledger and Ainsley like I do, and thank you for the incredible support! It doesn't go unseen, and I can never thank you enough for it.

ALSO BY

The Catalyst Series

The Beginning

Meet the women of The Catalyst Series a decade before the series takes place!

The Detour

Bea and Riggs

The List

Penelope and Andy

The Case

Larkin and Theo

The Vacation

Jane and Pierce

Be sure to join my newsletter to stay up to date on new releases and all other things me!

http://www.samanthamthomas.com

If you enjoyed Second First Impression, please think about leaving a review! I would be so grateful to you!

Review Here

www.ingramcontent.com/pod-product-compliance
Lightning Source LLC
Chambersburg PA
CBHW021220310726
48971CB00006B/1632